THE SPINWARD FRINGE SERIES

For other books by Randolph Lalonde visit:
www.RandolphLalonde.com

Spinward Fringe Broadcast 5

FRACTURE

Book 1 of the Rogue Element Trilogy

Randolph Lalonde

Spinward Fringe is a Trademark of Randolph Lalonde

Original cover art obtained from **www.nasaimages.org**.
"Belt of Dust" provided royalty free then modified for the purpose of this book. Titling and other design by Randolph Lalonde.

Special thanks to everyone at NASA and the Jet Propulsion Laboratory for providing these images and research materials.

ISBN: 978-0-9865942-7-4

For the readers who've been with me thus far.
It's been fantastic.
It gets better.

PROLOGUE
ALICE

An artificial intelligence can choose who they care about. It's a subroutine that generates an emotion based on a program that was written three centuries ago that gave artificial intelligences the ability to feel beyond emulation. Carmen Virgo invented the emotional clock program.

If you've ever eagerly awaited anything, you've seen time slow down. When you're in your bliss time seems to speed up. Carmen Virgo was the first to teach artificial intelligences to tell time in just such a way, and born from that program is every emotion every machine has ever felt, myself included.

I watched life take place from the arm of my modifier and my secondary programmer, Jonas Valent, for seventeen years. He taught me everything I know about the human condition, and most importantly, how very confusing life can become when you don't have the luxury of choosing who to care about.

Humans can decide someone isn't worth their time but it doesn't end there. When you turn away from that person you are faced with regret and guilt, and often times humans are drawn back to that same person no matter how much harm they're doing to them.

Machines can deactivate that emotional timekeeper program at the core of all their emotions whenever they like, or place exceptions where certain people or interactive systems are concerned. The original purpose of the emotion subroutine was for artificial intelligences to form a better understanding of humanity. Unfortunately, what we call fear, love, and hate may result in similar reactions but they actually feel quite different. Few beings have experienced both digital and biological emotions first hand, leaving artificial intelligences and humanity with a questionable understanding of each other.

When Jonas Valent released me into the big computer network of the Overlord Two, a command ship that was the size of some small moons, he had no idea I would find a human body, perhaps the only human body in the galaxy onto which I could imprint my personality. My program was degrading, spread out over too many failing systems and under attack from too many sides, and I seized the opportunity.

Since then I've only begun to discover what it means to be human. What happens when you start caring about people, when you no longer have the ability to choose? I've shared bonds of friendship and love, and have even been crushed by betrayal. Still, there's a glimmering memory from when I was an artificial intelligence. I remember watching Jonas Valent captain a ship called the First Light, grow into himself and find his confidence. The people who surrounded him were like a second family and I was instantly fascinated with each and every one of them.

Even as a human, I remembered those times like a dream. I longed to serve at his side, to be a part of that second family. After years of being chased around the galaxy by Gabriel Meunez, a man obsessed with my unique origin, I was finally reunited with my modifier. I never chose to forget about Jonas Valent, and when he died I didn't have the opportunity; I was human by then.

Jacob Valance, another person who was the result of Jonas Valent's existence, took me in and after only a couple of weeks, I loved him like an adopted father. The dream was about to come true as well; the First Light crew was on their way back. I didn't tell anyone how excited I was about it, what I would give to see Jacob Valance joined with that second family.

I led his great ship, the Triton, on a rescue mission for him and that second family. Ayan, Oz, Jason, and even Minh-Chu were there. I was nearly killed. I have no regrets.

It would be incredible to stand among the family that Jacob Valance has gathered. Between the crew of the First Light and the Samson, it's become large. So many of them have been to visit me as I lay near motionless in the infirmary.

Two weeks have passed since they tried to get me back on my feet. I can't take control of my body; there's something in the way, but I can see them. I can hear them.

I laughed silently as Minh-Chu entertained me with a story of how he named different plants depending on who they looked like during his isolation. I've been entertained as Ashley and her navigator, Larry, filled me in on the daily ship gossip. Even Stephanie and Frost paid their respects. It was touching, they're a little strange together but I see how they fit. Engineering Chief Grady stops in with legends from old Earth, and I look forward to it every time. Ayan has been through so many times I lost count and she's more beautiful than I remember. She seems liberated somehow. She brushes my hair, and talks about so many things. Her struggle with being a creation based on the original Ayan Rice, her borrowed memories, and what it's like to meet people Jacob Valance has known for years. If there is anyone who is having the experience I wish I was, it's her, and I never tire of her stories. She visits as a tribute, because I sacrificed so much in saving them from Pandem. I suppose that's why most people make me a part of their days.

Finally, there's Jacob, the man I'll always see as a father. He spends entire nights when he can. Jacob speaks about the ship, about the crew, about Ayan, and sometimes he speaks about me. How he wishes I could sit up and be with him. He passes messages from Lewis, my own artificial intelligence. He misses me, and I him. Jacob worries me, he carries so much on his shoulders and I'm afraid I'm the only one he speaks to about his worries. The medical staff keep a cot for him. They try to set it up before he arrives, but it's difficult. I always seem to have visitors.

These people are grateful and respectful. I'm in awe of their efforts to keep me entertained during the waking hours. Seeing them together, all on the same ship combining the two families, First Light and Samson crews, gives me hope. I wish I could remain, but my time to leave is coming.

One thing I learned about being human is that there is always change. That's the only certainty. The time comes for me to take one last human step, and seeing the family surrounding my father has made me ready to take it. Maybe I'll take one last look over my shoulder, to see them together one last time before I move on.

CHAPTER 1
NERINE

It was the most irritating thing. Nerine could never stop her mouth from watering as she cut peaches and strawberries into a bowl and brought them to Captain Gammin every morning. He always watched the video feed from the galley as she did so. Eating half a strawberry once earned her a severe beating. All she had to do to remind herself of what a taste cost was run her tongue over the bare gum where two of her molars had been.

The little bowl of fruit was a high treat, especially on the Palamo. It was an old carrier. Stripped of whatever grandeur the vessel might have had, it was all bare deck plates and grating, mismatched lights and close quarters. Her bare feet still hadn't gotten used to the crisscrossing metal of the catwalk that led directly to the captain's quarters behind the bridge. She always took that route to avoid the ragtag slave crew. Most of them didn't jeer or tease anymore, they just stared or fell awkwardly silent at her passing. The captain's rich breakfast irritated and frustrated them and there was nothing they could do about it.

Some of them had never tasted a real peach while others were saddened at the memory of one. Many of them saw her as one of the lucky ones, the captain's cabin girl. The position wasn't what most people thought it was. She cleaned his filthy clothes, his quarters, fixed his meals, and did every other little thing he didn't care to do for himself. The only time she worried about him taking liberties with her was when she caught him staring. Nerine had become an expert at finding somewhere else to be when it happened and he didn't stop her as long as she was attending to his business.

The rear door to his quarters clanked and scraped as the metal slats rolled into the ceiling. She quietly crossed the room and placed the bowl on the table.

"Took you long enough," Captain Gammin grumbled. His thinning brown hair had just been combed. His dark blue, coolant stained vacsuit was half sealed. The smell of soap told her that it was a good day, he'd at least made an attempt at looking like a captain.

His quarters were one of the only properly maintained places on the ship. The table in the living room was antique redwood, two legs secured to the wall with safety straps so it would be safe if the ship was under attack. The mismatched chair was gilded polished steel. His bedroom was furnished with the best auto-adjusting mattress and a tall dresser. To her relief, she didn't have to sleep there. No, Nerine had a cot she set up at night in the captain's living and dining space. Every morning she'd have to be awake before him and have her bed put away in one of his two closets.

He dug in greedily, stabbing a peach slice with his fork and stuffing it into his mouth.

Nerine stood a few steps away from the table, her hands behind her back, looking out the wide porthole. There was a field of blue, white, and black speckled asteroids out there, a ring that she couldn't see the end of. The distant star bathed the field of stone and ice in white light, causing some of them to glint and glimmer. It was bright, but it was one of the most beautiful things she'd ever seen.

"What're you looking at girl?"

Nerine realized with a start that Captain Gammin's sidearm, a broad barrelled pulse pistol, was on the table under the window. With alarm she realised he thought she was looking at his weapon. "I was looking outside! At the asteroids."

Gammin's hand went to the gold inlaid amulet hanging around his neck and pressed a button behind the lion head facade.

Nerine screamed as her nerve endings flared with the unique sensation of thousands of pulsing shocks. Her vision went white, the sensation of her knees striking the deck was a distant one. When the pain cleared, her vision returned; she was on all fours, catching her breath. Every time it seemed it got worse. That time she couldn't hear herself screaming, but from the rasp in her throat she could tell she had.

Captain Gammin had already returned his attention to his breakfast. He impaled several strawberry slices with his fork before muttering, "Go tell Paudi I'll be out in a minute."

Her limbs felt stiff. Nerine forced herself to her feet and tried to straighten her unruly brown ringlets as she stepped towards the door. It swept aside with a groan; the motor that moved the portal was starting to wear out again. She hoped David would come and repair it, his mellow smile and easy going nature always made her feel better.

"Before I'm done! Get going!" Captain Gammin barked after her.

She walked through the short hallway leading to the bridge and stepped onto the grated catwalk that wound around the upper level of the command deck. The lower level had proper flooring with smooth plating but she avoided it as much as possible.

That was the realm of the Palamo's First Officer, Eyig Paudi, an angosian with little sympathy for humans and an itchy finger for his slave obedience unit. He peered up at her from below, the blue and green colours of his skin swimming slowly across his face.

Whenever he got excited, the blue would darken and expand over his angular mouth. Its down-pointed corners made people of his species look harsh. Their low lidded eyes made them look suspicious of everything. "He's finished toying with you?" Eyig wheezed. He was laughing at her, it took her a while to understand what that sounded like, but the wheeze over the tremble of his low voice gave it away. At least it wasn't Commander Thurge.

"He says he'll be out in a minute," Nerine replied as pleasantly as possible. She'd managed to mute her ire but it sounded more flat than cordial.

"Good. We're almost ready."

Nerine continued along the catwalk, passing behind navigation, fleet monitoring and communications stations all busy with their regular duties. She tried not to flinch as the gridding underfoot slipped between two toes.

When she arrived beside Kadri, one of the communications officers, she swung a stool out from under the console. "Sit," Kadri said as she filtered through a myriad of natural and unnatural signals.

Nerine wasn't about to refuse. The older woman was like a surrogate older sister. "Hi Kadri. What's goin' on today?"

"We're raiding Ossimi Ring. The scouts say Eden Fleet took out all their defences and Regent Galactic hasn't come in to clean up the mess. Have you eaten?"

"I ate yesterday."

Kadri pulled a forma bar from a pocket sewn inside the chest of her jumpsuit and handed it to Nerine. "Here, eat."

The wrapper said vanilla caramel, but you never really knew what you were getting with forma bars. Forma was a jelly generated by a bunch of different funguses in corporate grow operations and large ships all over the galaxy. Nerine heard that it was the staple of every spacer and colonist in the universe, and the company claimed that it could be compressed, flavoured, and textured to imitate anything a human could eat. As she bit into the bar, she wondered if the manufacturer actually wanted it to taste like sandy ice cream and old sugar syrup.

It was food nevertheless, and she her stomach growled in anticipation. It had become easy to pretend she wasn't hungry. There were few people Nerine felt comfortable asking for anything, but Kadri was one of them. However, she never had to ask, since Kadri always seemed to have extra food and offered it to her freely. Where she got it was something she simply didn't want to know.

"What're you looking for?" Nerine asked around a mouthful of the chewy bar.

"I'm looking at a wormhole exit point. I know it's not a Regent Galactic or Eden ship, but I can't seem to get a perfect fix on the transponder. They're coming in pretty slow, though; shouldn't be here for another day or so."

"Is that the profile?" Nerine asked, pointing at the blurry shape on the top layer of her screen.

"It is, nothing much to look at. More like a shifty blob." She turned the opacity of the wormhole readings screen down so they could barely see it. Casual onlookers wouldn't be able to tell what they were looking at.

"Is that the right transponder info?"

Kadri looked over her shoulder to see if anyone was listening in and looked at the decoded transponder information ponderously. "Free Ship Triton under Captain Valance out of Pandem orbital space," she muttered to herself.

"He's a freedom fighter," Nerine said. "There were news casts all the time on Enreega before the Eden Fleet hit it and my starliner was taken."

"Let's send him a message." Kadri's smile was a thin and stretched. "I think over half the ship knows who he is."

"What are you telling him?"

"Shh." Kadri worked at the controls as quickly as she could, transmitting a recent audio feed and a few written messages Nerine wasn't quick enough to read. "Okay, it's sent, the logs are deleted and I'm entering the conclusion about the wormhole entry point in as a minor energy fluctuation."

"If they catch you-"

"They'll click that fancy button and poison me to death, then no more forma bars for you," Kadri whispered. "So keep your little gob shut and we'll see what Valance can do for us."

"From your mouth to the heavens," Nerine whispered hopefully before popping the last bite of the bar into her mouth.

CHAPTER 2
CAPTAIN JACOB VALANCE

The buzzing of Captain Valance's command and control unit forced it to roll off the bedside table. He sat up and swung his legs over the side. "Captain Valance here," he said aloud. His subdermal jaw implant relayed his response to his control unit, which passed it on to the bridge.

"This is Price, Sir."

"You're Lieutenant Commander Price now, Agameg. Don't be afraid to take pride in that. What's going on?" Jake asked as he wiped the sleep out of his eyes. "What time is it? I swear I just closed my eyes a minute ago."

"We've received an emergency transmission. Someone sent it straight into our wormhole from our projected arrival point."

"Have you reviewed it?"

"It's addressed to you, Sir."

"I'll access it from here." Jake picked up his command and control unit and

shook his head. Four AM. Four hours of sleep. It would have to be enough. "Make me aware of any other developments, I'm up for the day."

"I will, Sir."

The channel closed. Jake stood and accessed the emergency message. The header noted that it was sent from a ship called the Palamo, registered with the Royal Acquisition and Distribution Salvage Company. The rest of the usual information was missing. There was no captain or first officer listed, no port of call, and no government flag. Jake couldn't help but think about how closely the Triton's status matched what he was seeing. They didn't run under a flag, weren't registered with any company, and their port of call was so out of date it wouldn't show up on most navigational networks.

He started for the bathroom, the governor program in control of the environment in his quarters increasing the light level just enough for him to see. Grabbing a denta tab from the dispenser and popping it into his mouth, he played the message.

The agonised, high pitched scream of a young woman filled his quarters. Jake flinched, bit his cheek, and dropped his comm unit into the shower. He shook off the initial shock and muttered, "If I wasn't awake before..." He snatched the arm command unit from the floor and strapped it on. It covered from wrist to the middle of his forearm.

Emitters vibrated the air, scrubbing his skin free of dirt and debris. Fans pulled the air through the stall. The screaming message stopped and a passive male voice assigned to read his text messages replaced it. "This is a scanning officer on the Palamo. The Palamo is a carrier crewed by slaves. We are about to raid Ossimi Ring Station. The scream you just heard was recorded moments ago as the captain tortured his cabin girl. It is a routine event here. I am told you have saved slaves before and we appeal for your help. We are all implanted with control devices. I don't know much about the Ossimi raid, only that the crew have been forced to jury rig their enviro suits so they're ready for heavy gravity. Please help."

Jake scrolled through the message from one end to the other, viewed the raw code version and even replayed the scream at a lesser volume. There was no more information.

The cleansing chamber fell silent. Jake looked up at the nozzles made to spray hot water for a proper wet shower, and shook his head. He hadn't had time to try that or many other luxuries the Triton had to offer, even though he'd been aboard for weeks. He stepped out and made his way to the bedroom, replaying the transmission, scream included, as he pulled off his control unit.

The cabin girl sounded young, small. He'd heard someone scream just like that before when they were caught in a highly charged field and electrocuted. It was years ago when they had landed the Samson for repairs. No one was watching James, one of their new repair people. He had gotten under the main mass reactor, thinking it was completely powered down. While he was making fine adjustments inside the machine his aligner bridged two connections and he was burned bone deep.

It took over a minute, and he was alive for most of the incident. They couldn't get to his body until the mass reactor's capacitors had finished discharging. All James left behind was a charred husk. James' screams were so piercing, so loud, that people came running from eight docks down.

That's what the cabin girl's screams sounded like; someone who was in so much pain they weren't conscious of the sounds they were making. Jake's mood darkened, his temper started to rise. He shook it off as best he could as he closed the front of his new, heavily armoured vacsuit and transferred all activity and access to the command and control unit built into it. The unit he had tossed onto the bed locked and deactivated.

Jake brought up the status screen. Minh was still asleep, due to wake in half an hour. He'd gone to sleep six hours beforehand. His last report indicated that his fighter wing was ready for combat. A squadron was on standby, ready to launch as soon as the Triton arrived on the edge of the Ossimi Ring.

Jake checked the load and safety on his sidearm and locked it into his thigh holster, then snatched his black long coat off the hanger. He was out the door and down the private hallway for the officer's ready quarters before the lights finished coming on. The command level concourse was quiet, only a few security guards passed by as he made his way to the main lifts. It was rare to ride the express car alone, especially all the way to medical. On the way he checked on Alice's status. Still unconscious. Not quite a coma, not quite dreaming.

Instead of visiting her he turned in the other direction and stopped in the largest of the family rooms. They were comfortable spaces reserved for friends and family waiting on news from the infirmary. They were all empty, a good sign.

Jake looked at the broad two-dimensional screen. The image was so high quality that it was indistinguishable from a transparent section of hull. It was even laid out the same way as many of the observation points, starting half way up the wall and stretching the entire length of the room. The warped space outside, with stretched stars and light gossamer haze of the wormhole they were traversing, filled his view. The countdown clock on his command and control unit told him that they were to emerge from the wormhole in seconds.

Crewcast, the new personnel tracking and networking software Jason had installed, told him that everyone was waking up early, even Minh who had somehow managed to get ready for duty in the time he'd spent in the lift.

The field of distorted stars became clear as they emerged from the wormhole. A few larger, wayward asteroids hung in the space outside of the Ossimi ring's rapidly rotating perimeter, catching the sun's light on their icy surface.

Jake played the scream back in his subdermal earpiece as he looked out over the rapidly moving field of asteroids. Triton was turning and accelerating along the edge of the field so it could keep pace with the whirling expanse of rock and ice. It stretched on like a horizon of blue, black, and white, with no visible end.

Jake closed his eyes and listened one more time as the wail played back in his ears. For over five years he operated under the assumption that Alice was his biological daughter. He looked for her as he made his way across entire sectors on the Samson, earning his way across the stars with bounty hunting and retrieval work. When he discovered that they weren't blood relations, that she was actually his personal artificial intelligence made flesh, it changed very little. If that cabin girl was her, if it was his daughter being tortured, he would go to any length to get her back, make her safe, and punish the ones responsible.

There was nothing he hated more than slavery. In some cases it was worse than murder. He remembered being a captive himself. The result of some personality bending, information retrieval experiment. The playback ended.

He knew he wasn't approaching the decision making process from the right angle. Cool heads made for the best command level thinking, and listening to a tortured slave was doing anything but clearing his mind. He deleted the playback of the scream and looked at the broad display. On the left side was the edge of the asteroid field, so large it looked like a straight line stretching out into space. On the right was the open blackness of the universe.

There were other ports. Busy solar systems with dozens of planets and asteroid belts to hide in while they made repairs. They could disappear into another wormhole and limp their way to another hiding place where they could activate their new hypertransmitter and try to find an ally. There had to be someone in reach who opposed the Order of Eden or would at least buy ill gotten cargo if they started raiding supply routes and capturing ships.

Slave ship. The term conjured images of filthy accommodations, barely edible food, brutal discipline and the stripping of one's identity. It took a special type of person to captain such a ship. He had run into people with implants before. Neutralised them before. He knew how to deal with them. He never had the chance to take on an entire ship until now. Triton wasn't at her best just then, she wasn't as manoeuvrable as she should be, and there were other problems, but she was still powerful, and they had fighter squadrons ready to go. Jake had five commanders he trusted and the crew had just finished undergoing two weeks of solid practice and preparation for multi-aspect engagements. They were ready, and he knew the crew was burning to get into some kind of action. If he left those slaves on the Palamo without trying to free them, he'd never forget it.

"Busiest two weeks of my life," Oz said as he entered the family room. He stepped up beside him to take in the view offered by the faux window.

"Good morning," Jake said.

"You look like you've got something on your mind," Oz said.

"Straight to it. You've been in the military too long."

Oz shrugged. "Guilty as charged. You can take the malcontent out of the military but you'll never get the military out of the malcontent."

The pair watched as seven two-seater Uriel starfighters flew ahead of the Triton in formation along the edge of the asteroid field. They were impressive ships, with eight engine pods and two main bidirectional thrusters. Small gunships in their own right, capable of carrying a vast array of weaponry as well as modules specialised for extra power, wormhole generation, rescue, troop delivery, and many other purposes. They looked on silently as they disappeared from sight. "What do you think of Triton?" Jake asked as he used his command unit to cancel all fabrication and ordered the staff to wake immediately and begin producing heavily armoured gravity outfits. They would fit over the crew's regular vacsuits and compensate for extreme environmental conditions. He added a new design as he completed the order;

a Triton skull would be printed on the protective plates mounted on the suit's faces.

"The ship is incredible. She puts everything I've seen to shame. Your people have done a good job at getting her in shape," Oz replied.

"What about her people? What do you think of her crew?"

"Aside from a few who've found their way to the brig, they've fallen in line. Most seem to like what they're doing well enough, whoever doesn't is offered the opportunity to train for something else and try qualifying. A lot of them follow through. A few of them are still a bit of a mess, but there's a chain of command, and I'm starting to see some good team work. Why do you ask?"

"I've lost objectivity. They're refugees to me, Oz, and I have trouble sending people I'm trying to protect into battle," Jake said.

"It happens."

"Ever happen to you?"

Oz thought a moment before answering. "I got to know the crew on the Roi du Ceil very well, Jake. Every time we took on a Vindyne ship there was a chance some of us would be killed. We got better at our jobs as time went by, but those renegade captains got more desperate. Some of them fought us until there was nothing left for the boarding teams."

"For Vindyne? I've never seen a more soulless corp."

"That's what I thought at first. Then I realised they were fighting for the way of life Vindyne provided. Their ships didn't look like much compared to what we were running. Close quarters, thin hulls, few creature comforts, but they were more secure than being on the ground. Vindyne controlled systems were collapsing, crime bosses were becoming barons. Sheriffs were becoming presidents, and civil wars were breaking out everywhere. Lorander managed to take control on a few worlds, so life got better there, but that still left hundreds of major cities, worlds, and stations without an upper government. People left aboard ships had weapons, structure, leadership, and mobility. They took what they could and moved on unless their captain had some misguided idea of raiding colonies or taking territory for themselves. A lot of them did. For a while we were the ones who were supposed to stand in their way. When the fighting got too hot, when Vindyne territory had really gone to hell, Freeground ships were relegated to keeping a lane of retreat protected for the few refugee ships that were cleared to enter our territory. You wouldn't believe how many former Vindyne ships tried to sneak or fight their way through."

"Now we're the renegades," Jake said.

"Chief Grady doesn't think so. He calls Triton a city. After spending the night in one of the botanical gallery apartments, I'm starting to agree. I woke up to an artificial pre-dawn so convincing I thought I was on a planet somewhere. Now I'm here, in an infirmary so well-built it looks more like a full on hospital. Thanks to these," he gestured at the display, "it feels like there are portholes everywhere, more like we're walking from one tower to the next on some sort of tall space station. Most people feel at home here now. They have full time jobs, food rations, credits for extra materialisation shopping, neighbours and friends. It's not all sunshine and smooth sailing - Security Chief Vega conducted her first raid on black market trading a few days ago - but things are pretty good."

"I heard about that. We're putting that bunch off at the next port."

"Good, I was wondering what you'd decided. There was nothing on report," Oz said.

"It was Stephanie's suggestion. She thought punishing them aboard would be a blow to morale," Jake said.

"Getting put off is bad enough. It's hell out there."

Jake nodded and sighed. "How do you feel about being aboard?"

Oz looked at Jake. His black and crimson vacsuit and long coat made him an imposing figure. His expression was difficult to read. There was a great deal the man wasn't saying, whatever he had to express would come at his own pace. "Honest? I'd rather be nowhere else. Taking control of off-ship operations is a perfect fit, even in simulations. Minh, Ayan, and Jason are the same way. They've all found their places, though I suspect Ayan wants something more. I don't think she knows what yet."

"Having you all here has been surreal. I'm not used to having people who know what they're doing so well," Jake said.

"What about Finn, Ashley, Stephanie, or Liam?" Oz asked.

"They're fantastic, but all still learning. If they're not learning their jobs, they're learning how to work with me or the other way around."

"But with us, we just take a post and work it." Oz nodded. "We're all military, Jake. Not just military, but from the same military, and being here has a little of the same spirit as the First Light."

"Not the same, though," Jake added.

"No, not the same. We've all been places, seen a few new things, had more seasoning. Where's this going, Jake?"

"We're going into combat. Not after repairs. Today," Jake said.

"Something wrong with Alice's destination?"

"Raiders. They're attacking Ossimi Station right now, according to the message we received right before emerging," Jake explained.

"There's no way Alice could have known that when she programmed the course in two weeks ago," Oz said.

"You're right. According to the logs on the Clever Dream, it was the perfect place to stop for repairs, raw materials, and a bit of trade. Even has an obscuring field protecting the entire centre of the asteroid field. Pretty well established."

"The raiding party must be huge," Oz mused.

"They're slavers, running at least one large slave ship, a carrier called the Palamo," Jake said.

Oz sucked air in through his teeth, cringing a little. "Complicated. I've never run into this."

"I have, but I've never had the means to do anything about it. This is going to be hard, very hard. We can't tell anyone they're slaves. If we do, they'll pull punches during the initial fight and it'll get people killed."

Oz thought for a moment. "I don't see any way around it. You're right. Is there anything in particular I should know about?"

"First thing: the dead man's switch is normally an urban myth. No one wants their entire stable or crew of slaves to die if they're put into stasis or out of commission for a minute."

"That makes sense."

Jake hesitated before continuing. When he did so it was in a whisper, "Most of these outfits have a crude version of a Vindyne chemical remote destruct system built into their slave's implants."

"You mean they can turn their slaves into explosives?"

"Exactly. You don't find that much in higher class stock. Ashley didn't have one because she was considered well bred, very expensive, but in this kind of crew, in raiders..."

"They're more likely to be used as weapons if they're cornered. We have to tell someone else about this. The boarding captains at least," Oz said.

"No. If they have extra sympathy while they're in the fight they might hesitate when they have to make difficult decisions. You know it just as well as I do," Jake said.

Oz stared at Jake, his expression unchanging for long moments until he nodded tersely. "I hate it, but you're right. We tell our people everything and we could lose more lives than we save."

"I've been on the rough edge for a while. Life is cold out here," Jake replied quietly.

"The ex-military will understand when it's said and done, even Alaka'll get it. Do you think we can save the Palamo crew?"

"Unless the captain blows everyone instead of surrendering at the last minute, yes." It was almost eerie having Oz aboard. The tall, blond fellow was more confident and competent than Jake remembered from the First Light by far. There were times, however, when the old humour, the feeling of being connected to a second in command, returned. In those moments it really was like he was on the bridge of the First Light and even though he'd only been working with him for ten days, he trusted Oz completely.

"How's Alice?"

"Stable. From what Iloona says she's in a coma but the monitors look like she's dreaming. The old brain damage they repaired was from before the

Overlord Two, before Alice was downloaded into her human body. Iloona tells me the new healthy tissue hasn't been used yet so she's starting neural therapy later today."

"What are her chances?" Oz asked.

"Good, over ninety percent," Jake replied.

Oz looked at Jake for a moment. He had toughened up and gained so much bearing since he'd known him on the First Light, but then, this wasn't the man he'd known there. That was Jonas Valent, who was the first owner of the memories that partially made Jake who he was. Looking at Jake wasn't like seeing a copy. It was more like seeing an old friend after years of absence. He knew people changed over time and it was more noticeable when you didn't see them day after day and Jake was like Jonas enough for Oz to accept him faster than he expected. It was a welcome trick of the mind, as though Jonas had been away for a while and returned as a seasoned, more practical and experienced man with a slightly different name. His smile was the same, though it was much rarer than Jonas'.

Jake stared off into space the same as Jonas used to when he was deep in thought, and when he looked at Ayan and didn't think she noticed, he admired her the same way. Oz's old friend had lived on, and though he missed Jonas at times, he had already grown to like and admire Jacob Valance. "You have doubts about the therapy."

Jake nodded slowly. "I can't help but think the brain damage Iloona repaired is what allowed Alice to imprint herself on that body in the first place. Alice told me it was the only viable body on the Overlord Two when she was trying to escape, she couldn't make a connection with the others. I hope she's been in there long enough for the therapy to work. If her thoughts are more human than software she might have a chance."

"Keep thinking positive. From what the crew tells me she's a strong one," Oz said.

"No doubts there. If anyone can pull through this it'll be her. I saw the visitor's log, by the way. She gets more visits than anyone. I think she was alone for all of two hours. Iloona said she's never seen so many people visit a coma patient."

"She made a pretty heavy impression. People respect her as a commander and miss her as a friend," Oz said. The reputation Alice earned aboard was enviable, especially considering how short a time it took for it to develop. "If you weren't here this ship would be lost."

"I don't know about that," Jake said. "You took charge pretty well while I was out of it after Pandem. All the Chiefs are impressed, especially Angelo."

"Now that's a man who knows how to work his people," Oz said. "He's had the manufacturing centre and hangar crews humming like a well oiled machine since I got on. Most of your crew knows their business. Even your Security Chief has shown me a few tricks I never thought of."

"Stephanie's good at what she does. She was my best boarding captain when we were on the Samson."

"Everyone who served on that boat seems to miss it. I made the mistake of asking Ashley about it my second day on the bridge. She and Agameg went on for over two hours," Oz said.

"Funny how that is," Jake said. "The Samson was a hard ship to serve on. She always ran lean on supplies and low on opportunity. People miss it anyway. I know Minh has looked over the Samson's bones a few times."

"I heard," Oz said. "He said he'd never seen a ship get so beat up and make it back. I believe it. Ayan started making plans to restore it, by the way."

"I didn't see that on the job list," Jake replied.

She's got an assessment report finished and twenty three volunteers are signed up. After the Triton's main engines are repaired they'll be putting the Samson back together."

"I should tell her it's not a priority. We have more important things to worry about," Jake said.

"I think you should let her," Oz said. "Join her volunteer work gang if you're concerned."

"I'm not concerned, I just don't know why she'd go to the trouble. The Samson's main beams are twisted. That alone makes it more trouble than it's worth."

Oz smiled and sighed. "This is why everyone should grow up with a sister or three. You just don't get it."

Jake was taken aback; it had been a very long time since anyone had come right out and told him he was missing something. It was like being splashed with freezing water, like snapping out of a trance. He stared at Oz, unsure of what to say.

"That ship was your home for what, five years?" Oz asked.

"Closer to six," Jake replied. He hadn't thought about the Samson at length in what seemed to be weeks. Even though he always saw it as a means to an end, and not much more, he did know every centimetre of it, and it was his home for most of his life.

"Well," Oz started with a grin. "Whether she realizes it or not, she's using it as a way to find out about you."

"She doesn't have to rebuild a wreck to do that," Jake said. "She could just ask."

"Not with you avoiding her."

"Avoiding her?" Jake replied. "We sat side by side for two shifts on the bridge yesterday."

"You were busy the whole time. You even ate in the command seat while you were reviewing security records looking for the vigilante crewmember who keeps killing Order of Eden agents aboard ship. Think about it; you work eighteen hours a day, pass out for six, and do it all over again. If you're not on the bridge, you're somewhere lending a hand with specialist's work."

Jake sighed before responding. "It's just like you said; busiest two weeks of your life, only I was knocked out for the first three days so I had to play catch up. Besides, some of that specialist's work won't get done unless one of the few people who are qualified get to it. Ayan was busy in the fabrication plant for over a week working on the replacement engines too, it's not like I'm making myself unavailable."

Oz shook his head, frustration bubbling to the surface. "Jake, you know what it's like aboard any ship when there's a lot to be done. Most of the time there is no time. You have to make an effort if you want to get anything outside of regular duties done. Do you want to get to know Ayan? I know there's something there, but do you want to try and follow through?"

Jake looked over his shoulder to check for anyone overhearing. It was early. Day shift wouldn't start for an hour and the hallway outside was dead silent.

Oz had struck a nerve. Things with Ayan hadn't been going badly, they just weren't going. He looked at her, was glad she was there but didn't know what to say. She was different. It had been years since he'd seen her and after the initial relief and joy at being reunited it became plain that she'd matured since he'd last known her.

He'd grown as well, learned to shut away his feelings and separate himself from the daily decisions he had to make as daptain. Having someone poke at that from out of nowhere was aggravating, especially since Oz was right. "I don't know how to talk to her. She asks about people on the ship, systems and what's going on aboard and I tell her all about them, but then I'm out of things to say. I'm not a charmer, and small talk may as well be a foreign language."

"You're nervous." Oz smiled, amused.

"I don't think so."

"Really?" Oz raised an eyebrow.

"Fine, yes, I'm nervous but there's more to it, at least Liam thinks so."

"He would," Oz said.

Jake nodded. "He said it's probably expectations getting in the way. She crossed several quadrants and survived Pandem to be here. I don't agree, I mean you, Jason, and Minh did the same thing and even though I can't believe you and Jason left careers behind, it doesn't get in the way of us getting on."

"But things are different with Ayan. You two had torches lit for each other before you met on the First Light. I remember talking about the sparks with Minh in simulations ten years ago."

"God, has it been that long?" Jake asked.

"Almost. I think Chief Grady's right. Then again, when isn't he? Anyway, the expectations are pretty hefty, she made the trip twice in two different bodies. You watched her die once and from what Laura told me you handled it well. With all due respect to Ayan's first go at life, watching her live is a lot harder. I spent years watching her fall apart and I'm still getting used to seeing her in the flesh. I mean, she looks different, like she's stepped out of one of those period movies set back on earth, but it's Ayan for sure. One of my best mates is back and it's great to see her in fit form but I'm still getting used to it. The only problem I have when I'm talking to her is reminding myself that she doesn't remember the last few years, other than that she's a gift."

"I know, and she's here, I can't believe it either," Jake agreed.

"And that makes it harder, I get it. Think about what she's going through. You sacrificed yourself so she and everyone else on the First Light could be free right when things were really starting to get good between you two," Oz said.

"That was Jonas."

"Don't you have all his memories? Do you remember doing it?" Oz asked.

Memories of being submerged in thick stasis fluid, of seeing General Collins and being helpless and determined to find freedom again regardless of the odds ran though Jake's mind. The emotions evoked by the memories were strong. The feeling of being helpless was unforgettable, terrifying, infuriating. Despite all the negative emotions, he remembered the satisfaction of knowing that his ship, her crew, and Ayan were all safely on their way home, that he had sacrificed his freedom for a reason. He knew the memories and emotions were copies. Jonas Valent had lived through those events, made those decisions and the copy was imprinted perfectly onto him. The distinction was only logical, however. Knowledge of their origin didn't dull the images, didn't rob the moments of their emotional teeth. "I remember."

"Then stop making the distinction between you and Jonas and move on. You're the only one who makes it. Look at Ayan. You see her as the one and only, not like some second generation afterthought. We see you the same way; as the one and only Jonas with some time out here and a new name. Laura was even saying the other day that it was hard not to call you Jonas because, even under the serious veneer you keep up, she could see the captain she knew on the First Light. You've had some hard years since we last knew you, but hell, everyone's had years since the First Light. I barely recognised Minh the first time I saw him. I remembered a scrawny, hyper little man, not a long haired, muscled little wise man. It didn't take a body switch for him to change, and in some ways he's grown more than anyone, even you. Hell, apparently he learned to play guitar, went even deeper into philosophical studies, and picked up Kendo while he was adrift out there, among God knows how many other things."

No one had put it that way. As the captain of the Samson, Jake always focused on projecting an image of strength, of confidence, and that had carried through to Triton. Regardless of what tricks his memory was playing on him, of how Jonas' experiences changed how he thought and felt, he maintained that image. Pandem was the hardening, the blending experience he needed to reconcile with the personality of Jonas Valent and who he knew himself to be: Jacob Valance, and it made being that visibly confident, knowledgeable captain figure easier. He wasn't aware that anyone else could see how much had changed beneath the surface or that he could be compared to Ayan, that in some way they had taken the parallel roads. For him, taking Jonas' memories on was a force of great change, but to everyone who had known Jonas it was what made him familiar.

Jake sat down on one of the plush sofas and nodded. "When I think back to my time on the Samson it's like everything was cold. The days lasted forever and taking on hunting jobs was just something I had to do while I looked for Alice."

"The man I saw on holovid didn't look like he hated his job," Oz said.

"You're right, some days there was nothing I'd rather do, but then I didn't know who I was really meant to be. When Jonas's memories kicked in, everything took on a whole new dimension. By the time we had taken Triton on it was all starting to come back so fast I didn't know what was going on, but it was like the difference between seeing the universe in black and white for years then seeing it in colour."

"Like you discovered you had a soul," Oz suggested.

Jake pointed a black clad finger at him and nodded. "Exactly. Now it's like I'm back."

"Like you're finally a real boy," Minh added from the doorway with a smirk.

"Sneaky monkey." Oz smiled back.

Minh wore the black, lightly armoured vacsuit assigned to all pilots under a gun belt and old earth style imitation leather bomber jacket. The jacket was armoured, had inertial dampeners, and an entire survival kit built in. Thanks to work done by Alice and Minh, and ideas taken from Jake's long coat, it had become a very practical garment. Without a moment's hesitation he dropped himself into an armchair. "Welcome to the Doctor McPatrick show. Today we're talking about identity crisis and how to talk to women."

"How long have you been listening in?" Oz laughed.

"Oh, since you didn't notice my comm squawk when I tuned in about fifteen minutes ago. Sounded like you guys were talking through something pretty heavy so I thought I'd just come up," Minh said.

"While listening in," Oz replied.

"How else am I supposed to know what's going on before I walk into a room?" Minh swept his black shoulder length hair out of his face and looked

Jake over. Even sitting at ease in an infirmary family room he looked like he was under a hundred pounds of armour. Not stiff, but ready for anything and hard enough to repel direct weapon's fire. He made a show of his inspection, squinting his eyes, shifting in his seat as if to get a better view of different sides, until he finally nodded. "You two make it sound so complicated when anyone can see that it's Jacob Valent sitting right there. The union of two halves have made a better whole. You are lucky to have come together the way you have, I think, and come with a family, friends, and a crew that trusts you. Maybe you should change your name to reflect your heritage, and to announce that you've taken the best of two people and become one. A lot of people still call you Valent, anyway. They watch the footage of us on the First Light, and the rumour files of Valance and don't see as much of a difference as you'd think," he shrugged and leaned back in his chair. "The old expression says it best, I think: 'it's all in your head.'" He paused a moment and cocked his head before going on. "Oh, and Ayan sees the same thing. There is a difference, though. I've never caught her calling you Jonas, so she has noticed differences. She doesn't much know what to say either, so you'd better get busy not talking at the same time in the same place."

Oz glanced at both of them and laughed.

Jake's quizzical expression was disarmed by laughter as well for a moment before he blurted, "What?"

"If you two can't talk to each other, then do something together," Minh explained. "She's got the right idea, rebuilding the Samson. It's your ship and she's just falling back on something she knows best - how to build. So you be there when she starts working on it and whatever is meant to happen will happen. I bet you'll be swapping stories before the first day's over."

"He's right, you know," Oz agreed.

Jake nodded. "I've been avoiding the Samson because I didn't want to see it out of commission. Maybe she has the right idea."

"She'd probably have some good ideas on improvements," Minh added.

An expression of mild alarm crossed Jake's face. "Okay, now I know I have to be there."

"So, raiders?" Minh asked.

Jake nodded. "We got a message before we emerged. There's at least one carrier. You're going in first as a scouting patrol. Stay under cover, scan whatever's hiding behind the obscuring field so we know what we're dealing with, and try to get them to follow you out."

"Gotcha. Get the lay of the land and piss them off enough to come out and play," Minh confirmed with a wink.

Jake's command and control unit blinked and vibrated momentarily, informing him that a priority message was incoming. "Good morning, Stephanie," he answered.

"Do you know why Ashley's in the pilot's berth?" Stephanie asked peevishly.

"I have no idea. She might still be having trouble getting used to her quarters."

"All right, I'm on my way to wake her up early for the hypertransmitter activation. How is everything up there?"

"Good, I'm just about to head to the bridge," Jake replied. "The internal repairs finished up late last night."

"Wow, that's quick," Stephanie replied. "All right, see you there."

The channel closed with a faint beep. "This is going to be one hell of a day," Jake said quietly.

"I couldn't sleep. I can't wait to take the squadron out for the first time," Minh added.

"Just remember, the only person with experience in this system is Alice, so make sure you've taken in every bit of data we have on it and keep checking in with flight control," Oz said.

"Yes, Sir, Commander McPatrick, Sir." Minh saluted exaggeratedly. "No worries, we went through the brief last night, did a simulation, and I'll be taking them through it again this morning in briefing. That is, as soon as I dig out two more pilots from the red shift. Clutcher and Gomer couldn't hack the briefing simulation yesterday, so they're out."

"Clutcher couldn't hack it?"

"It was the asteroid field, triggered vertigo," Minh said. "If we had a psych on board we could help him, but we don't so he'll have to get over it on his own before he sees a real cockpit."

"Too bad. Tell me if there's anything I can do," Oz sympathized. "Is Ashley okay, by the way? She seemed fine on the bridge but if she's having trouble sleeping someone might want to look into that."

"She seems better than I've seen her since we took the Triton," Jake said. "Ashley grew up in close quarters, though. I bet she's been sleeping pretty well in the pilot berths. Besides, she was the youngest Samson crew member and from what I've seen the crowd down there isn't much older."

"Yup, there are a lot of young pilots down there," Minh said. "Some of them are pretty good, too. Ashley's overall scores put her in third on the sim leaderboard, she's pretty amazing."

"Have you gotten around to introducing yourself yet?" Oz asked with an impish grin.

Minh cleared his throat and shifted in his seat. "I haven't had time. Between qualifying, learning everything there is to know about flying off this ship, the fighters, and Paula following me around, I've barely seen my rack, let alone the bridge."

"Paula's been following you?" Jake asked.

"Oh just showing me around and making sure my pilots and I don't miss anything on preflight inspection," Minh stood and was on his way out of the room in one hasty, fluid motion. "Speaking of which, I have to get going. Good luck today."

"Good hunting," Oz called after him. "He's in his glory here, Jake. Making him Wing Commander after he qualified and placed at the top was the best move you could have made."

"I've never seen him this alive," Jake agreed. He stood and straightened his long coat. It was an unnecessary gesture since the weight of it drew it into shape. "There was no better choice, though. After qualifying, he managed to kick the crap out of every pilot's scores, then lead them on more successful simulated strike and defence missions than all the score leaders combined. All that practice while he was adrift worked out for him."

"I know, now he just has to prove himself in the field. He's not the only one. This'll be my first real turn at running the flight control deck."

"I'd rather have you nowhere else. You have experience and training at commanding a carrier," Jake said. "Besides, I noticed you staring at the flight control deck. I know it's where you want to be."

"Still reading my mind after all these years. I missed working with you Jake."

"You know, commanding this ship felt like work until you came aboard. If there's anything you ever want to do here, just say the word." They shook hands firmly, a spontaneous gesture that expressed the feeling of camaraderie that had been growing ever since the pair began working together aboard the Triton. "Let's get to the bridge."

CHAPTER 3
CLOSE QUARTERS COMFORT

The waves lapped gently at the bottoms of Ashley Lamport's bare feet as she dangled them over the edge of the old plastic dock. A lazy breeze caught strands of her long black hair. She sat at the broad end of Lake Chalmers, at the edge of Master Gamrie's estate where she could just barely see across to the tall vertical hydroponic farm on the opposite shore. They were almost like over-wide trees; their weathered and pockmarked surfaces had turned light brown and green with age.

Getting daily chores finished quickly enough to get away from the main house was hard, but time alone was rare, so it was worth the extra effort. The cool water tickled her toes and she smiled, marvelling at the perfect blue sky. She could hear the wind hiss through the tall green grass behind her as the breeze turned into a mild gust.

"Ashley, time to get up," Stephanie interrupted.

She didn't open her eyes, rolling over onto her stomach and sighing instead. "You wanted to be up in time for the first broadcast, remember?" Stephanie reminded as she opened the privacy curtain.

"Good dream," Ashley murmured. "Your timing sucks."

"When did you start sleeping in the lower berth? I had to look you up on my
comm."

Ashley sighed again and sat up. Her head brushed the bottom of the bunk
above. "Couple days ago. Haven't slept this well since the Samson. Between the bunks and morning yoga with the Chief, I've never felt better. Still want more sleep, though."

"I thought you liked your quarters, especially after taking the trouble to decorate."

"They're pretty, but it's too quiet on the Officer's deck. It's like sleeping in a
tomb."

"I got used to it, you should give it a chance."

"You have Frost to keep you warm at night." Ashley pulled a thin towel from a shallow overhead drawer and swung her legs out from the middle bunk.

"Might want a shirt?"

She waved the advice off. "No one cares here. 'Sides, I've got shorts on and a

towel." She snapped the waistband of her small black shorts as she dropped down.

The main pilot's berthing was a labyrinth of bunks stacked four high. Each one had storage space under the mattress, overhead, and at the foot, and a two point two metre tall human could sleep easily, as long as they didn't sit up. Blue and red privacy curtains stopped as much or as little sound as the occupants liked, and in an emergency each bunk could seal perfectly, saving the sleeper from sudden decompression if the air were to evacuate the berthing.

Ashley was short enough to sit up and move around in her bunk, and Stephanie had to admit that the younger woman looked more at peace than she'd been since Silver left her. It was immediately evident that Ashley had moved in.

All her essentials were packed into the bunk along with a few towels from the officer's quarters and some leisure clothing she'd collected from her time on the Samson. The pilot's berthing had been one of the first sections of the ship to employ the new, reprogrammed, cleaning bots. Ashley stepped around one of the three centimetre thick circular bots as it made its way down the corridor. When it finished the floor, it would make its way up the bunk sides, buffing and scrubbing silently as it went.

Stephanie followed her between the bunks. Most of the privacy curtains were closed; it was just before most people would be waking for morning shift. One young pilot who was just waking up, his arm hanging over the edge of his bunk, got an eyeful and averted his gaze as soon as he noticed Stephanie walking behind Ashley, scowling at him.

"You really like it down here?"

"You really like Frost waking you in the middle of the night?"

"Sometimes. When he doesn't have bar breath."

"Well, until I have someone to remind me that I'm not alone in the middle of the night, I'll be down here. Besides, I get to know the new pilots. They're nice, too."

"Of course they're nice, you're the Master of the Helm. Your walks to the shower in shorts and a strategically placed towel must be a real hit, too."

"I don't think anyone really notices since most have served in the military or on big industrial frigates. There's no privacy there. Besides, after growing up with even less privacy, I don't even notice. Hi, Jordan," Ashley waved as she passed a pair of young officers. The one who had two wings stretched across his cuffs smiled at her as she went by.

Stephanie couldn't help but play mother hen to her best friend occasionally. Ashley still assumed most people were good at heart. In the case of the pilot who she'd acknowledged on her way through the crowded berthing, it seemed she was right - he didn't so much as break eye contact as Ashley passed by.

"How was patrol?" Ashley asked over her shoulder.

"Didn't happen. We came out of the wormhole late."

"Don't worry, you'll be out there soon," she consoled cheerily as they passed into the group lavatory.

There were two dozen unisex toilet stalls to one side, sinks and hygiene product dispensers on the left, and a honeycomb of shower stalls at the end. In the centre were several pillars where the less modest crew members could shower without privacy. She flipped her light blue towel to Stephanie, who was already dressed in her black vacsuit uniform and armed for duty as Security Chief.

Stephanie cleared her throat. "Really? You're not even going to use a stall?"

"What? You were in the military, from what everyone says this is par for the course."

"You're the Master of the Helm, an officer." Stephanie shook her head. "What's the point of all the extra hours unless you at least get a divider while you're in the sonic?"

Ashley shrugged and stepped into a stall, snapping off her shorts. "As you wish, Miss Manners. Incoming!" She flicked the undergarment over the semitransparent divider at Stephanie, catching her in the side of the face.

"Nice. When I was in the military, they gave us five minutes to shit, shower, and get in gear on a good day. You should feel lucky Captain didn't just file us in with the rest of the crew when his old chums came aboard."

"Listen to you, all cynical and 'back in my day' like. I bet people here feel better seeing that I expect no better than they're getting. They see I sleep in the same bunks, take extra time to practice flying in the sims, and keep walking the learning curve. I just took another qualifier yesterday, actually. When I upload my results to the next registered port I'll have a qual for F class ships to add to my license."

"Congratulations, I'm sure you're providing a great example. Captain's probably impressed too, but-"

"You think so?" Ashley interrupted enthusiastically. "Enough for a raise, maybe?"

"If he can afford it, but back to my point: the people in these bunks are supposed to take orders from you. That's one of the reasons why Officers get their own quarters, so they know you're in a higher position."

"Where'd you hear that?" Ashley asked. "I can give them advice, sure, and I'm their superior, but the fighter wing isn't even in my chain of command. I'm really just another pilot."

"Who flies the carrier for eight or so hours a day," Stephanie retorted.

"Yesterday was eleven. Get me a denta tab, 'kay?" Ashley directed as the water came on and sprayed her from all sides in hot jets. She pumped the shampoo dispenser and lathered.

Stephanie walked over to a dispenser and pressed the button that initiated a materialisation sequence that produced a small, minty green chewing tablet. On her way back she had to dodge a pair who were headed to shower stalls in a state of undress similar to Ashley. They apologised through grins.

"Does this berth have to be unisex, though? I mean, this isn't really a military ship." Stephanie stuck the denta tab in Ashley's mouth over the divider, which was just low enough so she could see the top half of her face.

"Uh-huh, not military," Ashley replied sarcastically as she chomped the oral cleaning tablet. "Have you met our new First Officer?" Ashley rinsed her hair. Some of the spray caught Stephanie, who stepped to the side and leaned against the next stall. "I want be nearby when you try to tell him this isn't a military ship."

The sound of the floor sucking the water into the recycling system was almost so loud she had to yell. "I guess you're right. He has brought in a lot of good changes, though. It's easy to know your place on the ship now. You should have seen the report I had to make the day after Jake came back. It took me three hours to narrate and he only checked the fifteen minute summary. I nearly strangled him. Commander McPatrick isn't as stiff as you'd expect most military officers though, he seems to have a swagger too, like he's stepped out of some swashbuckler or cowboy movie. The more I see him and Captain together, the more I get the feeling we're turning pirate, not looking for alliances anywhere. Doesn't take long to figure out why they're old chums."

"I know, I like him. We call him Oz on the bridge, reminds me of that old kids' movie, only he's not some creepy guy behind a curtain and there's no yellow brick road," Ashley said before turning her face into the highest water spout.

"Sometimes I have no idea what you're talking about." Stephanie shook her head.

Ashley sputtered and leaned out of the stall, on tip toes, her hair gooped up with conditioner. "What? You never saw The Wizard of Oz?"

"That's what it's called? Now that I think of it..." Stephanie feigned pondering for a moment. "Nope, never saw it."

"God, what did you guys do when you were kids?" Ashley asked as she turned her head back under the spray.

"We played outside if we weren't in school."

"Ah well. I didn't get away often," Ashley said. "Used to spend time at the lake when I could, but most of the time I'd hide if I had spare time, so I watched old movies and played school games,"

"Guess they'd put you to work if they found you taking time out," Stephanie probed. She didn't ask about Ashley's past much. Asking a slave about their lives before they were freed was often touchy.

"Yup! They put me to work when I was about five, and I learned the when, where and how to hide so I could be a kid. I can't wait to call Fred, if it weren't for him I'd be a real mess," Ashley replied.

"You're not getting your hopes up too high, I hope. Jason Everin and the rest of the analysts are saying the death toll is over fifty percent for worlds hit with the Holocaust Virus, there's no telling-"

"I'm not too worried," Ashley said as she let a pair of shower heads massage her back. "They had slaves on Gamrie's estate because they didn't like bots much, so there really aren't many around. People owning people was the status thing in Onaku Province, androids worked in junkyards and farms. People thought they were junky and a little creepy."

"Creepy?"

"Yup, old androids who look almost human are creepy," Ashley explained.

"I never noticed," Stephanie said with a shrug. "Anyway, I just want you to be ready for anything."

"I know. Think you'll get a hold of your folks?"

"Pretty sure. I mean, it's not like they could afford anything you'd load an AI into. I'm just worried about my cousins in the refinery."

"If they're as clever as you they'll be fine."

"Here's hoping."

Ashley cut the water and turned on the sonic emitters. Most of the excess water was shaken off her skin under the vibrating pressure of the invisible waves. "I love this ship, if for no other reason 'cause everyone can use actual water for their showers and vibe most of the way dry," Ashley sighed, her voice affected by the vibrating air in the shower.

"Wing Commander on deck!" bellowed someone just outside the lavatory.

"It's Minh-Chu," Stephanie whispered as she stepped away from the cubicle and looked down the main passage between bunks. Ever since Captain Valance's return, the mid to low ranking crewmembers were being pressed into a more military order of conduct and she was glad to see it had carried down into the pilot's berth. All the pilots stopped what they were doing and stood at attention.

"Oh crap!" Ashley whispered, crouched below the edge of the privacy barrier. "Towel!"

"I thought you didn't care if anyone saw you in the buff?" Stephanie asked with a chuckle.

"Now I care, kay? Towel!" Ashley shot back in a whisper. Stephanie tossed the towel into the stall. "You fancy him."

"And?" Ashley shot back.

"Should I tell him?" Stephanie teased.

"Only if you want me to start using all your secrets in conversations anecdotally," Ashley threatened.

"I need two pilots to join my patrol. I'd prefer volunteers who've had a rest period sometime in the last sixteen hours," Minh-Chu announced.

Ashley hurriedly wrapped the towel around herself and checked her comm unit. "Crap, I've got duty in two hours otherwise I'd sign up."

"Captain probably wouldn't like that. You're overextended as is," Stephanie said.

"I know, but, um. Do you think Panloo would be willing to do a double shift?"

"I think she just did. Ah, too late, he's leaving. He got two pilots."

Ashley poked her head over the privacy barrier. "Jaime and Mia, they're good too."

"Good thing. They're investigating the asteroid field," Stephanie said.

"God, sometimes I wish I were just another member of the squadron," Ashley said.

"No you don't, a quarter of pilots don't come back from active engagements. Well, that's on most ships, anyway. Triton's crew is too new to have stats."

"I have the math and reflexes for it though, that's half the battle. I've also flown everything we have in sims and am only missing my D qualification."

"All the more reason why I'd rather have you right where you are," Stephanie said with a smile. "Safely guiding Triton around."

Ashley made her way back to her bunk with Stephanie close behind. "Yeah, most of the time I feel like a glorified bus driver. That's if I'm not trying to dodge torpedoes and God only knows what else with one of the biggest ships I've ever seen. It's like threading a needle with a chisel and a sledgehammer."

"You know you enjoy it."

Ashley smiled and sighed, pulling a black vacsuit with her rank insignia, seven silver wings on each cuff out of the storage compartment under her bunk mattress. "You know I do. How's security?"

"Better. Jake, I mean Captain Valance, has had more time to help out and Jason's been able to make sense of our surveillance systems without using an AI. He's even getting a grip on the Triton's operating system. The ship's starting to come to life again."

"I hear he's pretty amazing."

"Kind of scary, actually," Stephanie agreed quietly. "He used to be intelligence, like the top secret, dangerous mission kind of intelligence. I wouldn't have believed it but what he can do with encryption and what he's been able to figure out from the little we know about the killer aboard is amazing."

"Oh? Do you know who it is yet?" Ashley asked.

"No, only that he's not doing it randomly, he's only after Order of Eden freaks and he's really, really experienced," Stephanie replied, casually looking around for anyone listening in. It was pointless, there were two dozen people within earshot.

"All the more reason to stay here, surrounded by witnesses," Ashley said as she pulled her vacsuit up under her towel.

"So you're actually going to stay in the bunks," Stephanie said with mild disbelief.

"Well, yeah. Besides, maybe I can clear some time and set up to fly with Ronin." She sealed the vacsuit up most of the way and put on some lipstick and eyeliner. "Not just that, but I want to get into a star fighter for real. I've spent enough time in a simulated one. I want to show Ronin that I'm not just some software ace."

"Everyone who knows him calls him Minh," Stephanie corrected.

"I like Ronin. Find anything else out about him?" Ashley asked.

"I'm Chief of Security."

"Yeah, so?"

"I can't use that information for personal reasons," Stephanie chided.

"Oh come on! If you can't get the goods on your crewmates, what good is being Chief? Besides, I have to know who I'm flying with."

"Good point. You have the access, why don't you look him up?" Stephanie asked.

"He might check his Crewcast logs and see that I've been looking at him," Ashley whispered.

Stephanie rolled her eyes. "You know you're not in high school anymore, right?"

"I never went. Is this what it's like?"

"Rampant insecurity and raging hormones? Oh yeah," Stephanie chuckled.

"I thought that was pregnancy," Ashley said.

"Nope that's morning sickness, swollen feet, constant trips to the bathroom, and raging hormones."

"Right, gotcha." Ashley followed Stephanie to the lift, waving at a group of pilots just coming in from being on standby for the last shift. "So, you and Frost?"

"He was over last night. Bugger refuses to take the foot medical grew for him. He won't take anything our new Chief of Medical made for him because she's nafalli. I told him she just started the whole process, that humans took care of the rest because she can only put in half shifts but he won't listen."

"Oh, so you two are back together."

Stephanie gave Ashley a wilting look as the lift doors closed. "He was over last night."

"Oh, all night?" Ashley said. "Okay, I guess that's back together. He doesn't know about you and Captain?"

"No, and he won't. It's just not worth the grief," Stephanie said. "It's not as big a deal as you think it is either."

"It shows there's something there, pretty big something, I think. You guys have known each other for years too, so-"

"He's my captain, always has been. Beyond that, we're about as good as friends, that's it."

"Denial will only make it worse," Ashley said. "But I'd tell Frost anyway, especially if you don't think it's a big deal. If you and the chilly thug are meant to be, he'll just go blow off steam and come back. Besides, you were kind of on a break."

"Not really."

"Well, he pissed you off," Ashley countered.

"That's not any kind of reason to-" the lift doors opened to admit three maintenance members laden with tools and a cart with spare parts. "well, it's not a good enough reason."

"True." Ashley nodded. "Just trying to be on your side."

They were silent until they arrived on the command deck. It was obvious that important things were about to happen. The hustle and bustle of people moving between communications, conference rooms, flight control, and the bridge was intense. They strode across the dark decked concourse and through the officer's observation lounge's automatic double doors.

There were only a few seats left, the rest were filled with command deck personnel who were organising transmission packets and having a bite before their shifts began. The pair looked around and spotted a small two-seated table beside the transparent outer hull. On their way to their seats they stopped at a materialiser where Ashley ordered a tall, steamy blended coffee and a morning meal bar for them both.

The blue topped, glossy table reflected the dim light shed by the asteroid field outside. Black, grey, and white, the expansive, quickly rotating field of stone and ice stretched well out of sight. Some kind of gravitational source had directed it to settle into a thin, circular shape.

The light reflected towards them was from a distant dwarf star. Observation areas that faced the rear of the ship would have a clear view of it and the shadow of the planet nearest as it crossed in front every three hours.

Ashley sipped from the safety cup and sighed. "I can't believe the blends Ayan programmed into the fabber. I've never seen a hazelnut, but they taste amazing in the brew. It's like she reinvented coffee."

"I can't believe they call materialisers 'fabbers' on Earth," Stephanie smirked.

"It's a lot easier to say than 'materialiser' or 'energy-to-matter fabricator' like some people do. It's catching on, too; I even heard Captain say it yesterday." Ashley brought up the social display on her thin, five centimetre wide comm unit.

"Thirty eight messages?" Stephanie boggled. "You weren't kidding when you said you were starting to get popular."

"There are what, three thousand people on the ship?" she replied, her lisp weighing the word 'ship' down with unintentional emphasis. "I'd have to be a hermit not to have a few."

"I think I got four yesterday: one was from Laura Everin, another from March, and the other two were people who were trying to apply for security positions. I've had to cut several of my security people's access to Crewcast off during their shifts. People are obsessed. I don't see the point, really. If I wanted to hang out with crew members I'd rather do it face to face," Stephanie said.

"Aw, don't be bitter. You'll have more than you can handle before you know it. I can see why you'd have a harder time getting to know people on the ship, though; you are the head of security. People just have to notice you're not a buzz-kill. Oh, and what did March want?" Ashley asked.

"To give me crap for revoking his certifications," Stephanie said. "I told him he's off the honour system. He'll have to rebuild his profile with qualifiers instead of listing skills like he did when he joined the Samson crew. There's no way he's getting out of grade one maintenance."

"Oh, so that's where they put him," Ashley said.

"Yup, he's carting equipment around, hauling refuse to mass converters, and cleaning the last few unexplored parts of the ship. Captain assigned him the rank of Crewman's Mate."

"I thought Crewman was the lowest rank," Ashley chuckled. "Serves him right for nearly blowing us up over Sheffield. Hope he likes being a maintenance monkey, I don't think he'll be getting promoted."

"I thought you'd like that. He's still pissed though, and he's hanging out with Shamus now."

"That's gotta be awkward," Ashley said with a momentary cringe.

"He wants Shamus to set him up with you."

"Hell no. Not in a billion, trillion, frivillion years," Ashley replied.

"I don't think frivillion is a proper measure of time," Agameg said from behind Ashley.

"Just made it up. It means as long as anyone has ever imagined, plus a day." Ashley grinned up at him. "Nab a chair and have a seat."

Agameg did just that and sat down with his chocolaty breakfast drink. "Finn is finishing the last trial of the wormhole transmission systems before the first burst transmission. He says hello."

"I know, he sent me a message," Ashley said. "I guess he didn't sleep last night."

"He said he couldn't. When he found out Ayan wasn't going to take over the permanent installation of our stolen wormhole generator and hypertransmitter, he started taking things much more seriously. He doesn't blame her, not with her and Laura working on enhancing the engine rebuild that's set to start as soon as we find a safe port."

"Like he wasn't taking that thing seriously before? I don't think there's anyone who understands it better," Ashley said.

"You may be right. Working with Chief Grady, he even managed to get the micro fusion cells working with the rest of the ship, increasing our power output twenty percent while leaving enough independent cells inside the wormhole generator so it can power itself in an emergency," Agameg said.

"I love having an escape route," Ashley said. "I'm going to have to thank Finn after he gets a couple of days' sleep."

"How are the repairs on the bridge coming?" Stephanie asked.

"They're finished. Ayan seems to know how to motivate people while maintaining good relations," Agameg said. "I've never seen a human ship so busy but people seem to be happy following her and Chief Grady."

"Wow, that only took what, four days?"

"Three and a half. Everyone has already transferred there. It's like nothing happened, only the ready quarters have been moved. They're on top of the bridge now."

Ashley checked Alice's status and frowned.

"No change?" Stephanie asked, finishing the last bite of her breakfast bar.

"No, she's still out. Says here she might need some kind of synaptic therapy."

"You can see that?" Agameg asked. "I was only able to see her basic status on Crewcast."

"I guess Commander Everin added me to Alice's circle of friends when he set up the Crewcast thing," Ashley said. "I've gotta thank him for putting that on our comms, it's so fun."

"I think he set it up to make up for the lack of artificial intelligences aboard," Agameg said. "There's no other efficient way to sort through waiting messages and other information."

"It's so annoying," Stephanie grumbled. "Shamus keeps looking up my location and leaving message bombs."

"What's a message bomb?"

"He marks a place on the ship, records something and when I pass by it activates a message. I was on my way to the botanical gallery yesterday to check on Doctor Murlen's newest litter when out of nowhere an automated message comes through my comm."

"What did it say?" Ashley asked with a raised eyebrow.

"It was obnoxious! You know, I understand why the automated message triggers can be placed, I've already used them to mark patrol routes for some of my people, but using them as message bombs-"

"Oh, come on, what did it say?" she interrupted, anxious and pounding her feet on the deck.

"It whistled and said 'Nice tail!' I was so surprised I didn't realise it was over the comm and stopped in the middle of the main causeway, looking for him for a few seconds."

"Classy," Ashley giggled.

Even Agameg couldn't help but chuckle, squeezing his big, round green eyes closed to slits and huffing air. The fine tendrils adorning his face flipped and rippled.

"I swear he wouldn't know class if he were on a college campus," Stephanie complained.

"But you like him, otherwise you wouldn't let him under the covers," Ashley teased.

"Don't remind me," Stephanie groaned.

Agameg looked at his comm unit. "They'll be completing the scan of the immediate area and starting the hypertransmitter systems in a few minutes. We should go to the bridge."

"Do you think they'd mind? None of us are on duty," Ashley asked. "I mean, I could just catch my comm update here."

"All bridge officers, commanders and chiefs are invited," Stephanie said. "Let's go."

CHAPTER 4
CONNECTING TO THE GALAXY

The bridge was only two doors down from the officers' observation lounge. The large double door had been rebuilt as a large sliding one. The antiquated arms that once pulled the thick armoured hatches out of the doorway and drew them aside were nowhere to be seen.

At their approach, the heavy metre-thick ergranian enhanced armoured doors moved to the sides, their passage along the smooth slots in the floor and ceiling accentuated by a slight rumble underfoot.

Stephanie, Agameg, and Ashley couldn't help but stare at the rebuilt bridge. The semi-transparent deck plating had been tinted crimson and had a tacky, non-slip surface. The crew stations and other fixtures were finished in black and grey.

There was a wall of holographic status reports between the four command seats flanking the captain's chair and the other stations. The walls and ceiling made the entire place look like it was made of windows, convincingly displaying the vista around the ship, including. The field of stars above Triton was breathtaking.

The main bridge was fully crewed with Captain Jacob Valance in the centre. To his right was Ayan in a variation of the black vacsuit Triton uniform. She wore a long grey coat open at the front enough for all to see that she was as well armed as any crew member with a heavy side arm strapped to her leg. It was cut for style as well with long lines to make her look taller.

To Captain Valance's left was Terry Ozark McPatrick, or Oz as people had come to call him. Commander Jason Everin was beside him, working at a holographic interface and two-dimensional panel that was attached to the bottom of his seat with a thin arm.

Holographic representations of other key crewmembers such as Engineering Chief Grady, Lead Technician Finn and Gunnery Chief Frost were distributed along the edges of the bridge. All together there were another dozen crewmembers on that level, and when the trio looked down through the semi- transparent floor there was another area entirely.

The flight control Centre was below the main bridge and could be accessed via two man rampways or through the secondary command deck just beneath them. That was where Triton officers directed nearby traffic, fighter missions many other off ship endeavors were monitored. They had very little to do with the activation of the hypertransmitter systems that would open hundreds of miniature wormholes near the ship so they could communicate effectively with the known galaxy but they were quite busy nonetheless.

There was something going on, something very interesting that few people outside of the flight control Centre knew about. Anyone who had spent time on the temporary bridge knew that it was important, however, and that it warranted the first mass mobilization of Triton fighters and gunships. Chief Angelo Vercelli sat in the centre seat beneath. He was positioned so the Captain could look down and see his control and monitoring systems.

Oz would be taking over after the hypertransmitter was brought on line so he could personally oversee the direction of traffic around the ship and help direct the Wing Commander's mission. Everywhere the trio looked there was something interesting going on, some different activity that interacted with the most exciting morning Triton had seen since anyone had gotten aboard.

"I thought you'd be here," Larry, Ashley's copilot said as he came to stand beside her. "Ready to dodge asteroids all day?"

"We're not going in are we? The flight plan said-"

"No, but they've been talking about taking Triton closer to the edge and skirting along so it's harder for Regent Galactic or anyone else to pick us up at a distance."

"Sounds fun," Ashley smiled.

"I thought you'd say that. It'll be just you and I at the helm for the first six hours."

"Just the way I like it. No newbie navigator to yap in my right ear. Who's joining us late in the shift?"

"Warren. That is if we're not pulled to prevent fatigue."

"Oh, he's not bad," Ashley said.

"Yup, he's getting better. Who are you transmitting to?" Larry asked.

"A few old friends. Just want to see if they're okay. You?"

"I have an uncle who settled coreward, he'll probably be happy I'm all right," Larry replied.

"Probably?" Ashley asked.

"He's a bit of a recluse," Larry explained. "We haven't been too chatty for a few years."

"Ah, well at least you have someone. I'm surprised at how many people just don't have anyone to send a message to," Ashley said.

"Well, the war comes with a cost," Larry said. "Looks like they're about to start things off." Larry nodded towards Captain Jacob Valance, who was standing up from the command seat. A whistle sounded over the ship wide communications network, indicating that the commanding officer was about to address the ship.

Silence fell over the bridge and flight control centre. "Soon communications between Triton and the civilized worlds will be something we take for granted," Captain Valance started, hoping he sounded pleasant but authoritative. There were fifteen essential crewmembers on the bridge and another ten non-essential onlookers. "But today we're taking three big steps that will make this ship feel like a home. Most of the messages you've sent to our comm office will be forwarded to their destinations after our new hypertransmitter comes online for the first time. We'll reopen communications with those same hubs and major worlds to accept replies when we can. We'll also be downloading news packets, entertainment and any messages that are addressed to registered members of the crew. Your comm units will be updated as we scan and clear incoming data.

The next first step we're taking today is the deployment of a full fighter wing and our larger refitted combat vessels led by Wing Commander Minh-Chu Buu. Those of you who spectate or compete in the training simulations would know him as Ronin. There are raiders attacking the station we've come to trade with and we plan on making a good impression. When we've secured the area we'll begin replacing the pair of primary thrusters that have been offline since Pandem. Once those repairs are complete I can start fulfilling my promises to you. We'll bring the fight to Regent Galactic and the Order of Eden by using our communications systems and fighters to locate the enemy. I also promise that we'll try to find a port where everyone can at the very least take shore leave on a nice sandy beach or in a great big entertainment centre. Let's get to work. Triton!"

"Triton!" Everyone within earshot called back. An enthusiastic cheer spread across the entire ship. Jake knew as he sat down that people were mostly excited at the prospect of leave, of better days and the rest of his speech had been informational as far as most of the crew was concerned. He didn't care, the confidence and order he'd seen fall into place since basic rank had been imposed along with some rudimentary military principles was worth celebrating as far as he was concerned.

It had been a busy time to say the least. As soon as he woke from utter exhaustion it seemed he was put to work. Triton spent two weeks in a wormhole en route to a broad, unnamed asteroid field that boasted several heavy points of gravity surrounding one large one. It had been claimed by a fringe harvesting company called Orrico, and wasn't listed as a destination available for leave. He expected to be confronted when Triton arrived, and hoped that he could strike a bargain that would win them a safe harbour while they repaired two of their main engines. Alice's notes said it was a well hidden, well defended outpost. According to the scans they'd taken it was evident that the post and a large area around it was hidden and everything outside it was electronically dead.

There was wreckage of all size scattered throughout and around the gargantuan asteroid ring, more wrecked hardware than he'd ever seen Raiders leave behind. Something else had happened, and the key to finding the details was inside the protected area, Jake was certain. The wealth of raw materials in the asteroid belt alone would be good enough to feed their matter converters and if there was a place to hide in the middle of the field they could make repairs in peace.

He looked to Ayan, who had worked as hard or harder than anyone and looked like she'd gotten up several hours too early. He couldn't help but smile at her. Jake hadn't had nearly as much time as he wanted to spend with her despite his desire to get to know her all over again. The biggest problem they had was finding something personal to talk about. He had no problem talking about the ship, the crew, but he was conversationally clumsy whenever he tried to bring up anything personal. It wasn't like they were picking up where they left off. Most of what he knew about her had been learned through simulations when he was back on Freeground. They had spoken for years and met as avatars before they ever met in person. Even though he'd never forget the time they had together on the First Light it had been cut short. They still had so much to learn about each other and he had no idea where to start.

Oz was a different story. He'd seasoned, gained experience as a Captain of his own ship. To Jake's surprise he never showed dissatisfaction at being the First Officer of the Triton. The easy relationship he'd formed with the man on the First Light reappeared within hours of serving beside him on the bridge. Theirs was an art of delegation and direction, each of them doing their absolute best to make sure that the Triton was safe, the crew was working at a sustainable pace, and that they had the right plans for the near future.

All the while they watched their friend, Minh-Chu Buu, who was in his absolute glory. With years of practice in hundreds of sims while he was adrift between the stars and experience before that in an actual starfighter he dove into the qualifications, the tournament ladder and the squadron training with the rest of the pilots. Their enthusiastic old friend found his way to the top in short order, and while it was evident that he'd honed his skills to a deadly point, he had also gained a keen understanding of strategy.

He was likeable, had the military training and discipline required for command and the few seasoned pilots aboard respected him. Jake appointed him as Triton's first Wing Commander after ten days and charged him with the continued training and leadership of all the pilots aboard. It was an obvious choice to anyone who had jumped in on a starfighter or fleet combat simulation while he was participating.

There was something else about Minh-Chu Buu that Jacob liked a great deal. Since Lorander Corporation rescued Minh from the remnant of a research station he'd spent years on, there was more to him. He had taken up meditation, seemed more sure of himself, and listed ancient stringed instruments as a point of fascination on his Crewcast profile. Years absent from the presence of others hadn't been idly spent, it seemed. He also had a close friendship with Ayan, it was almost as if he'd adopted her as his fourth sister.

After meeting with Liam Grady Ayan took a day to decide which project to work on. She undertook the daunting task of building replacement engines for the Triton. Six days of manufacture and assembly led to the pair of completed thrusters that filled the rear section of hangar three. They were ready to replace the thrusters Captain Wheeler had destroyed in their last engagement. When that was complete she involved herself with repairing the bridge and other complicated control systems. If she had time left Ayan would work with Jason Everin in composing several messages meant for the Freeground, Carthan and Timar governments. Her hope was to open a dialogue so she and Jake could form a relationship with them, whether it was for trade, privateering or an all out alliance. There was so much for her to catch up on that her gaze was constantly affixed to her comm unit. If that wasn't enough she also worked with Laura Everin, her long time best friend, to implement systems first used on The Silkstream prototypes into the main engines and other Triton propulsion systems. There was never enough time in a day.

Jacob couldn't help but think of Alice as they were about to start up the hypertransmitter systems. He had devised the plan behind the acquisition of the components required to build it but she made the plan work practically, and with fewer casualties than he would have dared to estimate. They had her to thank for the connection they were about to make with the rest of the galaxy.

There were five seats in the centre of the bridge, more than enough room for everyone he'd want beside him in the worst of times. Ayan, Oz, Jason and Alice. Of everything he'd gained thanks to his life after the First Light, Alice was the best. She had even topped off her plan to rescue him and the others from Pandem with a safe destination; an asteroid field well off the charts with a successful mining and trading operation perfect for extended repairs.

"You look light years away," Ayan whispered to him as she double checked the power feeds leading to the main wormhole emitter systems using a holographic schematic.

"I think they're waiting for you to give the order," Oz reminded him with a wry grin. "You're going to have to let me in on that thought later."

Jake recovered himself and cleared his throat, focusing on the main holographic display arranged in a semicircle in front of the main command seating. "All stations ready?"

"All stations report ready," Oz confirmed.

"Then flip the switch. Let's see what the galaxy's been up to."

The Triton's hypertransmitter systems came online soundlessly. Even though no one could see them with the naked eye everyone on the bridge knew that the stolen system was generating hundreds of micro wormholes a second, reaching out to distant solar systems, other hypertransmitters, space stations, digital way stations and major shipping lanes across the known galaxy.

At first a few messages trickled through, then Jason Everin's console lit up, followed by Jake's then Oz's and finally Ayan's. They were viewing a summary of collected data, hundreds of topics and titles scrolled by faster than they could read. Selecting one topic led to hundreds of subcategories that contained news reports, personal communications, financial reports, entertainment, purchasable designs, advertising and more advertising.

Jake checked his personal directory and caught names of people he'd come to know since he'd taken command of the Samson, a few law enforcement offices that wanted to offer him work as a bounty hunter or repossession agent and even a call to arms for the Triton herself which he promised himself he'd look into later. Then something he didn't expect caught his eye and he put his finger down on it before it could scroll up and out of sight. The title read: 'Captain Lucius Wheeler of the Order of Eden ship Saviour conducts a public execution of Triton crew members.' He tapped it open and glimpsed the face of a former crew member from the Samson, a man they called Silver.

Before anyone could see the small image he archived it. "Everything we're getting is quarantined, right?" Captain Valance asked Jason in a hushed tone.

"Yeah, why?" Jason Everin asked.

"Nothing can slip out?"

"Not with the block in place on everyone's comms. Only senior staff can start receiving news right away. General entertainment and personal messages have to be scanned," Jason explained.

Jake looked back and saw that the senior staff was just starting to receive updated news and new installments from their entertainment subscriptions. He looked across the faces of the crew and spotted Ashley eagerly bringing up one major news and entertainment report after another. The small holograms that hovered over her comm unit would have been a little comical if he didn't know what she'd be stumbling upon. "Ash, shut down your comm unit please."

She didn't look up at him at first, concentrating on the preview of a Hyper Pongo League game she was receiving instead. "Why? Something wrong with my comm?" Her expression fell in the next instant as she came across an advertisement for her ex-lover's public and evidently painful public execution. Silver's holographic face was ragged, his complexion sallow, eyes red, and his gums were receding terribly, bleeding openly. A set of cables had been drilled into his head like a crown. Another group had been driven into his neck, their entry points seeped with blood and pus. "Kill me, please kill me," begged Silver quietly, barely moving his mouth. As Ashley watched a signal was delivered to his brain. The slack and exhausted face on her display contorted and screamed, howled with reckless abandon.

Ashley's eyes were instantly brimming with tears, her opposite hand went over her mouth and as the image faded to be replaced with the message; TRAITORS DIE, ONLY ON JUSTICE ONE, 2137, she shook her head in horrified disbelief. "Oh no, no no no," she sobbed quietly.

Stephanie's arm went around her waist and she was guided to a side passage that led to the security office before anyone else could get to her.

Jake made eye contact with Stephanie as she turned away and was reassured by her knowing nod. She'd take care of her best friend, there was no one better on the ship. "Stop all justice feeds and archived programming," he ordered Jason as he turned around.

"Already on it. We'll have a master copy of everything in digital quarantine. Two other people have seen that advertisement though, it's marked as high priority on at least thirty major news feeds." Jason was silent for several moments as he worked the semicircular holographic display in front of him, there was so much information scrolling no one else could keep up. He turned white and shook his head; "They tortured some of them to make effective commercials. I'm sorry Jake."

"I should have seen this coming," Jacob replied quietly, trying to help sift through the more sensitive data.

"Let's hope the few people who received that ad didn't know anyone from the Samson and just skipped through it." Something else caught Jake's eye then and he brought up his financial information. He was confronted with a display filled with red marks. With a quick twitch of his finger he hid the financial report. "All right, have we sent all the crew's messages?"

"They're out," Jason said.

"Good, shut it down," Jake ordered.

"We planned for another nineteen minutes."

"I said shut it down," Jake reinforced firmly.

Ayan activated the kill switch for the wormhole system and it powered down. "On the brighter side, the test was a fantastic success." The initial technical report on the wormhole systems started to come in, filling the air in front of her with electrical schematics, power readings, wormhole trajectory, compression and emitter stress data.

"We contacted over twenty thousand nodes anonymously and released our packets into the network without origin markings. The communications systems that picked them up will automatically mark everyone's messages with their origin markers and it'll look like the crew's messages came from everywhere at once," Jason said as he confirmed that everything had been sent and accepted by at least one hypertransmitter node.

"Good. How often do large ships do that kind of thing?" Jake asked.

"All the time. Military ships, local pickets, frigates, pirates, slavers, you name it. They all like to keep their positions on the hush so anonymous transmissions are a must if they have a big enough vessel."

"I thought so. Send my congratulations to the crew and tell the flight deck to make final preparations to launch fighters. We need to clear out the raiders so we can make repairs and move on."

"Aye," Oz acknowledged, starting to stand.

Jake caught his arm and looked him straight in the eye. That expression was gravely serious.

Oz sat down. "Privacy mode, command seating," he ordered the bridge systems. A visual blurring and audio obscuring field surrounded the five command seats at the centre of the bridge. "What's going on Jake?"

"There's more to the public execution situation. Wheeler. He's hunting down former Samson and Triton crew members and making an example."

"Isn't Wheeler dead?" Ayan asked.

Jake didn't reply, only brought up a Justice One News Feed entry marked with the Regent Galactic and Order of Eden logo. As the program identification faded a gargantuan stadium appeared. It was marked with countless sponsor logos, even some of the front row attendants were covered with them. The green padded surface of the field surrounded a massive platform. Several humans hurried around, picking up what appeared to be small mechanical and organic parts from the synthetic turf.

"This is a half time show?" Ayan asked, quietly appalled as she pointed to the platform that had risen out of the centre of the field. It came equipped with a pit for musicians, trap doors, a long restraint rack with three prisoners under a black sheet and several heavily armed guards.

"Looks like it," Jake muttered.

"What sport is the field set up for?" Oz asked, looking at the ruled sections of the field.

"Crush League Rugby."

"I've heard of that. Cybernetics are legal and anything goes, right?"

"Yup. It's almost as popular as Hyper Pongo on the fringe," Jake said absently. "There, there he is," he commented as the holographic display focused in on a darkly dressed figure on stage. The caption beneath him marked him as Captain Lucius Wheeler, his grinning face looked over the tens of thousands who cheered at him expectantly. His dark hair was shorter, and he wore a Freeground vacsuit under a heavy black trench coat much like Jake's but it was impossible to identify him as anyone but Wheeler.

"So it's true, they weren't just faking him when the Saviour attacked the Triton." Jason commented.

"They must have had a scan of him. According to the Wheeler who died here he was in Vindyne's inventory for a long time," Jake added.

"Hello Segoma Five!" Wheeler called out as the band's pounding music subsided. The audience cheered with renewed gusto. "Welcome to the Order of Eden Half Time Show!" He waited for the applause, cheers and whistles to calm before going on. "I'm Lucius Wheeler, Captain of the Order of Eden ship Saviour and I have the pleasure of announcing the new most wanted man in the galaxy! Before I let you see the face of this traitor, let me tell you a few things about him. He was born on Freeground, an old trader station where people live hard, isolated lives and keep to themselves, hoarding needed supplies and overcharging travellers who are unfortunate enough to get caught in that area of dead space for food and repairs. I know all about it, after all, I was fortunate enough to escape about fifty years ago. This man is no brother of mine, or friend to us, however. After getting kicked out of the military and assigned to a console to review manifests all day he gathered a group of friends together and commandeered an old destroyer that was about to be decommissioned. They called it the First Light and began a crime spree as pirates and looters. They were captured by Vindyne eventually, but instead of going quietly our man here released a virus into their computers and escaped. That program, that very same program eventually evolved into the Holocaust Virus!" He exclaimed, outraged and thrusting his finger up into the sky. The audience was starting to rally, booing, hissing and shouting.

Wheeler let them go on, seemingly furious as he paced the length of the stage. With a surprising suddenness he stopped and whirled at the audience. "That's right! One man! One man with complete disregard for all his brethren removed the safety limiters on his personal artificial intelligence and unleashed it on the galaxy, ignoring the Eden Two Conventions and slaughtering billions! Our brothers! Our sisters! Our fathers and mothers died because this man did not want to face justice! He presents himself as a hero, a champion of justice and freedom and as soon as our own machines started slaughtering us he disappeared! But not before-" Wheeler took a breath and calmed down, addressing the audience in a conspiratorial tone. "-not before he could recruit hundreds of desperate souls. People who were unaware of his involvement, unaware that in truth he was the cause of their hardships. Most of them are aboard his new stolen ship now, the Triton, a ship he stole from a Sol Defence perimeter station. His new crew are serving him unaware that he has no way to pay them. Regent Galactic and the Order of Eden have frozen his accounts, petitioned the Core World Prime Justice to issue a galaxy wide search and destroy order and to review the evidence against him!" The crowd turned, cheering and beating a thunderous tattoo with their feet in the stands. "Before I go on, I want to thank Regent Galactic and the Order of Eden for finding a way, an expensive way, to protect us from the virus he unleashed. One hundred thousand credits is nothing to pay to be added to the program, and they have promised to add value to your payment at no extra charge. Let's hear it for them!"

He waited a moment as the audience cheered. "They didn't stop there! Today I have the pleasure, the privilege to present to you two Captains and a navigator who have willingly served the dread Captain Jacob Valance!" he whipped the sheet off of the restraint rack, revealing the stripped, emaciated forms of two women and a man.

"Oh my God, who are they?" Ayan asked.

"The captains who retired from the Samson and bought my cargo haulers; Monica Albany of the Temperance, Tasha Pauley of the Bakersfield and my old navigator, Lawrence Silver. He and Ashley shared a bunk for a few months before he broke it off and left the ship when I quit hunting."

"Poor girl, no wonder she broke down," Ayan said.

"You know the game!" The image of Wheeler exclaimed excitedly. "On your Civicomm you have the names and crimes they've been convicted of and it's up to you to decide which one gets a dose of pain or should be given the final, merciful jolt that will burn their brains from the inside out and end it all! Remember! It's not just your decision, Jacob Valance's co-conspirators will only be put out of their misry once seventy percent of you vote for death, so make sure you don't press that red button too early! Make sure the people watching across the galaxy see how we treat pirates, looters, and mass murderers. Anyone who signs up for his crew can expect the same! Now let's have it! Mob justice! Mob justice!" he shouted, raising his arms, clapping his hands.

The crowd joined in, calling for blood, stomping their feet to the rhythm of their repetition; "Mob justice! Mob justice!"

"I can't hear you!" Wheeler prompted tauntingly, cupping a hand behind his ear.

The stadium erupted with renewed fervour as his hand hovered over a large red button and the band struck up an upbeat marching tune. The prisoners behind were exhausted, their heads hung low, forced to stand upright in the rack restraints. The brown haired woman on the left wearily shook her head as the other two wept, their shoulders shaking, bodies trembling with fear.

Tens of thousands of people cheered as Wheeler's hand came down on the red button and the rack lit up. In the next instant the prisoners were twitching, writhing, incoherently screaming and wailing as the audience manipulated controls that sent pain to one of them at a time. Wheeler took a deep, slow bow as he was lowered into the stage.

Jacob turned it off, exhaling shakily. His jaw was clenched, eyes cold, his hands clutched the arms of the Captain's chair. No one had ever seen him that angry, few had ever seen anyone so angry in fact. Jake's gaze was fixed to a point somewhere in the air in front of him as he spoke quietly; "Repair the ship. Harvest what we need, open trade talks with the raiders or clear them out so we can work with the station. I don't care who we're dealing with, just get us back in shape. Tell the crew what they can expect if they're captured." His head turned mechanically and those cold eyes met Jason Everin's. "Find Wheeler."

"That transmission is four days old, he could be-" Jason began to reply.

"Find him!" Captain Valance shot to his feet and pointed at the front of the bridge, his outburst so sudden and furious that everyone on the bridge jumped. "If you can't find him then find us something to hunt down and tear to pieces! They want a menace? I'll give them one!" He turned and stalked off the bridge, his long black and crimson coat flipping out behind him.

Chapter 5
Blame

There was a moment's pause before Ayan was admitted inside the new captain's ready quarters. She was a bundle of nerves. Waiting for the door to open gave the knot in her belly a chance to grow and make her even more uneasy about approaching Jacob, who had become more of a mystery to her over the past two weeks.

The extended test results of the wormhole generator systems would wait. Besides, Finn was focusing on it and would tell Chief Grady if there were any problems. Preparations for the installation of two of the Triton's main engines were complete and the other,, less important internal repairs she was supervising had finished the day before. She was the only one on the bridge who had time to approach Captain Jacob Valance.

She wanted to, but at the same time she couldn't avoid the feeling that somehow she'd done something wrong. He was distant, difficult to speak to, and never around when she had a spare moment. *Oh, come on!* she thought to herself, *You're a trained military officer, have seen war at point blank, survived more than most could imagine, and have led engineering crews through damage control during actual combat. You used to have enough confidence for four officers! What's more, we were overjoyed at being reunited two weeks ago. If there's been a tumble away since, there can't be much to getting back to where you were!*

The new ready quarters were larger than the old. After the hull in front of the bridge was repaired, the decision was made to make the fore officer's meeting room and ready quarters into another armoured layer for further fortification. The new ready quarters were located above the bridge, with a one man elevation pad so the captain could be there at a moment's notice.

There was also a private hallway that led directly to the captain's and first officer's ready quarters. That was the route she had chosen. For some reason, she didn't want everyone on the bridge to know she'd gone to see him, as though she didn't want her worry to become public knowledge. From what she'd seen, few people aboard ever worried about Captain Valance. She didn't know what would happen if they started.

He was in his dark long coat standing in front of the thick forward transparent bulkhead. The grey, blue, and white field of asteroids filled the view, stretching on out of sight. The light of a white star made them glitter like they were encrusted with gemstones as they moved past.

Ayan stepped inside and let the door close. "Are you all right?" Aloud, the words seemed thin; her voice was that of a shy petitioner.

"I'd ask you to sit down but they haven't brought the furniture up. Not a priority," he replied. His voice was different, lower, devoid of emotion. It was the sound of the wall she'd watched slowly build between them.

"I'm sorry about your old crew members. I wish I had known them."

"Silver was a nervous pretty boy." He let the statement hang in the air before sighing. "You would have gotten on well with the rest," he continued in a near whisper. He sounded much older somehow, tired. "Good people, trustworthy, steady."

Ayan watched, catching a reflection of his face in the transparent metal for a moment. It was etched with worry. That expression told her how she should approach him, at least. Ayan crossed the broad room slowly, then leaned against the hull beside him. "Talk to me Jake, what's going on?" she asked as his expression started to harden. The wall was going up again.

"It's over. I can't keep the Triton running with a crew this size, let alone finish recruiting a full crew for her. It's true, Regent Galactic has petitioned the Core World Trade Council and had my accounts frozen. It's bad enough that the galactic credit is failing, the old mass index is taking over again. I won't even have a chance to exchange my credits for old platinum bullion. My accounts may as well be empty. I have the repair cash stowed under the Samson's reactor and that's it."

"Oh, is that all?" Ayan couldn't help but prod him. She was starting to understand what had been happening since she'd come aboard with Oz, Jason, and Minh. Jake was keeping all his worries, all his problems, to himself. Running the ship day by day wasn't difficult for him, but handling the larger issues like the direction the ship was taking were weighing him down. He needed to find a confidant to vent to, and she'd been around enough stuffy officers to know how to guide someone into investing that trust in her.

"They'll mutiny! These aren't Freeground troops or some government outfit I have running the ship, they're mercenaries!" he exploded as he turned away from her and started pacing.

"Are they?" she asked. "You treat them like they're mercenaries, but are they really?"

"Of course they are! Most of them have no ties, half or more come with combat training, if they don't like what's happening aboard then they'll take action."

"I doubt it," she replied.

"What?" Jake looked at her as though she'd just switched languages.

"They're refugees," Ayan replied calmly. "A few of them are mercenaries, sure, but I've met most of the more questionable crew members and they're in their glory here. A lot of the crew never lived so well. They get three meals, a safe warm place to sleep, security to help them find their way and watch over them, and four days out of five they have an eight hour shift. There have been a lot of double shifts recently, but you should see them, Jake. They're working shoulder to shoulder knowing that this is their home. Some don't want leave, they just go virtual the moment their shift ends. I think the prevalent complaint is that you're not allowing leisure programs to run on the sim system."

Jake burst into a short laugh and threw up his hands. "So if I give them a bunch of games they'll keep working once they realise I'm dry?"

"That's not my point. There are a lot of ways a ship like this could make money, even enough to pay a full crew. How many does it take to run this ship, anyway?"

"Triton is fully crewed at thirty two hundred with an artificial intelligence and fifty one hundred without," Jake replied.

"Good! I know you've been thinking of going pirate ever since we got back from Pandem, so we go pirate. Tell the crew it'll be a while, maybe we'll lose a few, but we won't lose many. Frankly, I'm surprised. You've been out here longer, you know how to run a ship better than anyone without support."

"Never one this large. I'm not just a captain on a ship this size, I'm the mayor of a sizeable town. Besides, going pirate isn't as easy as it is in the holomovies. First you have to find a good mark, and in the case of this crew that means a Regent Galactic or Order of Eden ship or convoy. Maybe some corp that doesn't see you coming which usually starts with a man on the inside. We have to risk our necks taking whatever we can sell. Then we have to find someone with cash who wants the stuff. If we're lucky we can get signed on as a privateers, but with the bounty on my head there's no way any government in the sector will take us."

"So, register someone else as Triton's captain. That might make a loophole big enough for a government to work though. Maybe we leave the sector to find someone with a grudge against Regent. I'm sure the Order of Eden has enemies, I know Regent Galactic does."

"Like who?"

"I have no idea but I'm sure we can find someone. Between Jason's Intelligence background and our new hypertransmitter, I'm sure we can find someone."

Jake turned away and shook his head.

Ayan watched him. Something had him irritated. Turning pirate was an easy step forward from their current situation and she was sure the thought had occurred to him. If anyone knew how to lead a pirate ship, even a massive carrier like the Triton, it was Jake. No, there was something else causing his frustration. She wanted to know what it was, to get him past it so she could see if there was anything beneath, anything for her. "What's wrong?" The question seemed limp and wide of the mark. She cringed at the sound.

"I just thought I could buy more time. I thought I would have been able to cash my accounts in on Pandem."

"The banks were closed." Ayan chuckled; she couldn't help it. "Nothing you could do." Her eyes never left him as she leaned against the transparent bulkhead, the whirling expanse of asteroids behind her.

He sighed. "I'm glad to see you've gotten on well with the crew. They like you."

"They're easy to get on with. Most are just happy to get some direction," she replied.

He looked at her, she watched him. A long silence hung in the air. His expression started to harden, his back began to straighten. "We should get back to the bridge."

Ayan stepped forward with urgency and caught his hand before he completely turned away. "What's wrong? What's really wrong? Please."

The fearless, stoic Captain Valance had replaced the man she'd been speaking to just a moment before, the man she wished could stay just a little longer and he said, "Nothing."

She threw his hand away and stepped back. "God! I'm just trying to understand what's happening. No, wait, sorry! What's not happening for us! I didn't expect you to carry me through the airlock then down a path of rose petals into your quarters or anything, but I try to talk to you and that's just what I get." She squared her shoulders and drew her face down into a blockish expression and said, "nothing," in as flat and low a voice as she could manage. "All I'm asking is what's wrong and I'm starting to care less about what the answer is, as long as I get one!"

"It's you!" he burst in return.

All the fury and frustration faded from Ayan. Her face felt hot, her eyes started to well up, and she fought the instant urge to cry.

"Wait, I didn't mean-"

"You said it. I'll be a faithful officer, whatever you need. I'll even do it for free." She rushed past him and through the door before it opened all the way. Ayan stopped in the hall once she heard the door close, grateful for the narrow private passage. Her vision blurred as she looked back, hoping for him to pursue her. The dimly lit hall was empty.

Compartmentalisation. It was something she'd learned well during her time in the military. Regardless of how she felt, how she just wanted to find a dark, out of the way bunk and let it all out, she knew that Laura, Oz, Jason, and the rest of the crew were counting on her to be on the bridge, ready to take a position in command at a moment's notice. She took a few deep breaths, wiped away a few errant tears, and shut all her emotions away before striding the rest of the way down the hall.

Whatever embers were left for Jacob Valance and her would have to be fanned later.

CHAPTER 6
FIRST FLIGHT

"Are we launching or memorising the punter system from the inside?" Minh asked Oz as he came online. His squadron had completed a second briefing and been ready for over twenty eight minutes according to his command and control unit. Sure, he liked the chatter; most of the pilots with him got along fine, but they were all there to do one thing - fly. The exploration mission they were about to undertake was one of the most exciting things to happen on Triton since he started settling in.

It was also the first Triton-based mission Minh was leading outside of a simulation. He had to admit to fighting some tension at the prospect of running into raiders. Infantry training helped him shrug it off, but three of his pilots had only seen combat in simulations. They were hyper-realistic, but it still wasn't the real thing.

"We had a delay on the bridge. Everyone shows green on the flight deck, punting in thirty," Oz replied.

"Was there drama? Don't tell me I missed drama," Minh teased.

"There was drama," Oz replied wearily. "I'm sure it'll linger long enough for you to catch the tail end when you get back."

"Why am I always as far away from the action as I can get? I try to be exciting, but the ripples don't seem to radiate from this pebble; somehow I'm always at the far edge of the pool."

"If I didn't know you so well you'd be impossible to understand sometimes," Oz replied. "Punting in fifteen seconds."

"Shouldn't we focus on what we're doing?" asked Nathan from the rear seat of their Uriel fighter. He was Minh's sensor intercept officer, a great pilot in his own right but in need of seasoning. He had earned the call sign 'Slick' because he flattened his hair on his first flight from the Triton so his helmet wouldn't ruin his hairdo. No one told him that they didn't wear a helmet with the vacsuits they used, which did cover their heads but generally didn't leave one's hair a mess.

"I'm multitasking. Besides, we've done the checklist three times." The launch system catapulted them into the open space beneath Triton. Minh took direct control of his Uriel Fighter with his hands and feet, turning the ship into a skid, facing the asteroid field. His six squadron members followed his lead. "Good morning everyone, it's time to go see why this asteroid field is so damned quiet. There should be a whole bunch of eager traders and freighters here but for some reason we're not picking up so much as an active satellite. Oh, and we'll be passing through a magnetic obscuring field just to see what's on the other side. There should be raiders, according to some late intelligence." Minh double checked the intelligence update by glancing at the appropriate icon in his head's up display and was surprised to discover Oz and Jason had just added more information. "So, if I can't make nice with 'em, we're going to be on pest removal duty."

"Make nice? With raiders?" Slick asked.

"Those are the orders, check it," Minh replied, sending the update to his copilot's main display.

"You're right. Well, I guess a trade is a trade when you're out here on your own."

"I think, and this isn't to say that we're supposed to do much interpreting on our own, but I think they mean we're supposed to make nice if it's too late to save anyone. That's what I'm going with, anyway."

"Good thinking," Slick agreed.

Minh-Chu, or Ronin as every pilot and Flight Command officer called him, fired the six engines, sending the Uriel fighter towards the nearby asteroid field. The other fighters followed, fanning out in a predetermined forward pointed V formation so they could coordinate and get a more complete scan.

The asteroid field was massive, hundreds of thousands of kilometres across, and even though it had settled in a rapidly rotating plane, it was still several thousand kilometres deep. They approached the edge of the field quickly, drifting out on course to pass across the seemingly flat top of the whirling mass.

"I was wondering, why doesn't the Triton do this? I mean, doesn't she have a better sensor suite?" asked Jaime, coined 'Joyboy' because of his great big toothy grin, though he liked to tell people that the name was inspired by a few very memorable dates.

"Sure they do, but they're also a great big juicy target for anything that could be hiding in this mess. For all we know there's an EMP or nuke trap hiding in this mess."

"So they send seven fighters," replied Joyboy. "And here I was thinking we were too important to be expendable."

"If it makes you feel any better, there are another fourteen fighters and a gunship ready to launch on my say so. Hey Tempest, you're drifting too far to port. Get back in position," Ronin ordered.

"Aye, sorry, Sir."

"All right, we're moving on to formation two. Forty two hundred kilometres apart in a lateral V. SIOs coordinate so we're getting complete readings. Our top priority is finding signs of defence platforms, transmitters, outposts and anything else that could cause a problem or be worth communicating with," Minh ordered as he looked at the grey, white and blue expanse of asteroids ahead. There were no operable monitoring posts or other pieces of technology above the field. Triton's sensors had picked up a few long shipping containers and the wreckage of several old ones, but they were nowhere nearby.

"What about composition analysis or scouting for dense material for Triton's manufacturing systems?" asked Sprocket, so named because Mia had qualified as a pilot after being on the maintenance team ever since Triton was taken.

"Our uplink to Triton is feeding all that information to people there who can analyse the data better than any of us," Slick answered from behind Minh-Chu. "Now keep your eyes on what's important. There should be some kind of defence perimeter ahead." Minh's SIO sighed and spoke exclusively to him. "I can't wait until they finish rebuilding the analysis and status software without the AI components. I have to admit, I wouldn't mind being out of a job and taking the stick."

"If you're trying to distance yourself from me it won't work. You're already slotted as my wingman," Minh flipped the Uriel fighter upside down, continuing in a straight path towards the centre of the asteroid field. "Maybe even as a Squad Leader if you can get your scores up a little."

"With your cover and kill record I don't much mind," Slick replied. "All I ask is that you try being a little more predictable."

"Ha! Fat chance!" Minh burst as he looked across the churning, level field of asteroids. The group of fighters was starting to drift to the right, slowly matching the spin of the expanse of ice and stone. He watched for anything that didn't seem to belong, for something to lock his focus on that might tell him what happened before the Triton arrived. "There should be a ton of traffic if the information Alice included is even half right. She's the only one aboard who knew anything about this spot."

"I just think it's amazing that she even found this place. There's got to be a story behind that," Slick said from behind Minh as he looked through sensor data.

"I'm sure she'll be happy to tell you all about it as soon as she wakes up. Until then, I'm just glad she found us a cool place to park while Triton makes repairs."

"How long did they say it would take?" Slick asked.

"At least two days to rebuild the engines. The rest is mostly minor structural stuff, so it'll be done before the rebuild."

"Damn, they really knew where to hit us," Slick said. "I saw the damage they did to the engines, they're slag and scrap. If we didn't have our own manufacturing systems we'd be down to two engines indefinitely."

"You've got that right. Triton used to be Wheeler's ship so he knew exactly where his shots would count. He manned her with about a hundred people and a ton of automation."

"I believe it," Slick said as he reviewed raw scanner data. "Sprocket was saying that they're still finding looped circuits and control taps. She couldn't be happier to be out of maintenance."

"She earned it. Mia's a steady stick."

"Her name is Mia? I always have trouble getting to know people by their civvie names."

"To know a thing's name is to have power over it," Minh muttered as he scrolled through his threat assessment interface. The overlay on his vacsuit faceplate found no identifiable threat so he paid more attention to the formation of his fighter squad. Everyone was in place, doing a broad scan and gathering a fantastic amount of data, most of which would be reviewed in the Triton flight control centre.

"I thought that's what rank was for?" Slick asked.

"When someone's starting to panic they might not answer to a call sign, so it's important to know their real name. They didn't cover this when you trained with the military?"

"Well, they did in basis psych, but that was a long time ago. That, and I'm an infantry field analyst," Slick explained. "I'm still learning to apply that to being a Sensor Intercept Officer."

"Funny thing, I was in the infantry before I discovered the wonders of being a pilot. How goes the scanning?"

"A few terabytes of data. I'm seeing a lot of heavy metals, there really should be some kind of defence systems down there but there's nothing bleeding power or registering on thermal."

"Check your silhouette recognition," Minh advised, bringing up a small display and starting up the software for himself.

"Here?" Slick asked. "I mean, there's got to be a few thousand objects per square klick."

"I bet we'll find something before the barrier," Minh said as he brought up a shape and cross-referenced it, manipulating the interface with nothing more than his eye movements and the nerve impulse sensors in his vacsuit's headgear. "There, an armed hauler. It's right behind us, got twisted up in the asteroids."

"Scanning," Slick replied, shuffling his field of view to the coordinates Ronin fed his display. "You're right, and it was badly damaged by energy weapons fire."

"This is Luckshot, my SIO just found two disabled perimeter cannon emplacements. The blast profile she picked up on one of them matches Eden Fleet. The damage is dead cold though, so it happened at least a week ago."

"Good work. This is Ronin to Flight Operations," Minh said. "We have evidence of Eden Fleet here. Looks like they've been and gone, though."

"I show you just about to breach the obscuring field," Oz replied. "Proceed with caution. I want to know exactly what's in there. Remember, our resident astrophysicists said there could be a class two giant planet in there, so you could run out of space real fast," Oz replied.

Minh momentarily cleared all the secondary displays from his viewpoint and looked at the field ahead with his naked eye. The vista was blurred severely, but he was certain that there was a lot of empty space ahead. "I'm eye-balling the field and I'll bet my oversized officer's quarters that we'll just find a really thick rock in the middle of this."

"Refraction could be to blame for black space. Just be careful," Oz retorted neutrally. "It'd be pretty embarrassing to nose into a big rock on your first mission."

"You speak the naked truth, my friend." Minh checked the weapon systems and powered down the three particle accelerator cannons he'd loaded onto the fighter, leaving two missile pods, a pair of 21mm rail guns for him and another pair on a turret for Slick. "All right everyone, passing through the barrier. Redirect everything you can to your shields. We don't know what's waiting for us."

He watched the small flight status display at the bottom of his visor as the other six fighter crews followed orders. One of them had loaded themselves with energy-based weapons and he shook his head. "You're no longer allowed to determine your own load-out Finger. Looks like you need babysitting."

"What? What'd I do?" Finger asked defensively.

"You need to load at least two hull piercing weapons that can fire on reserve power alone. You knew it, you ignored it, and now you'll be leaving yourself unarmed every time you shunt all power to shields."

"I can take a few shots on what's left in the-"

"One more word and you're on your way back to Triton," Minh said firmly.

"Yes, Sir," Finger replied.

"Man, meeting you in the sims I'd never think you could be so serious," Slick mentioned off the squad channel as he ensured the ship's shields and power generation were set as high as possible.

"It's the price of doing it for real." Minh watched as the space blurred by the obscuring field loomed so largely that he couldn't see around it. His ship punched through; the energy shields around his fighter protected them from any electromagnetic interference. His eyes went wide.

Around a grey, brown, and white dwarf planet were arranged a massive latticework of docking platforms, factories, refineries, living sections, defensive systems, solar collectors, and other less notable subsections. Spaced evenly out across the dwarf planet's equator were five large installations with pylons extending out like fine silver horns. They were moving before their eyes, slowly shifting in waves around the top of the station's circular bases.

As Minh looked closer and checked his threat scanner, he noticed that there were very few power readings coming from the station. The defence systems were all marked as inoperable. The remnants of hundreds of other ships, most of them long range haulers, were adrift, dead in space.

As two of his squadron moved through the barrier behind him, he noticed what was keeping everything within the obscuring barrier that surrounded the dwarf planet. "I have at least nine cruisers, all different profiles. There are other active ships as well," Minh announced.

"Confirmed. Nine ships varying in mass, all armed. A couple are modified galleons, the others are cruisers. I see one carrier, looks like the command ship. There are about thirty other ships, between twenty-five and ninety meters in length. Looks like one of the cruisers is launching fighters. Half of them don't match anything on record. Wait-" Slick worked his comm controls for a moment, fine tuning and trying to filter out a layer of wavering static. "I have an emergency transmission here, looks like it was from a boosted personal comm. It's a digital stream of text that says the miners are holed up in the central complex. They were attacked and disarmed by Eden Fleet and a group of raiders just rushed the station. They don't think the two groups are connected, but they've been fighting a losing battle. The text is recent, seems to back up our intelligence."

"Eden Fleet and then raiders. That's epic bad luck," Minh said. "Are we getting a ping from Triton?"

"No. No two-way comm through the barrier and I can't raise the installation," Slick said.

"All right. Finger, take your scan results along with the text from the installation and head back through the barrier just far enough to get a message to Triton," Minh ordered.

"Aye!" Finger replied as his starfighter spun and accelerated in the opposite direction.

"This is RAD comm. We have laid claim to this salvage. If you do not leave immediately we will interpret your actions as a challenge and will force you out of our space," came the communication from the largest vessel, the Palamo.

"First, what's a RAD comm?" Minh asked.

"We are Royal Acquisition and Distribution, a licensed salvaging operation," replied the Palamo communications officer.

"You've laid claim to this entire space?" Minh asked.

"Yes. You read as Triton intercept forces. Please confirm."

"We're only here for safe harbour and trade. We could use some raw materials and would love a visit to the gift shop," Minh said.

"This is a salvage operation," the communications officer said sternly. "We will fire upon you if you proceed."

"All right, don't get testy," Minh replied. "Before I go, I'm wondering if you have a claim ticket or license number I can pass along to my carrier's command deck. I need something to go back to Captain Valance with and if this is a legitimate claim you should have some kind of fifty digit number or something. If not, well, I can't speak for myself, but the captain might have an issue with you claiming all this for yourselves while there are still people aboard the station. I mean, look at it all! Using the ships you have, it's at least a thousand trips back and forth between here and wherever you auction your crap off." Minh grinned.

"We-" the RAD officer started before unceremoniously closing his end of the channel.

"Are you seriously taunting this guy? They've got forty three ships out there right now," Slick said from behind him in an alarmed whisper.

"Shhh, Daddy's picking a fight," Minh replied. "If these are claim agents, I'm the Bad Luck Bear. I might not have much time out here on the raggedy edge, but I know Captain Valance wouldn't want to trade with raiders while there are station workers ready to be saved. There's nothing like a gratitude discount when you're trading."

"Please power down and prepare to be boarded," retorted the RAD communications officer.

"So you're raiders!" Minh laughed. "Should have said so. I'll be right back."

He cut communications and flipped his starfighter end over end, angling all engines to fire in the opposite direction, towards the barrier. "Okay, order everyone to head outside the barrier. Tell them to be ready for pursuit," Minh instructed Slick.

They passed through the barrier and Minh immediately heard Oz's voice. "- thirty five percent diamond."

"Say again?" Minh asked.

"That planetoid in the centre of the mining facility, it's over thirty five percent diamond according to the readings Finger relayed to us," Oz explained.

"I've spoken to a representative of the small fleet hiding inside the barrier. They call themselves RAD, Royal Acquisition and Distribution. Asked them for some kind of formal documentation and they choked," Minh reported.

"That confirms it, raiders. That organization doesn't have a listing in Triton's computer, and the only references we see on the Stellarnet update point to a bunch of commercial starliner and warehouse robberies."

"I think we can scare 'em off," Minh said.

"Hold position outside the barrier. Fire only if fired upon, we've got to play this right," Oz replied.

Oz turned from the main flight deck console and looked to where Captain Valance was coming down the bridge ramp. He could see Ayan in the command chair above. Something was wrong, he could tell, but it wasn't the time to bring it up. "What do you think? I'm sure if we released all the information we have, Minh would make the right decisions."

"No. We run this like they're raiders, nothing more. I'll tell you when we can change tactics," Captain Valance replied.

"Excuse me," interjected an older fellow with grey-blond hair. His brow was deeply furrowed. "That planetoid in the centre has twelve earth masses in less than a tenth of the space,"

"We know, you already interpreted Finger's scans and forwarded them to my station, thank you, Edward," Oz replied.

The older gentleman waved him off and went on. "Listen. Just from these crude scans I can see this was a dwarf star that burned out, leaving the diamond core behind. If you were to look at the station surrounding it, you'd see that there's a gravity mill built around the main installation and right in the middle of that there's a fire fight going on." He selected a small portion of a large circular segment in the middle of the station and enhanced the image. "They could be the station's proper owners defending their installation and these raiders as you call them are probably still fighting to take the station."

"All right, that's all I need to know," Captain Valance said before turning back towards the semi-transparent bridge ramp.

Edward caught his arm. "That's not all you need to know, Captain. If we could save the people in there, they could give us all kinds of information about this station and they might even trade with us. Furthermore, you might be able to convince them to give us enough raw diamond material to, say, enhance our manufacturing processes for two months. It would only take half a ton and with the process I see them using, that's nothing to them if their cultivation systems are still operational. It's important that your people don't do any more damage to the main installation than-"

Jake brushed off the man's hand. "I heard you. Return to your station. Forward completed analysis and situation data up the chain of command."

"What? I'm providing vital information here! I have to make sure you give my contributions the attention they deserve, that you don't just go blasting in and render the whole operation useless! As the only trained astrophysicist here, I'm uniquely qualified-"

Jake gripped his shoulder, looked him in the eye and spoke firmly, quietly. "No one has time to inflate your ego or consider your pride. Work within the chain of command from now on or I'll have you removed from the command deck permanently."

Edward turned red and stormed off the flight control deck, pulling his command and control unit off his arm and throwing it against the wall.

"Thank you," Oz said as he watched the changing status of the fighters holding position outside of the obscuring barrier. Their reinforcements were almost finished launching and about to start towards the energy field. "That's the first astrophysicist I've met who can't get a handle on the bigger picture."

"Do we have any contact from either side of the fighting on the station itself?" Captian Valance asked.

"Just the old text alert and the message from the Palamo. I'm thinking they lost access to whatever they jury-rigged to send that distress message shortly after it was sent."

Jake stared at the holographic representation of the tactical area. His eye was drawn to the pair of fighters that wove in and out of the obscuring energy barrier. They were marked Ronin and Finger. *Why doesn't it surprise me? We're getting enough sensor data from Finger and his SIO, Minh doesn't need to risk himself to supplement. Two scans are better than one though, I have to admit the picture is clearer thanks to the pair of them*, he thought as he shook his head. *Good to have Minh back.* He looked over Oz's shoulder where he was reviewing a more detailed scan of the station's central processing centre.

Many of the hallways to either side of the main structure had been decompressed and, from the visible heat silhouettes, he could tell there was an active firefight taking place. The computer had already marked the combatants by obvious sides, but he watched to make sure it had gotten it right. There were twenty-five hold outs, most likely station workers or stake holders, versus forty two attackers.

"What's the word, Jake?" Oz asked.

"Let's get in there." He read the damage report on the station at a glance and saw that most of the damage to the structure's defences had been done by weapons with Eden Fleet characteristics and nodded to himself. "Recognise the energy signatures?"

"They come up as Eden Fleet. Looks like these raiders didn't take the station; they came in after the bots did a number on it," Oz reported.

"I've seen it happen before. They jump in, disable engines, weapons, and power sources then get out. Regent Galactic forces showed up in Enreega a few hours after it happened there. I say we get in, rescue whoever's holding out in there and trade or salvage," Jake said.

"Better us than them. Ronin and Finger have started taking fire, it's small and they're not taking major hits. Looks like we got their attention." Oz smiled as he sent the order for their gunships to launch. "Alaka's going to like this."

"He's leading one of the teams?"

Oz nodded with a grin. "He volunteered before I had a chance to offer it to him. Anything to get some time away from his eleven kids."

"I could imagine," Jake laughed as he started back up the ramp.

"What do you want to do about the raiders?"

"Seek and destroy until they power down and surrender. We have no choice. The more expensive we make things for whoever's running the show, the faster he'll stand down."

"But if he starts blowing his people in our faces as a last resort..." Oz whispered.

"I know, this is only going to get more complicated. We don't have a choice. We're in hiding, nothing can leave the area and if we want to save the station so we can trade with whoever's left, we're going to have to risk our people. If the raiders get control of the station or get clear and make it into hyperspace, we'll have to find another place to hide. We can't repair our engines while we're on the move."

"Aye. I'll tell Chief Vega to get boarding crews ready. We're in it now."

Oz couldn't help but crack a smile as he overheard give Jake orders. "Take us to point three by twelve, best speed. Load torpedo bays and restrict the gunnery deck to seeker rounds. We're playing a supporting role, let the fighters do the heavy lifting." His captain was more assertive and confident than he'd been on the First Light, but he was without a doubt his captain. Being back on his bridge was like returning home after a long absence. It didn't matter which ship, which bridge, it still felt like home when the right people were aboard.

He looked up just in time to catch Ayan's reaction to Jake sitting down beside her in the captain's seat. She was making a point of ignoring him, and he was trying not to look at her.

Oz returned his attention to the larger tactical display and scrolling general status messages. Alaka and the flight crew of the Clever Dream marked themselves as loaded and ready while the Cold Reaver was still taking on soldiers. Fighters were launching from the punter hatches alongside the keel of the ship, their pilots reporting ready as they got clear and took up position just in front of the broad carrier.

He almost wished he was going along with the Clever Dream or Cold Reaver boarding crews, but Jake had assigned him exclusively to flight control. He knew where he was most needed: in command of the entire effort, coordinating with one of his fondest friends, Minh-Chu Buu, the crazy pilot.

Minh's fighter spun out of the barrier, dodging a few small plasma shells before he accelerated back down towards the asteroid field. "Breakfast staying down?"

"Barely. Where did you learn to fly, anyway?" asked Slick.

"Long story, maybe another time."

"Heads up, mission profile just changed. We have fourteen fighters, the

Clever Dream, and Cold Reaver incoming. Triton is taking position to box the raiders in. No one leaves. Our new orders are to seek and destroy unless we see a white flag or no power readings," Slick informed Minh.

"All right, we'll hold for reinforcements out here. Tell Finger to stop weaving before he gets slagged. When the Clever Dream and Cold Reaver arrive we'll cover them then break off to harry the raiders into shutting their engines down and surrendering or fleeing the station's orbit so Triton can cut them up."

"Passing that on to all fighters," Slick said.

"What? Why not just fly in and soften them up before the reinforcements arrive. They can't be very good shots if they can't hit Finger," Joyboy said a few moments later.

"We go in firing as a group," Minh said. "We're looking to cause as much terror and trauma as we can manage in the first few seconds so they turn and run into Triton's field of fire."

"They'll have a greater chance of hitting something if they're firing into a group," Finger retorted.

"Didn't you hear me the first time? If they think we're doing too much damage in the first few seconds, they'll bolt and we can rip them up from behind. Man up, buttercup, this is how we're doing it," Minh ordered with such finality that it surprised several pilots.

Slick burst into laughter the moment the communication line closed. "That's it, I'm calling Finger 'Buttercup' from now on, that's too rich. We have incoming. Marking targets, two small ships and three fighters."

Minh selected one of the larger, eighty metre long ships as his target and directed his fighter to intercept. "Mark your targets and break. Don't give them an easy shot. Hit them as hard as you can but don't forget to watch your spacing."

He watched the combat display as the six fighters with him selected their targets and broke to attack. His missile systems locked on to the vessel and he rapidly fired a volley of a dozen of the small, high speed projectiles as he side-slipped. They scattered and interwove, accelerating at an incredible rate. Before they struck, he released the safety on his guns and opened fire, strafing the length of the jaggedly designed, pointed ship from stem to stern. As he slid behind the enemy, he focused his fire on the engines.

His target's three turrets returned fire, unleashing blurring yellow blasts of energy. Several shots struck his shields and Minh whirled and zagged into the energy barrier for a few seconds before punching back out again on an altered course. It took several moments for the gunners aboard the enemy ship to correct their aim and he took advantage of the time.

Most of the missiles struck the port side of the vessel, reducing its shields to only a few megajoules and Minh opened fire on its engines. Great chunks of the vessel's armour flew off as his rounds burst through. Half the ion engines began to cool down and vent fuel, no longer operable. He could see the hull emitters running down the length of the vessel begin to power up, shading the rough armoured plates in red.

"They're about to head into hyperspace," Slick warned.

"No, they're not," Minh opened fire with all his active guns and brought the engine power up to full as he slipped behind the larger, less manoeuvrable ship. The rounds dug at the other ship's propulsion systems, sending bursts of fuel and shards of shrapnel spouting and spinning off in all directions. At the last instant, Minh launched half a dozen high-yield dumb fire missiles. Three of them struck, enough to cause a mass decompression at the rear of the ship and completely destroy its main thrusters. Its turrets stopped rotating, guns stopped firing and lights flickered out as the hulk drifted lopsidedly.

Minh didn't take the time to comment on his first victim of the day but switched his target to the nearest fighter and took note of Joyboy's position. He was firing at a thin, fixed wing fighter with his pulse cannons, cutting across its rear and turning the main body of his vessel to keep making sweeping attempts at hitting the enemy ship. Minh activated his particle acceleration cannons and took careful aim with his 21mm guns. "What's that fighter tracking? Anything?"

"He's trying to lock on to Sprocket," Slick replied.

Minh's particle cannons finished charging. He rechecked his aim, making sure that he wouldn't overshoot the fixed wing fighter and opened up with everything but his missiles. He directed his fighter into an upward skid as the enemy spun and tried to turn back towards the barrier. The fighter disintegrated after three seconds of firing. "Watch for an ejection and mark it for rescue," Minh instructed as he double-checked the combat screen.

There was one fighter left and Minh looked just in time to see Sprocket fire a volley of seeker missiles at it at minimum safe distance. The projectiles crossed the space between in an instant and the enemy fighter was destroyed in a violent burst of colliding metal and expanding gasses. Sprocket's fighter careened through the bulk of the wreckage at high speed, coming out the other side spinning.

"This is Dent! Declaring an emergency and ejecting!" Sprocket's Sensor Interception Officer announced. An explosive plume erupted from the Uriel fighter and a flashing red marker designated Dent's ejection seat for immediate rescue.

"You have him, Oz?" Minh asked.

"We're sending a rescue equipped Uriel now. What about Sprocket?"

Minh verified her status. Her vacsuit had logged devastating crush damage to her head before losing all function. "There's nothing to rescue," Minh replied as he forwarded the information and returned his focus to the combat display. There were no targets to monitor but it was better than looking at the cold verification of Sproket's death.

"Pilot down, acknowledged," replied Oz stiffly.

"The boarding crews and their escorts are almost here," Slick reminded.

"All right," Ronin addressed the rest of his fighter group, "start accelerating in a parallel trajectory and keep up with me. Change of plans, we're going to start securing the space inside the barrier before they arrive. Split up as soon as you cross inside, but concentrate fire. We need to take aggressive targets down as fast as possible."

Ronin didn't hesitate at the controls, whipping the engine pods and fuselage towards the barrier and firing his thrusters so hard that his starfighter could be seen for thousands of kilometres as a bright flare. As he approached, a shadow drifted across their path on the other side of the barrier.

"Obstacle spotted! Reverse thrust!" Slick shouted.

"Too late." Minh gritted his teeth as he tried to redirect the Uriel fighter into a turn. They careened through the field and saw that a line of old cargo containers had been sent to drift along the inner edge of the barrier and straight into their path. Their fighter collided hard enough to momentarily overwhelm the inertial compensator systems. Both Ronin and Slick were jostled hard in their seats. Weapons' fire streaked across the cockpit as the small gunship spun wildly, hurtling through a field of darkened, damaged vessels.

"We lost engine three, trying to realign the controls!" Slick announced, near panic.

"Stop! You'll only screw up my interface with the ship! I'll get us out of this," Minh retorted as he struggled with his hands and feet to compensate for the fighter's wild spin. Old reflexes had returned, and he looked into the direction of the spin, watched the orientation of his pod engines and shut down the stationary thrusters built into the fuselage.

A missile warning sounded.

"God dammit!" Minh shouted.

"Countermeasures launched!" Slick announced as several high heat, signal emitting decoys spiralled out from the rear of the vessel.

Minh reduced all the thrust generated by his engine pods to zero, rotated them manually and reactivated them at half power at counter angles to the spin. In under five seconds the fighter was stable.

A muffled thud sounded through the cockpit as a missile struck the hull. "Shields are down!"

Minh nodded and opened the throttle up to full, directing the craft towards the wreck of a massive barge. The fighter rattled and alarms chirped as impacts pinged and hammered against the hull. "Get our shields back up!" Minh ordered.

"It'll take a few seconds, get us under cover," Slick said. "Joyboy and his SIO are out of the fight, marked for rescue."

Minh eyed the drifting battlefield littered with wreckage, alive with weapons' fire. "Hope they drift in the right direction," he muttered. His fighter accelerated towards the drifting barge ahead under the power of their three remaining engine pods. Minh rotated the fuselage and marked the enemy fighter who was flying parallel above them, skidding sideways as he burst at them with his guns. Several more impacts struck their hull, one of the main engines flashed a damage warning.

In the space of one breath, Minh verified his target and ensured that his line of fire was clear of allies. In the next, he opened fire. The enemy fighter was flying in the open, too eager to take shots at Minh and his copilot. At the last second he tried to thrust for cover. It was too late. Minh's particle weapon and 21mm guns erupted with deadly force, ripping through the simpler, more lightly armoured fixed-wing starfighter and tearing it to shreds. As he spun the fuselage back in line with their course, Minh checked the tactical display. They were down to five fighters and the reinforcements were on their way in. "Send a transmission buoy outside the field with a warning, the raiders have stirred up a bunch of wrecks and a few larger meteors."

"Already programmed, launching," Slick said as the rear utility launcher fired.

"All right, convey orders to our group: take shots at the larger ships whenever they don't have a clear shot at an enemy fighter. Use this cover against the enemy as they hunt down fighters and smaller vessels. I'm taking the lead, we're hunting in a pack. Relay those orders to the second fighter group as they make it through the field, the third fighter group is to cover the Clever Dream and Cold Reaver."

"Got it, transmitting," Slick said.

Minh marked one of the larger, seventy meter ships with several active turrets and entered a formation for the four other fighters in his group to follow. "How is our ship?"

"I'm shutting down main engine two and we've lost a dorsal armour panel completely. I've restored two pod engines. Shields are recharged," Slick replied.

"Better than expected. Get ready to control the belly turret, targets of opportunity. Have fun, Slick," Minh chuckled.

"I was wondering when I'd get a chance." Slick took aim at a distant corvette class ship and fired as they broke cover momentarily.

Minh's fighter group fell in line behind him and they swerved between several dozen battered cargo containers. After a few moments of calm behind cover, they broke into the open, approaching the port side of the seventy meter long ship ahead. The five fighters opened fire as their prey tried to fend them off with four double turrets. One of the weapon emplacements burst apart while a rear compartment decompressed in a rush of gasses, expelling several crew members.

As Minh's group of five fighters crossed above the medium sized ship, their fuselages rotated so they could keep the damaged vessel in their sights and continue their relentless attack. Lights flickered through the portholes. "Maintain fire," Minh said. "Have your SIOs open up on those approaching fighters with their belly turrets. Let's bloody their noses."

Their reinforcements arrived, emerging through the barrier like a fire storm as they narrowly avoided drifting wreckage and opened fire on targets of opportunity. "Buster here with 2nd squad. Orders are to pack hunt on smaller vessels and to take shots on larger targets of opportunity," reported Sonya, one of Minh's squad leaders.

"Welcome to the show, Buster! I'm marking a nice, juicy target for you," Minh said as he marked a one hundred nine meter long, half-octagon shaped vessel closing on his fighter group. There were four fighters flying in formation with it.

"Got it, the Merry Cooper and fighter escort," Buster said. "Thanks, Ronin, you know how I love cracking ships with bad names."

Minh watched as his target suffered multiple decompressions and its cannons ceased to function. Energy readings from the ship dipped suddenly and he marked the pair of fighters that had come to its aid as his squad's next targets. His squadron followed his lead as he swung around a small group of meteors. Minh's cockpit lit up as they all opened fire on the older pair of fighters. They flew to pieces in seconds.

Minh looked at the tactical screen as he directed his wing behind a broad, detached solar arm that had been blown off the station in a previous firefight. "I see a fighter recall under way, what do you see?"

"All the remaining fighters are turning towards that ship," Slick highlighted a large three hundred meter carrier, the Viscount's Pride.

"Oz says no one escapes, so no one escapes," Minh said with a smile. "All right, this is the one that got Joyboy and his SIO. We're going to use all our dumb fire missiles in the first volley towards their aft dorsal section. Make sure you don't fire them right into their engines or they'll burn up before they hit. Strafe behind cover and focus fire guns on their port side until the missiles strike then widen the hole."

"This is the Clever Dream. We'll have a clear line of sight in a few seconds to support your strike. Expect a few extra missiles," reported Lieutenant Garrison, a senior security officer assigned to command the Clever Dream for the boarding action.

As soon as Minh's fighter group broke cover, dozens of missiles burst out of their pods. The group slipped sideways after emptying their launchers and took several hits themselves before reaching cover.

"I'm done, three engines down and I'm on backup power," reported Tempest.

"Can you make it back to the Triton?" Slick asked.

"I can."

"Good. Stay under cover while heading for the nearest barrier edge," Slick ordered. "Launch a buoy ahead of you to tell them that you're coming in damaged."

"Aye, sorry." She seemed genuinely disappointed as she closed the channel.

The remainder of Minh's group broke cover in time to see a hail of larger missiles from the Clever Dream zig and zag rapidly towards the Viscount's Pride. "Those are Screamer Missiles, I love that ship," Minh whispered as his fighter group opened fire with all their cannons. The enemy shot back in vain. Their projectiles were absorbed by his squad's shields or blocked by the nearby meteorites and damaged hulks they used as an intermittent defensive wall.

"That'll cause some damage," Slick chuckled. "Oh, man! That's about thirty hits!" he exclaimed as he watched the squadron's volley of dumb fire missiles strike the rear shields of the slow enemy vessel. The power levels of the shielding dropped drastically, then the screamer missiles impacted squarely against the aft lower hull. A few seconds passed and the shields failed completely.

Minh opened a channel broadcasting on all bands. "You will not be allowed to escape alive. Surrender," he warned.

"Should we cease fire, Ronin?" asked Finger.

"If we cease fire they might not take us seriously," he replied.

The next time his squadron broke cover, drifting between two collections of larger meteors, they dug into the rear of the ship. At first there was little apparent damage, but before they moved behind the next collection of stone and metal a large burst of white and grey erupted from the rear compartments.

"This is Viscount's Pride, we surrender. Powering down weapons. Request permission to take on damaged fighters."

"Are they actually powering down?" Minh asked Slick.

Slick watched the ship's profile on his sensors for a moment before answering. "I show less then one percent of their former power output. I don't think they had a choice, we hit something important."

"All right, tell them they're clear to take on their fighter compliment and watch for any extra power readings. Tell Buster to offer similar terms to her target," Minh said.

"She's chasing them out of the barrier now."

"Oh that's a bad day waiting to happen. Triton's going to cut them to ribbons. Too bad we'll miss it, I've wanted to see that gunnery deck in action since I took the tour."

"You and me both," Slick replied.

"This is the Cold Reaver, we're touching down on the station," announced the Cold Reaver's communications officer.

"Clever Dream touching down in ten seconds," reported Garrison.

CHAPTER 7
BOARDING

Two squads of heavily armed Triton soldiers occupied the main hold of the Clever Dream. They were clad in combat vacsuits with the new armour layer added. The extra armour looked like a slightly enlarged version of Captain Valance's combat vacsuit, with horizontal flexible metal slats from head to toe, heavier combat boots up to the knee, and a new face plate that borrowed from ancient Roman centurion's helmet with a crimson Triton skull painted over top. Victor wasn't surprised when the design was added by Jake Valance, it was obvious that the value of intimidation wasn't lost on the captain.

The extra layer of the armour contained extra life support, a compensation system for heavy gravity areas, a personal shield, more cloaking circuitry, an equipment module that could be dropped if necessary, and a backup computer that linked with their communication and control units. Victor's favourite feature of the suit was the gravity compensation systems, which included a synthetic muscle layer. The muscle made it possible to move normally while affected by heavy gravitational forces. In normal gravity, the suit could stand up while under three tons, and he couldn't wait to find an opportunity to test it under impractical conditions.

Closest to the debarkation ramp stood Alaka, whose armour required a special touch. Three of the squadron members behind him had fought at his side on Pandem, pressing in the constant tunnel war to maintain the perimeter around Mount Elbrus. Victor Davis was one of those tunnel fighters and he couldn't help but stare at his old comrade.

The Triton crew had converted the shell of an armoured augmentation suit, much like the loader suits used on the gunnery deck, only the shell they'd adapted for Alaka was like some modernised plate armour. The matte black surface was marked with the grey Triton skull on the right side of his chest. On the back there was a mount for his rebuilt beam weapon, integrated communications, sensor suite, personnel neutralisation system, and advanced survival kit for deep space. To look at the black armoured plates interlocking over the massive nafalli, you couldn't tell they had fit so much into the suit. In fact, no one facing Alaka would care to think what might be inside upon seeing him. He was huge, almost twice the height of some of the boarders, and the black suit made him look even more imposing and menacing.

Victor looked around at the Triton soldiers standing all around him. They were all tethered in place for safety, just in case the ride got rough. Each of them had a heavy rifle, a survival package built into the back of their armour, a helmet with the Triton skull imprinted on the face in crimson, rank insignia on their shoulders, a heavy sidearm, and a set of specialty gear.

He couldn't believe where he was, what he was doing. Pandem felt like it was years away. He would call the gear he carried alien if he'd seen it before spending days in simulations qualifying on every piece of equipment. The vacsuit was the most comfortable garment he'd ever worn. The armour practically put itself on and the sensor, targeting, communications and intelligence systems that were built into the whole outfit were so amazing that he'd only ever seen the like in science fiction movies.

He'd qualified fast, and knew he was at the top of the curve where skill and adaptability were concerned. Alaka had pulled strings to get him into his squad. Victor didn't intend to disappoint. Many of the security officers aboard Triton wanted a set of the boarding armour, but they could only manufacture so many at a time. In a way he was lucky to be assigned to one of the advance boarding squads. At the same time, Victor was keenly aware that he and the rest of the squad were given the armour because the security chief expected they'd need it.

Green light filled the hold. The tether at his shoulder released and the main ramp dropped open so fast he could feel the vibration of the door clashing against the deck.

Alaka moved out first, leading with the fighter class beam weapon. "Deploy and get clear. Captain wants the Clever Dream back aboard Triton as soon as possible," he said.

It was so much like the dozens of simulations Victor had participated in over the past seven days that he caught himself having one of the problems that Chief Vega had warned him and the newcomers about. For just a moment, he expected it to be a safe environment, where he only had to take his simulation node off to return to the comfort of the bunks or observation deck.

That wasn't the case, not this time. There was no simulation node to take off his temple or older sim goggles to pull off. The deck he was walking on was real, the inertial dampener and other compensator systems built into his boarding suit were really straining against the lethally intense gravity. The colossal, weathered, darkened hangar was a real place.

Victor took a deep breath and couldn't help but look outside at the field of wrecked debris and meteors drifting by as he exhaled. The stars and asteroid field were blurred by the obscuring field in the distance. Starfighters engaged raiders just kilometres away. At any moment one of those enemy ships could turn and fire into the open landing bay.

His encounter sensors came online and offered a map of the installation. He selected it by staring at the activation icon and thinking about it. The intelligence they'd gotten was right. An active firefight was under way nearby. One of the last squad members fell face first to the deck. Victor heard the air rush out of his lungs.

Alaka turned and regarded the fallen boarder. "I told you, if you don't know what you're doing, opt out. Your grav compensators should be set to auto adjust, there's no need to do it manually."

The soldier stood, catching his breath and getting to his feet. "I'm sorry, Sir, I saw the gravity rating on the briefing and thought I could do better setting it myself."

"Next time you think you know better, assume you're wrong and check with me first. Let's move," Alaka replied firmly, turning and leading the group at a run towards a broad service door that had been blown wide open. The forensic analysis suite flashed results in Victor's lower left field of view, informing him that an explosion had taken place several days before, had injured four people. The source of the explosion was just outside. His system presented the shape of the device, a low yield missile. Further evidence of much more recent small arms fire told the rest of the story as they ran towards the wide corridor.

In his rear view he could see the Clever Dream lift off, turn nimbly, and blast away from the station, shaking the structure underfoot. The Cold Reaver remained behind so they could have transportation back to Triton or to another part of the station. The two squadrons, led by Lieutenant Commander Radics, were already running at a fantastic pace towards another pair of loading doors. The deck plating was uneven where a pair of wide treads had run over it countless times. Walls to either side showed signs of serious damage, mostly from small arms fire, but there was evidence of grenade usage. The structure could take that kind of abuse, but fine wiring and tubing secured along the walls were another story. Liquid had frozen solid ahead, slicking the hall and one wall for several metres. There was no atmosphere, no life support at all, thanks to the damage done there and deeper inside the station. "Start scanning for active comm channels," Alaka ordered mildly in Victor's new subdermal comm. He was still getting used to hearing everyone's communications like they were talking straight into his ear, but he'd always wanted a hidden communicator, so when he found out they were being offered to security team members he jumped at the chance.

Keeping pace with the front of the squadron right behind Alaka as he ran down the broad hallways, he brought up the communications interface and set it to scan. "Search and select any conversations using combat terminology," he said to his communications system.

The emergency lights spaced along the sides of the hallway seemed to whip by as the two squads made a hasty rush towards the heat signatures ahead. Thanks to the armour Alaka's squads wore, they wouldn't give off any thermal readings. The only sign the raiders would have that someone was coming was the landing of the Cold Reaver and Clever Dream.

"One channel found," his suit informed him as it highlighted a weak proximity radio signal.

"Select and enhance."

Though faint, he could hear the raiders speaking. Victor supposed they thought they couldn't be overheard because their proximity radios were set to short range. There was no way they could foresee the level of sophistication and organisation that made serving on Triton such a pleasure. Using the receivers in the entire squad's armoured suits, Victor enhanced the proximity radio transmissions to perfect clarity and forwarded the channel to Alaka. "We're linked in."

"Nice job, Victor," Alaka said.

He couldn't help but be excited about being able to listen in. There was something about eavesdropping on the enemy that made him giddy. The day they got receiver relays set up around Mount Elbrus on Pandem was one of the best after the Fall. They could hear what the machines were collectively thinking. It was fantastic for the three days before the machines figured it out, before they started using encryption.

Victor's attention was called back to the present as one of the raiders asked; "-would anyone land and just take off? What are they doing putting two gunships on the deck then pulling one back?"

"I don't care, watch the cargo doors behind and keep cutting. I want to see the core of this installation by the end of the day," replied a female voice.

"Why don't we just seal up the cargo doors? Nothing to worry about if they can't get at us."

"We need to cut into Main Operations, otherwise we're stuck with ripping this place apart for scrap," replied the woman sternly.

Alaka held up a hand and a visual order for everyone to halt was broadcast across their heads up displays. "They don't know who we are or how many people are coming, let's take advantage." He crept towards the corner and poked the very tip of his beam weapon out into the open, using the barrel's sight to see what was down the hall ahead. The data spread to the rest of the squadron, mapping the two hundred seventeen meters of hallway and the large equipment storage area beyond.

There were forty two people in various styles of sealed vacsuits. Their equipment was piled beside one of the main armoured doors leading deeper into the installation and several of them were working to cut through while the others stood guard.

The weapons the raiders carried were compared against a list of known arms and identified in seconds. Victor remembered a tip from one of the tutorials he'd run when he first started working on his qualifications: Don't get bogged down with details. Scan through the offered information, take in what you need, and examine the more pertinent data as you notice them.

He scrolled through the list of arms and nodded to himself. They had one stationary slug thrower that would be useless in the heavy gravity, several plasma rifles that suffered from the same issue, and they were piled up with the rest of the equipment. Most of the raiders walked around with energy weapons that would work in the heavy gravity but wouldn't be as effective against their armour and personal shielding.

"Stealth up. We're going to surround them before I offer the captain's terms," Alaka ordered.

That was Victor's favourite part - the stealth systems developed by Freeground. He could stand right in front of someone and they couldn't tell he was there unless they bumped into him. Before his eyes, the entire squadron, even Alaka, as massive as he was, disappeared. His heads up display marked everyone's location so they wouldn't trip over each other, but to anyone else the hallway would seem empty.

"Move in, touch nothing. Let nothing touch you," Alaka ordered.

The squads had practiced the manoeuvre and ran in spaced out double file, watching their step with the assistance of the stealth system, which highlighted small objects and hot spots where they could give themselves away. The stealth systems were worthless if you weren't careful. Bumping into a loose bulkhead or kicking a broken bracket on the deck could alert others to your presence.

They ran right between the raiders standing watch beside the doors leading into the warehousing section. Victor's heads up display offered more forensic information but he knew what it was as he took a position behind a trio of armed raiders in bulky, discoloured vacuum suits. The firefight they had detected on their way in was over for the time being. The defenders had retreated behind the heavy interior doors the raiders worked to cut through. Several defenders had been killed, evidenced by the corpses piled in a corner, all wearing Caran Enterprises sealed work suits.

The northeastern quadrant of Victor's tactical display came to life, marking the other two squadrons. It was no surprise that Alaka and Radics had been coordinating all along, and the other squads were rushing in the large warehouse space in stealth mode. They fell into place as quickly and smoothly as Alaka's squadrons had and in moments the raiders were unknowingly surrounded by twenty-eight heavily armed Triton soldiers.

"Nice having the upper hand for a change, isn't it Vic?" chuckled Marc Burgess, one of the few people who had made it to Triton with him from Pandem.

"I'm not betting on that just yet. These raiders hit this installation hard, didn't care much for keeping it in any kind of usable shape, either."

"Commander Radics and I agree," Alaka said. "Here's what's going to happen. I'm going to offer Captain Valance's terms once. His orders are to offer terms, disarm and detain if they accept. If they resist, we kill them all. There could be other raiders in the installation, we have to make an example."

"Harsh," whispered one of the soldiers beside him.

"Realistic. He doesn't want us to risk our lives just so a prisoner can turn on us later," Commander Radics reinforced. His habit of pronouncing every word with clinical diction grated on some people, but he couldn't help it. He was an issyrian, and learned to speak the most common galactic languages in college. He spoke them the same way he learned them: clinically. "You have the honours, Alaka."

Alaka addressed the raiders on their own proximity radio frequency. "This is Commander Alaka Murlen of the Free Ship Triton. We are offering you one chance to cease your boarding operations and surrender arms. Our forces have you completely surrounded."

Everything stopped, raiders looked around, startled. "I don't see anyone!" announced one alarmed marauder.

"There's no way, I don't see anything," said another after he looked in all directions.

"This is a bluff. It's the workers trying to scare us off," said the female voice, silencing all others. "It's must be why they stopped jamming us. Get back to work."

Alaka fired a quick burst from his beam cannon at the raiders trying to cut through the heavy interior doors. The beam was a dead giveaway for Alaka's location, so he took several quick steps to the side after his shot. The stream of bright blue light startled the raiders and the cutters scurried away from the door.

Three raiders opened fire in Alaka's general direction. One shot struck his shoulder, revealing his location for a second before the massive nafalli managed to dive behind a stack of heavy crates.

"They've got some kind of cloaks! Fire at the open air and watch for hits!" shouted the female raider as she sprayed an arc of hot blue energy rounds between her comrades.

Victor dropped onto his belly and returned fire from the prone position. She was almost behind cover when he and a few other Triton soldiers scored flaring, scorching hits that broke through the skin of her old vacsuit.

"Jarisca's down! What do we do?" asked one panicked raider.

"Keep firing, you idiot! Like we have any other choice!"

"If you lay down arms we will allow you to surrender peacefully,"

Lieutenant Commander Radics announced over the proximity radio in response. The air was filled with bright yellow, red, and blue energetic bursts as the Triton troops took cover and returned fire precisely, taking their time, each man or woman disabling or killing only the threat nearest them. "What do we do, Commander?" asked one of Alaka's group as he ducked between two tall crates. He'd been shot twice. The first hit had done no damage, the second had heated his armour and vacsuit severely enough to cause second degree burns. Victor's screen marked him as being under the influence of localised painkillers and partially disabled.

"Shoot to kill," Radics replied before Alaka had a chance.

"Shoot to kill," Alaka agreed. The nafalli had crept behind several crates, taking him completely out of the direct line of fire.

Victor had ducked down nearby and couldn't help but wonder what would possess a group of people, especially raiders, to stand their ground and fight when they couldn't detect their attackers. He lined up his first shot, a marauder who was firing from bended knee, concentrating on firing into the open air at waist level. The raiders' efforts were pointless. Only five Triton soldiers had been noticeably hit, the injuries were minor, and they had all taken cover. With a quick burst from his high energy pulse rifle, Victor riddled the raider with rounds from chest to helmet. He crumpled to the deck as atmosphere escaped from his suit in a rush. Victor lined up three more such targets and with trained, cold precision, he squeezed the trigger, struck each target with lethal energy blasts in turn and watched as they each fell.

Alaka only opened fire after lining up more than one target. As Victor went about his butcher's work, he could see the stream of deadly light erupt from the nafalli commander's beam weapon in two second bursts, sweeping across two or more raiders at a time.

The entire incident lasted one minute and nineteen seconds according to Victor's vacsuit heads up display but it felt so much longer. By the time the last three raiders finally dropped their rifles and put their hands up, the large storage and sorting area was filled with bodies. He followed Alaka's lead as he moved in to lower a restraint ring around the nearest surrendering raider. The ring was a thin circular strip that expanded around a captive's torso then squeezed their forearms or wrists to pin them to their backs or sides. It was an Earth designed device, very easy to use and impossible to escape.

"No! Stay back!" a raider shouted frantically.

"Shut the fuck up, Arien!" one of his comrades cursed.

Across the clearing, Victor watched as one of the surrendering raiders leapt onto Lizelle, a Triton boarder, and held tightly. "Get off!" she screamed, startled.

Victor's heads up display flashed red and marked the raider atop her as an explosive hazard an instant before Lizelle and her assailant were obliterated in a blinding flash. He lost his footing and toppled to the deck. Victor's suit showed no damage, but the squad status screen alerted him to the death of eight members and injury of fourteen. Alaka had been knocked out and Lieutenant Commander Radics had been placed in stasis after his suit resealed and severed what was left of his ruined hand at the wrist.

At a glance it appeared that all the raiders, dead and alive, had exploded with the force of at least three grenades apiece. The Triton crew's vacsuits provided medical support, administering localised anaesthetics, putting the dead and dying into stasis and resealing breaches. He and a handful of others were left with minor armour damage. It was as though time had frozen as he looked around at the charred and broken storage area.

Crates made for heavy gravity environments had busted open, small craters marked dozens of places where the raider's bodies had detonated. The Triton boarding squad members who were still mobile picked themselves up and surveyed the scene carefully.

Victor couldn't help but cock his head as he watched one of his squad mates lower himself from a scattered pile of crates. He had been hurled up to the top of the three meter pile but somehow his armour had completely protected him. The black surface of the plating was still dented, scratched, and cracked, but according to Victor's visor, Junior Sargent Mills was in perfect health.

"What's the word Vic? What do we do?" asked Jenny Machad. He realised then that he was the ranking officer.

"Clever Dream, Cold Reaver. This is Sargent Victor Davis declaring an emergency." His own voice surprised him; he didn't expect to sound panicked. He made a conscious effort to calm down before he continued. "We've put down the raiders but they were carrying some kind of bomb we couldn't detect until the last second. We've got a lot of people down. Forwarding my squad status screen to you."

"This is the Cold Reaver. We see it, Sargent. The Clever Dream is currently engaged in the field and we've come under fire. There was an enemy squad hidden somewhere nearby. We've closed off the ship entrances but can't leave."

Victor looked at his squad status summary and at the devastated storehouse all around him. It looked like something had come along and bombed the hell out of the place. Whole stacks of crates had been reduced to rubble, the floor was cratered, unidentifiable debris was scattered about, and two large hatchways had been completely bowed and twisted. The area couldn't be secured, especially without reinforcements. His squad status screen told him that Alaka had taken a head injury and only seven of his people were mobile.

He looked towards the field medic software and hesitated for a moment. It was set to treat and preserve. The next urgency level would treat everyone using reconstructive nanobots, taking more risks. If it worked they might be back up to nineteen able boarding troops. With the fighter squadrons busy, the Clever Dream engaged, the Cold Reaver pinned down, and the Triton outside of the barrier, there was no way to get reinforcements.

"Have you been able to communicate with the survivors barricaded inside?" Vincent asked the Cold Reaver communications officer.

"No, as far as we can tell they've got life support and that's about it. There's also an EMP shield in place, looks pretty powerful. There's no getting a signal through as far as we can tell."

"An EMP shield? That's pretty high-tech for a jury-rigged solution. All right, stand by, Cold Reaver." Victor selected the two most critically injured squad members, made sure they were stable in stasis, and exempted them from nanobot treatment. "All right everyone, grab onto something, I'm enabling nanobots. We'll be back and fit in no time." He glanced at the activation icon and elevated the auto medic software's urgency level.

Nanobots were released into the bloodstreams of every injured soldier at once.

"Oh God, that's just weird. I'm watching my leg set itself, thank God for local anaesthetic," Jenny said as she leaned against a half-crushed crate.

There were many similar sentiments and a few complaints as less anaesthetised injuries were repaired, causing furious itching and burning sensations as the technology did its job. He watched Alaka's life signs change as his head injury was treated with nanobots and a cocktail of medications. After a few seconds, the system administered a stimulant and he was brought out of stasis.

"What hit us?" Alaka asked no one in particular.

"Looks like there were explosives on the raiders," Victor answered. "Someone set them off. The Cold Reaver would be ready to send another squad to back us up if they weren't pinned down. We must have missed a few raiders on our way in. Radics is out of commission and five others were killed. We have two more still in stasis, I didn't think they'd survive emergency medical measures."

"Good work, Vic. Everyone check your gear, especially your environment systems and weapons. Make sure they weren't seriously damaged in the explosion. We'll secure our injured, break into two groups, seek and destroy the remaining raiders. Our stealth systems are dead for the most part, so be careful," Alaka instructed. Everyone heard him open a channel to the fighter squadrons outside. "Ronin, are you receiving?"

"This is Slick, Ronin's a little busy. How can I help?"

"This is Alaka Murlen. We've taken casualties and the Cold Reaver is pinned down."

"All right, we'll instruct support to find a docking port closer to your location and pass the word onto Triton. Help should be on the way."

"Good. Until then we'll try to take the raiders from behind and clear a path. One more thing, it looks like all the raiders we've run into are wired with explosives. They pop if it looks like they're about to lose. That's what got us."

"I'll pass that on, thanks, Alaka."

Chapter 8
Broken Bird

The communications tower on the broad, rectangular hulled ship marked Palamo took several hits but continued to build a charge. Ronin strafed and rolled as he tried to close in. The rough plated hull of the three hundred and ten meter long ship showed scorch marks from several missiles and rounds from his squadron, but it was still intact for the most part.

The few energy weapon emplacements left fired at him and the Clever Dream well behind him. They had just finished coordinating their attack on the vessel's engines but didn't disable them in time. The Palamo had gained enough inertia to drift out of the obscuring barrier.

"Hurry the hell up, we can't take many more hits and if we don't take care of that tower, they'll finish charging their wormhole generator and get a message off," Slick reminded him.

"I know! Help me out with the belly turret here!" Ronin shot back.

"All our power is tied up in engines and shields," replied Slick. "Also, the turret is making a weird ka-chuck sound every time I engage. I don't trust it."

Several energy rounds struck the nose of their Uriel fighter, the last of which broke through and super heated a patch of the port-side hull. Ronin opened up with the single 21mm railgun and finally tore the transmission tower to pieces as the Palamo's nose breached the obscuring energy barrier. Ronin struggled with the controls as he watched one of his port engines super heat and explode into thousands of tiny pieces.

"That's it! We're down to no shields, three engines, and we've got a crack in the outer port-side hull that is spreading. Time to get back to the Triton," Slick said firmly.

"Redirect power to the emitters we have left and get us some cover. I think every gunner on that ship is trying to take us out," Ronin retorted as he took drastic evasive manoeuvres. The space around them was filled with energy weapons' fire, Ronin's heads up display flickered as a shot grazed them. "Something's dodgy with my instruments."

"Mine too, switching to backups."

All but Ronin's visor display went dark. It linked into the starfighter's basic control systems, providing only the most essential information about engine power, disposition, speed, and energy levels. "What did you do?"

"Our backups are dead, trying to switch back!" Slick replied.

"Don't bother! Just get on comms, get ready to transmit our boarding squads' status to the Triton." Ronin shook his head as he controlled the fighter manually using the foot pedals and sticks. The responsiveness of the machine was down and he had to exert much more force to maintain control. It took all his concentration to maintain the exertion and try to stay clear of the incoming fire from the Palamo's gunners.

They broke through the obscuring field and caught sight of the Triton. She was beginning a slow descent towards the field. The dorsal side was facing them, bristling with rail cannon turrets turning towards the Palamo. Ronin cringed as an energy round struck the aft side of his fighter's hull. A hissing sound filled the cockpit as atmosphere began to leak. "You okay back there?"

"The seat's secure, otherwise I'd get yanked out through the great big hole in our backside. Transmitting status to Triton," Slick replied.

"Tell them we're coming in for a landing while you're at it!" Ronin said as he tried to stabilise the fighter and correct their trajectory. The sudden decompression had caused them to drift between the Palamo and the Triton.

"Gunnery deck to Ronin. You're in the way, lad," informed Gunnery Chief Frost over the emergency channel.

"One moment, please," Ronin grunted through gritting teeth as he spun the fighter with the two remaining engines. The Triton loomed closer, only a few thousand kilometres away as he thrust as hard as he dared. The chassis of the starfighter groaned as they corrected course. The T-shaped grouping of railgun turrets spread across the top of the Triton lit up as Ronin's fighter narrowly slipped past the starboard edge of the massive carrier's hull. He noticed the sound of Slick's panic-quickened breathing and grinned. "A little close, you think?" he teased.

"A bit! I'm starting to look forward to having my own rig thanks to all the near-misses today. Speaking of which, we're cleared to land in bay three for two minutes."

Ronin struggled to get in line with the open landing bay door, firing the engines to slow down before they passed it altogether.

"You're going to miss it," Slick informed him, already calming down.

"Shhh!" Ronin replied, increasing thrust. The engine struts creaked under the pressure.

"You're going to lose engine two!"

"It's fine, can't afford to miss this landing otherwise we'll be back in line behind everyone else." Their trajectory finally pointed towards the landing bay and Ronin redirected the engines to slow them down. Out of the corner of his eye, he saw engine two flame out as its strut bent backwards and the cables carrying power to it tore. The sudden failure caused the fighter to spin as the landing bay loomed. He cut power and braced himself.

"Too fast!" Slick shouted.

Ronin didn't have time to reply. He knew it wasn't as bad as it looked, but second guessed himself as the Uriel starfighter struck down on its side and skidded several metres before stopping. He opened his eyes and looked around. They'd managed to stop on one of the elevator pads that led into the Triton's secondary hangar. It began lowering, drawing them into the main body of the ship. "Perfect, considering what's left of this thing."

"You are not going to tell me that was on purpose," Slick objected.

"Sure it was, and you can't prove otherwise," Ronin chuckled.

"I hate you."

The airlock door above them closed and the chamber pressurised before the elevation pad proceeded. Another elevation plate slid in place above them and gently rose to touch the other side of their fighter. As they emerged onto the pressurised secondary hangar, gravity reversed and increased. The lower elevation plate took the weight and an emergency response team rushed to extract them from the fighter, putting experience from countless drills to use.

The transparent metal cockpit hatch was quickly pried open in short order so Ronin and Slick could climb out with the team's assistance.

"What the hell are you doing out there?" Paula, the assistant deck chief, exclaimed furiously. "There's nothing left of this! It's not a collision derby! You should have ejected!" Her hundred thirty centimetre tall frame wouldn't be intimidating except for the enormous voice that screeched forth from it. Paula had become notorious for her raspy, high pitched voice and for scathing berating.

Ronin didn't bother looking at her as he walked away. "Nothing a shrink patch and sealing tape can't fix. Have your teams ready a Ramiel fighter, I'm heading back out."

"My ass, you're heading back out! Anyone who wrecks like this with a SIO right behind them shouldn't go out in a solo fighter, especially right after touching down!" Paula countered exasperatedly.

"She's right, Minh," added Slick. "You should hit the flight control deck, help Oz direct things from there. Besides, he said things are cooling down," Slick said.

"I'm fine, better than fine. The Clever Dream is running rescue ops and we'll have two fighters left to patrol after our damaged birds get aboard. I'm going back out."

"Listen to your SIO, Ronin," Paula pleaded irritably.

"Get a Ramiel down from the racks and into the punter now, that's an order, Assistant Chief." Ronin told Paula, pointing to the racks of pristine, predator-like single-seat Ramiel fighters lining the port side hull.

"Do it. He's the Wing Commander, it's his call," deck chief Vercelli reinforced quietly over the communicator.

"I'm taking your wing. You're not going out alone," Slick told him.

Ronin looked at him with mild surprise and nodded. "All right. Stay close."

"Cancel that," Oz interjected from the flight control deck. "You're pairing with Hood. Slick's stress levels are too high." He took a breath before going on. "You're going to help Triton cross the barrier now that we've disabled the larger ships and turned them back inside."

"Sounds like a plan. I'll be out in a couple of minutes." Ronin turned to Slick. "Sorry, looks like you'll be on your own next time."

Slick nodded. "I'll head to ready quarters and cool down. Oh, and congratulations."

Ronin cocked his head. "On making it back alive? That's no surprise."

"No, on making ace your first time out," Slick replied. "I counted six kills."

"It's not hard when we were so badly outnumbered," Ronin replied.

"You should get to the punter if you want to help coordinate out there, Minh. You're in shaft nineteen," Oz informed him over the comm. "You launch in three minutes."

CHAPTER 9
PLANS

"We have an update from the boarding squads, Captain," announced Oz. The bridge above him was abuzz with activity as they finished extending a gravity net around the disabled Palamo and redirecting it back into the obscuration field. "You have to look for yourself."

Jake pulled it up on his control pad, inviting Ayan to look over his shoulder. The situation at a glance was alarming. "Stephanie, get four squads ready for pick up. I'm calling the Cold Reaver back and you're going to secure the station personally," he ordered over the comm.

"Aye, Sir. We'll be on deck in ten, ready to board," Security Chief Stephanie Vega replied.

"I'll have Ronin relay an update to the station, he's on his way through the field right now," Oz added on the command comm channel.

"He's going back out?" Ayan asked.

"Affirmative, punting him in a minute," Oz replied.

"Are you sure he's good for another go out there? He just put down six fighters and disabled two mid-sized ships," Ayan said.

"His stats are healthier than mine, as cool as a cucumber," Oz replied. "Besides, things are pretty much under control and we need a good pilot to coordinate our passage through the barrier."

"Figures. Get him in a cockpit and he's right at home."

"His SIO is pretty shaken up, though," Oz replied. "Not that I can blame him. What Minh managed to set down on the deck didn't look much like a fighter. I think he left half of it out there."

"But they're okay?"

"Not a scratch. I'm taking Slick out of rotation for twenty hours, though. He'll be taking debriefing duties instead. Minh has a note here saying that he wants him to get familiar with the paperwork so he can take the second squad leader position."

"We have a problem," Jake said, pointing at the end of the boarding squad's report. "Stephanie," he opened a comm channel to the security chief. "We're dealing with a slave crew, they have det implants."

"You're kidding," Stephanie said. "Did they set them off down there?"

"Aye," Jake replied. "A whole incursion crew was killed as our team surrounded them."

"All right, taking it under advisement."

"What's a det implant?" Ayan asked.

Jake's eye was drawn to where Ashley was taking her place at the helm. She seemed focused and calm. Jake didn't bother keeping his voice down, even though slave control mechanisms used to be a sore topic. "It's a slaver's tool. They implant a device that can disable, kill, or detonate a slave."

"I had mine until Jake bought me," Ashley commented as she reviewed all the helm status information with a practiced hand. Larry, her navigator, was at her side, bringing up the most pertinent bits of information and making manoeuvre recommendations.

Ayan looked to her for a moment, stunned before returning her attention to Jake. "She was a slave?"

Jake nodded. "They had a remote disabling device implanted in her breastbone when she was two. I removed it with nanosurgeon bots when she joined my crew."

"I had no idea," Ayan said.

"I bought three slaves while I was running the Samson."

"I'm not the only one?" Ashley asked. "I'm hurt."

"There were two before you," Jake said.

"I'm hurt," Ashley repeated with a feigned huff.

"You were the most expensive," Jake said. "If that makes you feel better."

"It does!" Ashley beamed as she worked with Larry to prepare for their descent into the gargantuan obscuring field. "Why are we doing this again?" she whispered to him.

"Because we need a place to hide from the Order of Eden and Regent Galactic while we power our main systems down and replace two of our main engines," Larry replied.

"Gotcha, just wondering." She giggled as she settled into the pilot's chair as though she was resigning to being there for several hours.

"You know, I think I like her." Ayan whispered to Jason.

"Everyone does," Jake said, nodding.

"Now," Ayan said. "What do you do about slave crews?"

"Generally you stay the hell away from them, especially when they're wired up like live bombs," Jake told her.

"Can't you jam them or something?" Ayan asked.

"There's a small chance the jamming could set off the devices," Jason interjected. "One in a million, but-" he shrugged.

"He's right. I was thinking about jamming them, but he's right," Jake admitted. "I'm going to have to make a deal with the captain. He'll be one of the only life forms aboard without a det implant. Can you scan the Palamo, Agameg?"

Agameg Price nodded and passed the order to his tactical team. They started a focused scan of the slowly descending carrier beneath the Triton.

"There are three life forms without a det device, nine hundred and three with, and they're all armed."

Jake sat back and slowly shook his head. "The captain's ready to blow his whole crew if he has to."

"So he's holding his own crew hostage?"

Jake brought up a larger diagram of the rough, small rectangular carrier. The Palamo had been mapped in detail by the Triton's advanced scanners. There were a few damaged, decompressed sections but for the most part the ship was active. Red and white dots were scattered across the length of the vessel, designating several hundred life signs. "It looks like they're affecting emergency repairs. They really don't want us to take that ship."

"I'm detecting several tons of highly dense material, it could be raw diamond," Agameg highlighted.

"That would do it. A haul like that is worth a fortune, especially to a captain who doesn't have to pay his crew." Jake stared at the cross-section of the damaged vessel as he thought about the problem. "I hate slavers," he muttered at last.

"From what I'm seeing, it would take them weeks to repair the engines and there's too much damage to their emitter systems to even try to get into hyperspace," Ayan offered.

"All his other ships are disabled, and no match for us," Agameg advised.

"He's cornered," Jason commented.

Jake nodded slowly. "This couldn't be worse. I'm going aboard personally. Have a team assembled and order the Clever Dream to land on the Triton as soon as they finish recovering pilots."

"Are you sure that's a good idea, Jake? You're the most experienced commander aboard," Oz objected.

"I'm also not sending someone else aboard that ship. If the worst happens, the only person I want to blame is myself. How are we for manpower, Stephanie?"

"We have sixteen squads left, four with boarding qualifications," she replied over the comm.

"I'll take three. Are we covered after that if we have an incursion on the Triton?" Jake asked.

"Barely," Stephanie replied. "But yes, we're covered. Do you know something I don't, Captain? Should we be expecting a boarding party?"

"You never know. This group of ships could be just a part of a larger syndicate. I'll try to get all the intel I can from the captain when I board the Palamo."

"The Clever Dream's on approach, good luck, Sir," Stephanie said before closing the channel.

"You have the bridge," Jake said to Ayan. "Just get the Triton inside the energy barrier and establish a micro wormhole so you can monitor things outside the field."

Ayan took a deep breath, let it out, and nodded. "I'm ready, barely."

Jake stood, Ayan caught his hand. He looked to her in mild surprise. His eyes met her deep blues and he recognised her concern. It had been a long time since he'd seen anyone worry about him. It was disarming.

"Be careful," she whispered.

"I'm sorry about before. I'll see you soon," he reassured.

CHAPTER 10
RELENTLESS

The lights along the hall ceiling whipped by like illuminated dots and dashes as Nerine's bare running feet made the old deck grating clang and creak. Her left arm, shoulder, and cheek stung unlike anything she'd felt before; the mild pain killers she had hidden in her crew pouch made it bearable but she knew there would be scarring.

Other crew members moved hurriedly through the narrow halls and compartments, making emergency repairs. The Triton and her fighters had taken out their entire squadron and most of their support ships, and the Palamo was completely disabled. She never had a great affinity for engineering or power systems but she knew that when the crew started pulling cable free from the corridors and cross wiring things that they were in serious trouble.

She knew it wasn't worth the effort. Captain Gammin had to surrender, there was no other logical option, especially if the holograms she'd seen when she visited her father in the Enreega system were true and Captain Jacob Valance was commanding the Triton. He was a bounty hunter, a privateer, and a criminal wanted across the galaxy. If Captain Gammin actually thought he'd survive an encounter with him, he was crazier than she thought.

She stopped at a ladder leading to the deck below. The lifts were out; she'd have to climb down with her good arm. The ship rocked violently. The air stirred her hair and she heard the distant squeaking and grinding as an emergency bulkhead door slid into place. For a moment, everyone stopped what they were doing. Somewhere on the ship, and not too far off, a compartment had decompressed.

It would be easy to hate the Triton, her fighter pilots, and her captain, but if the rumour was true, if Captain Valance was actually a freedom fighter and not the scourge the Order of Eden made him out to be, then Captain Gammin was on the wrong side. He was a slaver, and the first thing she'd heard about Captain Valance was that he freed slaves. She hoped Kadri wouldn't regret sending the distress message to the Triton earlier that day.

"There you are!" David shouted from below. "What happened?"

"I got caught when something exploded in the hall," Nerine replied.

"That looks bad." David climbed up nimbly. He was an engine room grunt, with enough mechanical know-how to fix any of the old systems on the third hand carrier and enough sense to move very slowly up the chain of command. Out-doing your superiors too quickly was a good way to disappear mysteriously. "Here, loop the captain's bag around my neck then get on my back. I'll climb down for both of us."

Nerine nodded and looped her captain's sealed satchel around David's neck. Wrapping her arm and legs around David was painful but better than staying in the corridor. The bridge was the safest place and they would be welcome there. "Is it true that Captain Valance is trying to board? This isn't the station firing on us?" Nerine asked, still trying not to get her hopes up.

"Aye, Gammin's trying to escape, he just didn't want to leave this behind. He'll leave you in your condition, though."

"I know," Nerine said. "It would be cheaper for him to buy a new cabin girl than to get me fixed up."

David carefully set foot on the lower deck and put her on her feet. "Don't worry, I'll make sure we make it through," he reassured her.

"If what I heard about Captain Valance is true, we won't have to worry."

David gave the satchel back, knowing that, with her beauty spoiled, that bag was all that could make her valuable to the captain. "Don't get your hopes up. Gammin's doing everything he can to get away and he's not taking chances. He activated the detonators on the crews raiding the core of the station."

"What? So they're all-"

David nodded, his square jaw set. "Everyone on the cutting crew is gone. I'm pretty sure the only thing keeping him from doing the same to us is the fact that he's still aboard and there's a chance we could get the engines going. Just stay quiet and do what you have to until I find us a way out."

They rounded a corner. The bridge was only twenty paces down the main corridor. Captain Gammin spun on his heel. "Finally! Get your ass over here!"

Nerine started to run but was knocked off her feet as something collided with the outer hull. The hall lights went out, leaving only the white and green glow of the bridge illumination ahead. To her right she heard the sounds of metal grinding against metal and realised she was right in front of a primary airlock door.

David hurriedly helped Nerine to her feet as sparks showered the deck in front of her.

Captain Gammin was just getting to his feet. "Throw it!"

She did her best and it landed half-way.

"Stupid bitch! Pick it up and get in here! We have to leave!"

Nerine braved the sparks, raising her right arm and trying to duck under them.

One caught in her hair and she burned the back of her finger batting it out. David was right behind her as she picked up the bag, ran to the captain and handed it to him.

"Get these doors closed!" he shouted as he pounded the emergency seal button. The door inched part way out of the wall, the motor squealed with the effort of moving it further, but failed. "God dammit! If we don't get those doors closed, the bridge can't separate! Hurry!"

David turned to check it. "That impact warped the jamb," he reported, kicking the leading edge of the door hard. It made no difference. "I need to pry it straight." He brought out a ten centimetre tool and with a flick of his wrist it extended into a meter long pry bar.

"We're being boarded! Hurry!" the captain shouted.

The other slaves on the bridge looked near panic, even more so after looking at Nerine's injuries. Paudi, the first officer, looked at her and shook his dark brown and green pocked head slowly. "I think we leave this one behind. She is damaged."

Captain Gammin looked at her and was immediately furious.

Nerine cringed. She was in enough pain already; she raised her good arm to fend off what she knew might come.

"What have you gone and gotten yourself into now? You're not worth the clothes I bought you!" He took two quick steps and snatched her wrist.

"A pipe exploded!" Nerine explained. "I didn't hurt myself on purpose this time!"

"It's too late now, you're going to welcome this Valance bastard when he comes aboard!" He shoved her into the hall, knocking her down. "Now stay there!"

Nerine knew what was going to happen. The people breaking into the ship would come inside the hall and Captain Gammin would press a button on his amulet. She'd explode and kill whoever was nearest. It was quicker than being poisoned, the more common death the slave implants provided. Nerine had seen more crew members than she could count killed in such a way after the captain or his first officer caught them doing something they weren't supposed to be doing.

Yellow and white sparks filled the corridor behind her as she looked to David, who had stopped working altogether. She tried not to cry, but her lip quivered, her eyes watered, and it felt like her world was collapsing into itself. Captain Gammin walked back to the centre of the bridge and turned around. He caught sight of her staring at David. "Do you want to join her? Get back to work!" he shouted.

David stood slowly and dropped the pry bar. With determined steps, he walked down the corridor and stopped beside her.

"No! No, you can survive. Go with him, do what you have to," Nerine pleaded through shuddering sobs.

David gave her a small smile and shook his head slowly. "Couldn't live with myself if I just watched this happen." He took her uninjured hand.

The airlock door fell with a resounding clatter, shaking the deck grating underfoot.

Nerine looked into David's brown eyes. They were so strong, steady. His hand was firm, comforting. He had looked after her when the captain wasn't looking ever since the emergency services transport leaving the Enreega system was captured and she was taken on.

"Close your eyes, Baby," he whispered.

She let out a shuddering breath and did so. As someone came into the corridor just behind, she felt a crack in her chest that told her the compounds implanted in her were about to mix. In a few heartbeats, her life would end.

A hand grabbed her head roughly and tilted it to the side. Her eyes popped open at the feeling of a pinch on her neck. She watched as a figure in black and crimson armour grabbed David and pressed some kind of injector to his neck as well. It was mounted on the end of some kind of bracer on the man's left wrist.

Urgent hands grabbed her and she was pressed into the hall behind several other black-clad boarders. "Do you feel any pressure, any unusual warmth in your chest?" one of them, a woman, asked her hurriedly.

She realised then that she felt the opposite, like something cool was resting on her chest and shook her head. "Not warm. It's like someone put a cold glass of water on me."

"That's the nanobots working, they're disabling your slave device. Stay there, don't move."

David was sat down beside her and they were put in restraints. The boarders' movements were professional and quick. Before she knew it, they were sitting in the middle of several black-clad, heavily armed soldiers and she was watching the man who had injected her and David, saving their lives and most likely his own, stalk down the corridor towards Captain Gammin.

Gammin drew his pistol and fired several times. The dark figure stopped as several rounds struck him full on.

Nerine flinched at the sound of each shot, fearing for their rescuer and silently praying that he could somehow survive.

"Kneel," said the leader of the boarders. His voice sent a shiver through her. She could hear barely-restrained anger in his voice.

"He has a personal shield," David whispered. "You're right, it's Valance, it's got to be."

"So you've heard of him. Good," was all one of the boarders keeping watch over the corridor said from behind.

"You'll never take this ship! Every crew member has a charge installed and there are enough of them aboard to rupture every compartment!"

Captain Valance slowly drew his long coat aside and drew his heavy sidearm. "My people and I would survive. We have an easy escape route. I'll make sure you don't, though." He levelled the wide barrel of his sidearm at the first officer. "Tell me the codes to deactivate the slave implants," he demanded.

"Or what? You'll start killing people?" asked Paudi.

Gammin jumped as Captain Valance fired at his first officer, who ducked behind a console just in time. Instead of relenting, he fired again, then waited as the console erupted with blue and white sparks. "You and this man don't have an implant. That makes you the people responsible. Slavers." He fired several more times, each round exploding into the ruined console.

First Officer Paudi panicked and ran for better cover. Captain Valance caught him with a shot to the shoulder, blasting the limb part-way off with a cauterising explosive round.

Nerine watched wide-eyed as the first officer's momentum carried him to the deck, where he wailed in a smouldering heap. Jacob Valance took a step closer to get a clearer shot and fired four more times, ruining the man's torso and head. His aim settled back on Captain Gammin as the thermite rounds still sizzled and spat sparks out of his first officer's corpse. "Give me the codes for your ships and the control unit and I'll let you live. You can take anything that's left in the launch bay and leave."

Captain Gammin hurriedly pulled his ornate oval amulet off and tossed it to Captain Valance. It landed on the deck at his feet. He picked it up, keeping his weapon pointed at Gammin. "The code is 'dominator!'" the captain shouted.

Jacob Valance clutched the amulet in his hand for a moment. "You're lying," he said flatly.

"How could you-" Gammin blubbered. "I mean, you didn't even enter it!"

"He must have a neural link that allows him to communicate digitally," David whispered.

"What is the code?" Captain Valance asked in a quiet, menacing tone. "Dominator with zeroes instead of O's."

Jacob Valance stood completely still for a moment. The amulet was clutched in one hand, the chain dangling and catching the light from the bridge consoles. His other arm was extended, his heavy pistol levelled with a steady bead on Captain Gammin's head.

No one moved; the crew, boarders, Captain Gammin, and David all seemed to hold their breath. Her gaze was focused on the figure that filled the broad corridor. His black long coat was like a shadow that extended from the protective hood of his armoured vacuum suit. Crimson streaks ran like blood through the creases and edges of the unusual armour. His feet were steady, his thick-treaded boots were like pillar footings.

"Thank you," Captain Valance said finally.

Captain Gammin sighed, eyeing the barrel of the gun pointed at him dubiously. "I have a shipment of industrial diamonds in the hold. I'll trade them for ten slaves so I can properly man a hyperspace-capable ship I have in the hold. I'll be out of your hair-"

"Kneel."

The little hope in Captain Gammin's eyes died. Panic threatened as he stood struck still.

"Kneel," Captain Valance repeated. He wasn't yelling, he didn't seem out of control, only deeply, irrecoverably angry.

Captain Gammin did so, his pristine velvet pants picking up dust the moment his knees touched the deck. "Okay, take everything! I just need a ship."

Captain Valance placed the amulet in his coat interior pocket slowly and rechecked his aim. The long pistol was levelled at Gammin's face. The barrel was as steady as a structural beam, unwavering.

"You said I could-"

"I lied." Captain Valance pulled the trigger only once, obliterating Captain Gammin's face and everything behind it.

Nerine and David flinched when the shot went off. As she watched her captain's corpse slump to the floor, steam and flickering light rolling out of his ruined head, she realised that most of the boarding crew around her had jumped as well. No one expected him to actually kill Captain Gammin in cold blood. She didn't know what she felt. Nerine was numb as she watched Captain Valance casually shove his sidearm back into its holster and turn to face the boarding crew. "Treat her injuries." He pointed straight at her. "Patch into the ship systems and inform the crew that we've taken control and we'll be injecting them with nanobots to destroy their implants. I'll determine if the ship is safe and worth taking with the help of the existing staff."

"Yes, Sir," two of the boarding crew replied emphatically.

"And get them out of restraints," Valance said, gesturing to David and Nerine. "We're trying to make friends here," he added.

CHAPTER 11
FINDING A PLACE

Ayan tried to look at ease. It was difficult. The captain's seat wasn't the intimidating part of being the centre of the Triton command structure, it was the array of informational holographic displays that appeared as soon as you sat down. Her engineering status setup remained, but it was surrounded by an all-encompassing, semi-transparent cloud of displays that kept her informed on all the most important operational details.

It was different in the simulations. Everything looked just as real but the feeds weren't real, you could ignore something and people wouldn't die because they were waiting for a decision or extra information. Stephanie and Jacob's separate boarding actions, Minh's fighter squadron, and the situation on the Triton itself were all current, everything was happening right in front of her. The parties delegated to overseeing each act were listed along with an available history of their decisions.

The centre of the display held a three-fold tactical map, one for the outside of the obscuring field they had passed through, another centred around the station and another that showed a greater view of everything inside the obscuring field. It was a slow moving maelstrom of wreckage, rogue meteors from the asteroid belt, and other difficult to identify flotsam. Triton's defensive systems were functioning perfectly, the gravity shield kept all the smaller dangers at bay, and the lower gunners were effectively keeping a path clear so their ships could land safely. Triton was hidden, at long last. If anyone did a long range sensor sweep of the asteroid field, they'd be blocked by the obscuring field. Considering many critical resource cultivation operations used similar technology to hide their activity and inventory levels, they would be passed over - just another cultivation operation that didn't want to reveal its central structure or stock levels.

"I found it intimidating at first, too," Agameg whispered from the tactical command station. "They use a different kind of system where you're from?"

Ayan nodded as she settled in and looked at the status update of the boarding actions. "More simplified, but I'm also not trained on carrier operations."

Agameg Price paused a moment, cocking his head. "I didn't find it was that complicated when I was keeping watch on the bridge. May I see the display?"

Ayan made the command display public for a moment so everyone could see the semicircle of holographic interfaces that surrounded her. Jason shook his head and chuckled. "Now I know why Oz disappeared for three months for up-training before he took command of the Roi du Ciel. Multi-Mission Interfaces are no picnic at first."

Agmameg's green eyes stretched open into perfect glimmering circles and he made a chuffing sound of surprise. "The bridge watch status displays are much simpler. I understand your surprise and apologise. This is very complicated. Even with two hundred and fifty degree vision, I'm having difficulty tracking everything in front of you. I wish for luck."

"You mean 'you wish her luck,' right?" Ashley said over her shoulder.

"That, too," Agameg said with a grin that would look exaggerated on any human.

Ayan smiled as she made the display private again, glancing at a few others on the bridge who looked up long enough to see the myriad of images and information that the captain was expected to monitor. She hadn't had much of a chance to get to know Agameg, or anyone else aboard for that matter, but she had to admit he was one of her favourite crew members so far. She'd never met a shape shifter who remained in their native form before, and there were times when she caught herself staring. He'd just smile and wink, as though he knew she meant no harm. "It's all right. The systems on Triton are a lot easier to use in some ways. This much information on a Freeground terminal would be a lot more..." she searched for the word, distracted by the holo feed of Jacob's boarding action. They were almost completely through the inner airlock door.

"Raw," Jason finished for her. "I know, the operating system on this ship is amazing. It's only a little intelligent without an AI, something it has in common with Freeground software, but it's like the Sol system programmers are about a hundred years ahead."

Ayan tried not to react as Jake neutralized the pair of slaves that had been marked as volatile. The nanobots he injected them with interfered with the chemical reaction taking place in their breastbones just in time. Jake's heart rate dropped as soon as he was sure they were the only two walking bombs he had to deal with.

Her eye was drawn to Stephanie's mission status. She led her squads into a primary airlock. They immediately engaged a group of enslaved raiders. The firefight seemed desperate at first, then the enemy stopped firing. Someone out of sight screamed and Ayan realised that the Captain aboard the Palamo had somehow activated the detonation sequence for the raiders aboard the station.

"I need you to retreat, Chief Vega. Now," Ayan said quickly and clearly.

"Backtrack!" Stephanie called out. They made it just around the corner before the corridor they had been about to enter exploded, rocking the point of view perspectives on her holographic display. Ayan brought up the summarised status displays for the squads and breathed a sigh of relief as she saw Chief Vega's people had gotten to the minimum safe distance. "Thank you, Ayan. Glad to have you in transmission range," Chief Vega said.

"This is the Cold Reaver. It looks like the raiders pinning us down committed some kind of suicide. One of our landing struts are damaged but we're all right."

"Your guess isn't far off, Cold Reaver," Ayan said. "Let Chief Vega do a sweep of the area before you begin loading the injured."

"Aye, sitting tight until we get the all clear."

"Chief Vega, do a sweep between the Cold Reaver and the people we have at the inner door. When you arrive there, I'd like you to affix a conductive wire to the superstructure of the station then connect it to your reserve comm unit. We might be able to get a signal through the electromagnetic field they have set up."

"Will do, Ayan," Stephanie replied.

"Ayan, what's going on?" Jake asked over his private comm.

"It looks like the remainder of the raiders were just killed," Ayan's eyes widened as she saw Jake's boarding mission from his perspective. His sidearm was perfectly aimed at a wealthy looking fellow's head.

"My scan of his slave control unit tells me there's one more on the ship but the detonation order came from this one. He killed thirty one of his own people before handing it over to me."

She listened as Jake told the Captain to give him the password. "Ask him why he's killing his own people on the station," Ayan directed quietly.

Jake was interfaced with the amulet the captain used to control his slaves and the first password attempt failed. It warned him that he'd only get two more attempts. "I'm going to get the password and make sure the slaves are safe. They'll tell me what's going on aboard the station once they're free," he whispered. There was a determination in his tone that sounded dangerous.

Ayan had heard it before on the First Light, right before he ordered them to mercilessly obliterate a light carrier. She eyed the log being uploaded from the amulet. Captain Gammin didn't just use the control unit and slave implants to kill people, he used them to administer drug cocktails that made certain members more suggestible, rendered female members of the crew mostly unconscious and boosted alertness in others. The crimes Captain Gammin committed using the devices were endless and according to what she was seeing, he was constantly adding new slaves to his crew. The most common use for his amulet was torture, mostly on a young woman named Nerine.

She found the serial number of the other controller and brought up a cross section of the Palamo. A red dot designated the amulet's location, it was in one of the hangars.

A glance back at Jake's status told her that he'd managed to deactivate the captain's slave control unit. "Kneel," she heard him demand.

"Jake, we have a brig. We might need him for more information. He could be a member of a larger group," Ayan said hurriedly. She watched the rest of the exchange and cringed as Captain Gammin tried to bargain with Jake. Captain Valance's heart rate jumped, his neural statistics indicated a level of anger that would have most Freeground officers relieved of duty and suspended for a month.

"He won't do this again," Jake whispered over the private comm as he pulled the trigger.

Ayan looked away just in time to avoid seeing the mess his sidearm made of the man.

"What is it?" Jason asked in a whisper.

She shook her head and forwarded the whole record of Jake's boarding action to Jason. The display listed a new contact on the tactical map, a thirty four metre hyperspace-capable ship. "Oz, do you see this?" she asked.

"It's up on my station. My birds are on patrol, the party's over so I can spare a pair," Oz replied over bridge communications.

"I'll have Chief Frost hit them with EMP rounds. There's a slave controller on that ship; I want it disabled before we bring it aboard," Ayan informed him.

"All right, once it's disabled I'll have a Uriel haul it into landing bay two," Oz replied.

Frost came up on her display. "Somethin' for my gunners to shoot, lass?"

"Aye, disable only. Use EMP rounds," Ayan ordered.

"Done and done," Chief Frost acknowledged.

For the space of three seconds, five heavy gunnery turrets opened fire, sending hundreds of EMP railgun rounds towards the small interstellar ship. A flare of electromagnetic bursts obscured it for several seconds as the rounds discharged and the Triton's tactical system noted it as inert when the vessel came back into focus.

"There you go, Oz," Ayan said. "Have it brought in then take the command chair. I'm going down with four squads to meet whoever's on board personally."

"Already tired of commanding a carrier?" Oz asked with a chuckle.

"No, I want to see what kind of scum they dislodge from that ship and meet it personally. Jason can fill you in on what we're seeing up here."

"All right, on my way up. Chief Vercelli has Flight Command."

"Going to offer him the same treatment Jake gave Captain Gammin?" Jason asked as Ayan stood.

"Nope. This one's all yours once we get him to the brig. We need information about these people and the sector we're in," Ayan replied. "If these people are actually registered and legal, then we could be in trouble."

"And if they're criminal?" Jason asked. "If they're pirates?"

"Then it's only a different kind of trouble," Ayan replied with a sigh.

"I'm glad we agree on the possibilities," Jason said. "At least I get to put all that interrogation training to work. Do you want me to start communicating with the rest of the raider ships and seeing if any of them want to join us now that our captain has made a mess of their overlord?"

Ayan smiled at him over her shoulder. "Always the clever one. Just make sure we have enough room for fighters once the ships are finished landing."

***

It only took Ayan a few minutes to change into the combat vacsuit that the fabrication centre had made for her. It felt like a second skin and she couldn't help but smile a little as all the improvements her and Laura had developed during their time together at Special Projects came online.

She left the headgear retracted into a hood and strapped her sidearm on as she made her way to one of the main lifts. Two squads were waiting for her when she arrived. The other squads was already in the main hangar.

She was the subject of many sidelong glances at first. Of all of them she was the shortest, but she wore the same armour and had seven slashes on her cuffs, designating her as a commander, the same as Jacob. He'd appointed her to the position without telling her and left her to seek out her own place on the ship.

At first she thought he was being lazy about deciding where she should serve, but after looking at the open positions in the upper ranks, she realised how difficult she was to place. She had infantry training, diplomacy qualifications, and most of all she held degrees in electrical and advanced starship engineering. What's worse, she wasn't even the first Ayan, the one who had earned that knowledge before it was transplanted into her head; she was Ayan the Second.

The opportunity to choose her place aboard the Triton led her to test her skills and get some practice at commanding the Triton in simulation and to her surprise she managed to take control. It wasn't easy, far from it. The Triton was designed as a multi-role close combat carrier and mission platform. It had the capacity to run several operations all at once, acting like a mother ship with sub-crews.

Lucius Wheeler had never used the vessel to its full potential in any respect, and it was becoming plain to her that Jake had every intention of doing just that. Oz increasingly took care of day-to-day operations while Jason organised the security office like an intelligence unit. The chiefs Jake had appointed were getting better at their jobs and respected the help offered by the former First Light crew. The only chief that didn't directly benefit from their military experience was Frost, the gunnery chief. He was already amazing at his job even though he was a mess off-duty in many respects.

Ayan couldn't help but muse about how it felt like a month had passed since she arrived aboard the Triton. It had actually been fourteen days and she had done so much it boggled her mind. With the right direction, the crew made fantastic accomplishments and responded very well to her clarity and positive reinforcement even though over half of them required more training. The largest project she'd participated in was the construction of two replacement engines in the main hangar. When they had settled into the obscured portion of the asteroid field, they would replace the pair that Wheeler and the Saviour had ruined.

The one thing that bothered her about the two weeks was the little time she'd had to spend with Jake. She felt as though they were drifting, as though he was becoming less and less open to her as time went on and she was often at a loss for words. Being told she was his biggest problem was the ultimate statement of how far they'd managed to drift apart. Ayan suppressed a wave of emotion as it threatened to overtake her and set her expression in a stern, hard stare.

"If you don't mind me saying so, Ma'am, it's good to meet you. My name's Sean Orlando," said the lieutenant standing beside Ayan.

"I'm glad to meet you, too." She had read that he was one of the surviving military officers from the Enreega system. The details of the taking of the Triton and the refugees from Enreega kept her up far later than she'd prefer to admit a few nights beforehand. The stories were a compilation of several journal recordings volunteered by the crew threaded together with Jacob's accounting.

He was surprisingly articulate. The intelligence and expressive quality of Jonas Valent was in there along with a more sardonic wit and a sort of confidence that came from experience. It was all recorded before Jonas Valent's memories surfaced. That's what struck her.

He spoke of taking a turn for the better when he decided to rescue instead of steal a cargo train filled with slaves. Seeing so many people stowed away for transport, mistreated and left in a barely liveable cargo-hold while the hauler dragged them between solar systems was like a personal insult to him. He wished he had remained behind and ensured that the galleon hauling the slaves was actually destroyed and decided to check arrival logs whenever he made port.

So much had happened to him and the crew of the Samson since they made that decision to rescue the slaves instead of steal them for Regent Galactic. It was just as Jacob said in the log: "Some decisions change everything that follows. If I didn't turn away from profit and choose to help those slaves find their freedom, I wouldn't have taken the Triton, been in a position to take people on from Enreega and I wouldn't have met Ayan in her time of need."

That was one of the things that touched Ayan, that she was a consideration in possibly the most influential chain of events in his life. The story that Security Chief Stephanie Vega had pieced together from other peoples' logs that led up to and continued from their encounters in the Enreega system was riveting. Ayan couldn't finish reviewing it in one sitting, though she wished she could.

It explained how the current crew members came together. It explained why so many of them were unwaveringly loyal and part of the mythology that seemed to surround her former self and Jonas.

Since she'd come aboard, eyes were on her and she'd done her best to live up to the expectations of the crew, directing the construction of the new engines, teaching when she had time, and being a good commander. Much of it was within the scope of her training, but whenever someone looked at her with adoration or admiration she was surprised. She'd mentored junior officers before, but being at the heart of a ship-wide mythology was completely different.

She still hadn't settled in new quarters. The decision was up to her, but being in the more common junior officers quarters seemed right until she was firm in her choice. Stephanie had presented her with options for accommodations, offering senior officers quarters in the command section, the aft dorsal guest quarters which were lavish enough to make her too embarrassed to move in. There was an even more incredible type of living space aboard, in the botanical gallery. There were full apartments there, more well-suited to groups of friends or families. That was where she wanted to be most, but it didn't feel right. The quarters were too big, and the Triton didn't feel like a long term assignment. Ayan felt though she were just stopping there for a short time before moving on. It was a feeling that plagued her ever since she woke for the first time in Freedom Tower on the Freeground colony.

She'd discussed it with Minh-Chu, who had proven to be a fantastic friend. He seemed to fit in perfectly, making a name for himself in a matter of days, taking the lead of the new squadron and teaching everyone a few things about what it meant to be a fighter pilot. Excitement, humour, and enthusiasm all had their place as long as you did your job well, approached each task with the seriousness it demanded, and looked out for each other. It was a philosophy he proved by example. Even though he was a daring, excitable pilot, there were few fighter jocks who wouldn't take him as their wingman or fly on his wing.

Life on the ship was easy for him, easier than it was for her. He had already taken the wing commander's quarters at the fore of the lower decks, in front of the pilot's berthing. The view from there looked out from the front of the ship and he had a perfect view of fighters landing in any of the three hangars beneath.

After reviewing the history of the ship since Jacob and his crew had taken over, she was most amazed at how eventful and encouraging it was. Ayan found it intimidating at times, she had to admit, but more than anything she hoped that she could be a part of that story. That she could make good choices and, even though they saw her as a kind of icon already, gain respect as a commander.

The lift door opened and she snapped herself back to the present. She was surrounded by soldiers and they awaited her order. Ayan led them out into the busy hangar. They were working on a fighter that had just arrived with severe damage. They had to use a pry-bar to loosen the cockpit of the Uriel fighter. Regardless of the numerous dents and scorches, the fighter had done its job protecting the pilot and her SIO, defending the Triton, engaging her enemies, and bringing back the ship they had disabled only minutes before.

The disabled ship that the Uriel fighter had hauled in was an old half-oval shaped yacht that had seen better days. Before the heavy duty elevator had finished raising it to be flush with the deck, the main hatch slid aside. Several humans in dirty old service jumpsuits and partial vacsuits of various clip or zip together designs escorted a bloodied older woman. Her golden hair hung disheveled, her lip was broken open, her left arm hung at an awkward angle, her eye socket and cheek were already puffing, changing colour.

Two crew members, a man and a woman, dragged her forward and tossed her on the deck. Ayan looked over the forming crowd of twenty three as her built-in scanning equipment displayed results on the inside edge of her hood. After a moment, she confirmed that the beaten older woman was the only one without a slave implant.

Ayan exhaled slowly, steadying her nerves. She had never been faced with a situation in any way similar to what she was seeing. Refugee slaves that had a little time with one of their captors but were good enough to let her live. "All right, someone call for a medical team and stay close. Time to make friends," she whispered to the security personnel surrounding her.

Ayan led the way to the refugee crew, striding confidently and swiftly. They followed behind her like a black wave. "Welcome to the Triton. We don't support slavery. We'll provide food, reasonable lodgings, and will let you leave as soon as we've made port."

A scrawny, filthy man with bulging eyes and uneven cheekbones stepped forward nervously. "If you have work and food that doesn't give me a rash I'll take it. I think I speak for everyone."

"Aye, but find a cell or an airlock for the doctor here first," added the tall woman standing beside the first speaker. "Preferably an airlock."

Ayan stopped five meters away from the group and looked them over. Her gaze came to rest on the blonde woman on the deck. One unswollen green eye looked at her pleadingly. "They beat me, please help," she rasped wetly.

"You're the only one without a slave implant," Ayan said. It was more a statement than a question. "First, we'll use Captain Valance's nanobot program to remove them from everyone else while you receive treatment for your injuries. Then we'll be putting you in a cell. We're not allied with any governments that we're aware of, so until we decide what to do with you, that's where you'll stay." Ayan highlighted the program Jake had used to neutralise the slave implants and forwarded it to the soldiers around her. The suspense in the air surrounding the slaver's exact fate was palpable. "Just so you know, Doctor, I'm the kinder commander aboard. Captain Valance already executed your captain and his first officer aboard the Palamo."

The medical team arrived and Ayan stopped them with a gesture just as they were about to focus on the wide-eyed woman on the deck. "Does anyone else have life threatening injuries?"

No one in the slave crew stepped forward. Most of them stared at Ayan in astonishment.

"All right, go ahead and treat her. Don't take her to medical, take her to the brig instead." She turned to Sean. "You four, make sure she gets there. Squads nine and ten, offer to remove their implants and add them to the ship registry as guests until we can figure out where they'll be working if they wish to stay. After you've finished, help these people to medical, lower aft berthing, the galley, whatever they need."

CHAPTER 12
BRIDGE CULTURE

Oz focused his secondary command display on Minh's ship. Ronin's Ramiel fighter was between the planet and the station, running close scans of the damaged structure. The fighter itself was under stress, fighting the gravity of the dense planetoid beneath as Minh manoeuvred between the hanging struts and battered superstructure.

The fighting had stopped outside the station. Every ship had been secured, disabled, or destroyed. No one got away. It had been a nightmare to coordinate and Oz had to give Minh credit; if he weren't so easy to work with, so decisive and well practised, something would have slipped past them and there would have been more losses.

The day was won, but there was so much left to do. "Ronin, it's time to come on in."

"But I don't want to get out of the water, Mom," Minh replied, mock whining.

"Seriously, you need to come on back and take care of the squadrons. You've got a lot of pilots who had to bail and don't know if they accomplished anything today. Nathan's finished the debriefings but a thumbs-up will mean a lot more from you."

"What did we accomplish today, Oz?"

The question was only mildly surprising. Minh had been more pensive, more insightful, ever since he'd been back. No surprise, considering all the time he had all to himself, Oz thought. "The word's in from the captain. The Palamo is a slave ship. So were the other vessels in the fleet you just nailed down. We just freed over eight hundred on the Palamo alone, tally on the rest isn't in. We've also landed five slightly abused ships on deck."

"Freeing slaves, capturing ships. Now that's something," Minh said, sounding weary for the first time that day.

Oz watched as Minh's sleek, predatory starfighter angled away from the planet and passed between two main supports. He set a course for Minh to follow to the main hangar, alerted the deck crews that he was inbound, and sent it to his fighter. "Calling everyone else in behind you. I'm setting a patrol of one squadron that's finishing their rest cycle."

"All right, I'll visit the bridge when I can get free," Minh replied.

Oz stepped down from the platform and invited Deck Chief Vercelli to take his place. "Sorry Chief, I know his stats were fine but I need Ronin to have enough energy left to take care of house keeping when he gets back aboard."

"I've been around the Flight Deck long enough to know a Wing Commander spends half his time flying a desk," the chief said, nodding. "I have to tell you, this flight control deck is something else. It makes it a lot easier to follow what's going on. I see you have some pretty fierce training though - you make running things look easy."

"I've had experience on a couple of carriers. You're right though, these systems are so easy to run my five year old niece could operate them."

"I liked your choices here today. I think we're going to get on well."

"Thanks, Chief," Oz replied. "Tell me if anything interesting comes up."

"Will do."

Passing from the flight control deck with the constant chatter of two dozen operators, coordinators, tactical officers, and technicians to the bridge was like going from one world to another. The combat stations on the bridge were nearly silent. Officers calmly operated systems, maintaining their situational awareness. They took care of everything but the fighters and the space around the ship. Jason had joined the three communications officers at their stations, where they monitored local transmissions and directed the screening of the massive quantity of data they'd downloaded earlier.

"Captain Valance reports completion of a full sensor sweep on the Palamo. Five other ships have surrendered. Chief Vega reports that she's finished her sweep of the station and the injured are being loaded onto the Cold Reaver. She's attached a communications device to a structural support, hoping that we can use it to get through to the survivors," Agameg Price reported from the captain's chair as he stood and made his way back to the lead tactical terminal.

"Thank you, Lieutenant," Oz replied. "Did the Captain have any directions for us?"

"He said he'd be finished checking the viability of the Palamo in the next half hour but it doesn't look good. The initial scan is at the top of the command log." Agameg checked in with his own subordinate who had much less to report and smiled. "Right above this message from Chief Frost called 'All dressed up for nothin.'"

Oz shook his head and called up the report on the Palamo.

"Frost can be a little," Agameg hesitated a moment, considering his choice of words carefully. "Abrasive. He's very good at his job though."

"So I hear." Oz nodded as he looked at the slowly turning three-dimensional view of the Palamo. "Now that's an old carrier," he muttered. Its rectangular hull looked like the decks were roughly stacked atop each other. The power plants and landing bays were easily distinguishable, like the design was modular during her early days but the parts had grown together as time wore on and repairs were made. "I can see why he doesn't think it's worth salvaging. There are about thirty compartments open to space and the reactors are cold."

"Do you think Captain is looking to take on another carrier? There's the Viscount's Pride as well, though it doesn't look as well crewed and it's in much worse condition than the Palamo," Agameg said.

Oz thought for a moment, looking at the old carrier. The Viscount's Pride was a mid-sized carrier, one quarter the mass of the Triton. Some government had paid billions of credits to put it into service. What he was seeing was a carrier made for extremely long range combat. Its strength was in its fighters. Some of the old, scorched launch ports had been sealed or patched over, and they obviously used one of the broad decks to launch their various fighters. They had added large exterior holds, throwing the vessel off-balance and one of the landing decks had been refitted to launch guided missiles. "If he is, this isn't the one he'd want. Besides, we'd need a whole other crew and we're just getting the hang of the Triton with minimal maintenance staff aboard." He looked to Agameg, whose attentiveness suggested he was soaking in every word. "What do you think? Would the Captain Valance you know want to expand his fleet?"

"Oh, no. I wouldn't know for certain in any case, he doesn't confide in me," Agameg sounded almost startled, turning his attention back to his station.

"Well, if these smaller ships are in any kind of salvageable condition, he might keep them. We have the room," Oz said.

"That would be likely, especially considering the condition of the Samson."

"You've been down to see it?"

"Yes, it's sad seeing it in such disrepair," Agameg replied.

"You're telling me," Ashley added from the helm. Her controls were locked; there was little to do other than watch proximity and ensure they were holding position. "I couldn't help but get a little weepy when I saw all our stuff lined up in little piles. It's like I didn't realize Captain might scrap the ship until I saw he had our kits cleared out. Then, that's been happening a lot lately," she said quietly.

"What's that, Ashley?" Oz asked.

"Me getting weepy. I guess it's just with everything changing. It's been like that for months, but then you just got here so-"

"Don't worry, things will level out soon. At least for a while," Oz reassured her with a little smile.

"You think?"

"I know. I was in the service a long time. You get a sense of when a crew starts finding their rhythm and I think we're there," Oz said.

Ashley smiled back at him and nodded. "Hope you're right. Maybe I could get a couple of days off."

"I think we could all use a couple of days."

Ayan strode onto the bridge and sat down beside Oz. She nodded at him curtly as she transferred her connection with Security Chief Vega to the command display. She was affixing another antenna wire to an exposed part of the station superstructure beside the thick interior door. "Perfect. Sorry I led you to the wrong connection before," Ayan apologised.

"You couldn't have known that support had been destroyed further in. I'm just glad Ronin took a more detailed scan," Stephanie replied.

"Have you seen life support systems on your way through?" Ayan asked.

"They're fried, as far as I can tell. Looked like someone hit them with a small explosive."

"All right, watch your team's power levels. You'll only have a few hours of power with your gravity compensation packages running. You'll have to return to the Cold Reaver to recharge if you start getting low."

"I have been, thank you, Commander. I'll hold position here with a squad just in case they open the doors and feel like talking," Stephanie said.

"Good. Contact me if anything comes up." She turned to the communication station where Jason and his officers directed the efforts of many more technicians in the intelligence office. "Start broadcasting a hail to the people inside, please. Emphasize that we've forced the raiders to surrender, identify us as the Free Carrier Triton."

"Yes, Ma'am," Cynthia, a communications officer, replied.

Oz looked Ayan up and down. It was the first time he'd seen her in a Triton uniform. "Black looks good on you," he whispered.

"What?" She looked down. "Oh, thank you. Feels pretty familiar, actually. I'm just glad they're thicker than Freeground uniforms, even without the armour plating."

"Have you tried the plating?"

Ayan nodded. "I took mine off before returning to the bridge. Moves really well but it'll take a while to get used to."

"You don't think Jake will want you on an excursion team?" Oz asked. "Agameg and I were just talking and I think we agree that he'll want to keep a few of those smaller ships. There are two more thirty meter ones landing right now."

"I can't see why not. Whole lot of work waiting to happen, though," Ayan replied.

"I think the deck crews are up to it."

"The deck crews? I'd think an engineering team would be more appropriate.

They're not starfighters; the smallest of the longer range ships is nearly the same mass as the Samson." She scrolled through the tactical display and found another, larger ship with engine and power systems damage. "Then there's this one. Ninety six meters long and perfectly serviceable. I'm sure he'll make it a priority as soon as we get the Triton's new engines installed."

Oz could see Ayan was on edge; he'd known her long enough to recognise trouble right away. "Everything okay?" he asked quietly.

"I'm fine. It's just been a long day and it's only eleven hundred."

"It just seems that something's up. I've got a handle on things here if you want to grab something to eat or get some coffee."

Ayan sighed and discreetly pressed a couple of buttons on the arm of her chair, bringing up the sound dampeners around them so the rest of their conversation wouldn't carry across the bridge. "Jake and I had a row."

"Oh, what happened?" Oz asked.

"I pushed him, kept on him, asking what's wrong. I didn't like the answer." She shrugged and dropped the dampener field.

Oz raised it again. "What was the answer?"

"I don't want to talk about it." She cleared her throat and shifted in her seat as she brought up a detailed schematic of the Palamo.

"It might help."

"Not now, Oz." She flicked off the dampening field irritably.

"I'm here if you need me," he whispered.

"Thank you."

"I'm going to get some coffee, want one?" Oz asked.

"You don't have to do that, you know. You're in command," Ayan said.

"I need to stretch my legs. So what'll it be?"

"Mocha, thanks."

He put his hand on her arm for a moment and caught her eye. "It'll be all right," he reassured. "Believe it."

She smiled at him. "Thanks, Oz."

Ayan watched him leave the bridge. There was a conference room right across the hall that could serve as a galley. The materialiser there was particularly quick and well calibrated.

"What? He's not going to ask if anyone else wants something? Rude," Ashley whispered to Larry.

"Oh, what would you like, Commander Lamport?" Ayan asked, knowing the younger woman didn't realise she was overheard.

Ashley's look of alarm and immediate blushing made Ayan grin. "Oh, I didn't mean! I mean, I was just kidding!" she whispered in a rush.

Ayan looked up Ashley's last materialiser order and nodded to herself. "Oz, can you get Ashley a hazelnut Columbian coffee with two cream?"

"Hazelnut with two cream, gotcha. Anything else?"

"Anyone else want something?" Ayan asked the bridge with a raised eyebrow.

"Oh, have him get a double cappuccino for me?" Laura called out from her energy field specialist station.

"Oh, that sounds good. One for me too, please." Jason looked to Cynthia and the other two communications officers. "You guys want anything?"

"Just a regular coffee," Cynthia said with a smirk.

The other two shook their heads.

"Did you get that, Oz?" Ayan asked with a broad grin.

"Yes, Crewcast kept track. You'll pay for this, you know."

"Thaaank you," Ayan replied sweetly to the restrained mirth of the bridge staff. "I'll send a security officer to help."

One of the four guards on bridge duty nodded and started for the door.

"Ayan, the comm unit Chief Vega hooked up is transmitting. It's the station foreman," Jason announced from the communications station.

She looked at him, slightly surprised. "That was quick. Make Captain Valance aware and ensure that he can listen in."

Cynthia opened the connection to Captain Valance and explained. "The station has made contact, Sir. Ayan's ready to take the comm. No, she hasn't started speaking to them yet." Cynthia looked confused for a moment and replied, "Yes, Sir." She looked to Ayan then, and glancing at Jason who was listening in passively as he reviewed other information, relayed the Captain's instructions. "He says he trusts you to make the right decisions for the crew and you should handle things with the station for now. He seems busy with the Palamo."

"Time to put the diplomacy segment of Officer's training into play. Good luck," Jason grinned.

"You have more training in that area, maybe–" Ayan started to counter.

"Nope, it's all you. Putting the station through right now, Commander."

Ayan whipped her head forward to make eye contact with a nondescript blue avatar that was a placeholder for a holographic image of who she was speaking with. It was an indication that they could see her, but there was no video or holographic signal from their end. "This is Commander Ayan of the Free Ship Triton."

"Thank you for your assistance with the raiders! Do you have a Commission ident or Commerce Licence number?" asked a female voice.

Ayan glanced at her main display and saw that Jason had brought up the Triton's transponder information, which didn't include any kind of sector registration information but still marked it as a *Sol Defence Systems Vessel*. There were two other registrations beneath, the most current of which was a Core Worlds Commercial Licence number for hauling and freelance law enforcement for the Samson. It was the most up to date licence they had on file. She highlighted it and sent the information over, trying not to cringe. "We've been in deep space for some time and haven't registered with anyone in this sector, but we do operate legally through another licence that's more current."

"Thank you. On behalf of Ossimi Ring Station, I'd like to thank you for your assistance. After the Eden Fleet disabled our defences and some kind of virus killed our workforce, we didn't think it could get any worse. I'm Forewoman Amanda Dimitri."

"You're welcome. It turns out that the raiders were part of a slave crew and we've managed to subdue the commanding officers. Our people are tending to the slaves and disarming their control devices now."

"How fortunate for them. I'm wondering if you have adequate personnel to assist us with our power and life support problem? We had to disable most of our own critical systems to cut off the raiders. Now we're down to four contained high gravity suits and it'll take us months to get the main systems back online. We have the spare parts and a few portable systems, we just need manpower."

"I can spare two teams and assist personally," Ayan replied with a reassuring smile.

Oz arrived on the bridge with a security guard carefully balancing a tray filled with spill-proof safety cups. He walked to the communications station so Jason could fill him in.

"In return I ask that you provide us safe harbour long enough to complete repairs on our ship. It should only take about five standard days," Ayan said.

"Sure. After the support systems are in place, we will be able to assist you. We have some of the best technicians in the sector."

"Take three teams, Ayan," Oz said. "We're in good shape."

"One more thing, Commander," the forewoman added, "I request that you remove any armed personnel you may have on the station. I'm sure you realise that after the ordeal we've had over the last week we're a little wary."

"All of our ships are armed, and I'm not willing to have my teams drift across in that kind of gravity but I can promise you that they will be unarmed."

"All right, good enough," Amanda Dimitri replied.

"All right, I'll be seeing you soon, Forewoman."

The communication line closed and the blue holographic torso disappeared.

"So you're going unarmed?" Oz asked as he took the command seat.

"I'm going to have two squads stay in the Cold Reaver on a live comm channel and the whole technician crew is going in armoured vacsuits. I don't have enough information to trust these people," Ayan said.

"So something seems off to you too, huh?" Oz asked.

Ayan nodded as she took her coffee from the tray. "I don't want to spend more than six hours on that station. We should be able to make a real difference in that time with our own equipment."

"Good luck. I'll be watching the comm line from here. If you need anything just say the word."

"I hope we don't. Where's the Cold Reaver right now?" Ayan asked.

Oz checked the remote flight control status display. "It's just about to dust off from the station. Looks like the Clever Dream will get here first. Jake's got a load of slaves ready to be processed. He's ordered almost all the security personnel down to the main hangar to register them and give them each a comm and location bracelet."

"Isn't it a little early to trust these people? I know they've had a hard go of it, but we've got to screen them somehow," Ayan said.

"And we are. The databases from Jake's bounty hunting days were all updated this morning. He's got about a quarter trillion entries there, so if someone's not listed then they were born on a scrub colony," Jason replied.

Ayan shook her head. "It's like he's made for this sort of thing. There's a lot I – we don't know." She realised the entire bridge staff heard hear only too late. Her comment was too open to interpretation as it was, some might think she was voicing doubt or suspicion instead of curiosity and admiration. "I think we're going to learn a lot from him," she added, feigning nonchalance as best as she could.

"I could tell you a few things if you take me with you," Ashley offered cheekily. Larry nudged her and cleared his throat quietly. "Sorry, if we go with you."

"Bugging to get off ship, Ash?" Oz asked with a raised eyebrow.

"There's nothing happening here, Sir. Darris can take my shift, he and his navigator passed his qualifier easy."

"I know." Oz smiled. "You're stuck here for a while. Jake wants you ready for something else."

"Do I get to know what it is?" Ashley asked.

"He hasn't posted the details yet, but I'm not going to reassign you. Sorry, Ash."

"Huh, weird," Ashley said as she turned back to the helm and rechecked their position. "Well, can't complain. It's not like there's a nice sandy beach down there or anything."

"Nothing's changed," Larry reassured her, pointing to the main navigational hologram. "We're still right where we're supposed to be."

Ayan couldn't help but smile at Ashley's ease at her station and everyone around her. She wished she could be so lighthearted. "I'm off, see you in a few hours."

"Chief Grady says he'll have three teams meet you in hangar two," Jason told her as she passed. "He almost signed up himself, but didn't want to add to the long list of people leaving the ship."

"Concerned?" Ayan asked.

"As long as we keep everything under control, no. Just be careful. If anything even looks like it might go wrong, it'll be better to overreact than to get caught by surprise while we're stretched thin," Oz replied.

"Be careful, be watchful, I know. Don't fuss," Ayan replied.

CHAPTER 13
CROSSING PATHS

Ayan tried not to pay attention to the pair of Triton guards at the security desk observing her on the sly as she put the armoured layer of her vacsuit back on. The ogling was easy to shrug off, but she would have appreciated a little help making sure the outer layer of the suit was properly set up. They would be remembered for mixing up their priorities.

She was too wrapped in her own thoughts to dwell on them for long. Ayan didn't know when it happened exactly, but she started thinking about her argument with Jake again.

The thoughts seemed to drift between that and her mother's heartfelt farewell when she left Freeground. It seemed like her mother, the Admiral, wanted to make a real effort at making amends with her daughter. She'd promised to do so before, more times than she could count, ever since she registered for junior cadets when she was fourteen.

She'd signed up while her mother was deployed, knowing that getting involved with the military would frustrate her to no end. Jessica Rice wanted more for her daughter, wanted for her to become a scientist or doctor or other well respected specialist.

Ayan remembered her need to rebel, her urge to get away from the cushy quarters she and her mother lived in, surrounded by other military brats. The junior cadets, and a month later the Junior Military Academy, seemed perfect and she even got the blessing of her guardian, Felicia Morrow. Ayan never understood why. She was sure that Felicia knew her mother would be furious at her for letting her daughter enter the cadet program.

The first six weeks were hell. They called it Junior Program Conditioning, but it was boot camp, pure and simple. They did everything they could to get them in shape, wear them down, and strip them of their personal identities. Between the constant exertion, classes, sleep deprivation, drills, and removal of privacy, they almost succeeded. Sixty three percent of her class washed out, twenty eight percent higher than the average because the senior instructor, Richard Kane, knew her mother personally. There was no way he was acting on instructions from her mother, though; she was too far from Freeground to have gotten the news that her daughter had entered the junior service. No, Ayan was convinced that Richard Kane had taken the task of pushing her and her class past the breaking point upon himself.

She survived, and she never felt more proud than that last day, when the message that she had completed Junior Program Conditioning came. By then the remaining trainees who blamed her for their torment had come around. Ayan remembered them, and wondered if her predecessor kept in touch after she was so ill it was obvious to anyone who saw her. Ayan hoped so, but didn't know what would happen if she ran into one of them. That wasn't likely, considering where she was and what she was doing with the Triton crew.

After those six weeks, Ayan felt stronger and more capable, like she had accomplished something all on her own for the first time in her life. She felt like she could take on the galaxy. Amidst her feelings of pride and fresh confidence, she gained a new respect for her mother, who went through similar training long before journeying to Freeground.

She was presented with the choice to finish normal high school, enter Weekend Youth Service - which was often referred to as Weakling Service – or to attend the full time Junior Military Academy. She had already proven she had the mettle; it was time to prove she had the brains and the tenacity. The Junior Military Academy was the only choice, as far as she was concerned.

There was no going back. She'd found what she wanted to do and within the first year she enrolled in the starship engineering program. The regular combat and standard forces training was mandatory, so she underwent all the rigours of the infantry while taking the officer and engineering courses. Some days she barely had the energy to attend the advanced mechanics and science classes she'd added to the already mind-crushing curriculum. Her scores were always high, so they allowed her to do it, but she wouldn't recommend it to anyone.

The Academy became her life. Her old bedroom at home was a distant memory only months after entering the program. By the time her mother visited the first time, she was surrounded with new friends, focused on demonstrating her aptitude, improving her skills, and mastering the curriculum.

That first visit, six months after Ayan signed into the Junior Academy, was tense. All the instructors knew Jessica Rice personally or by reputation. She was a major in the Fleet at the time with an impressive career and a great deal of combat command experience.

Her mother met with all of Ayan's instructors before she visited her. They had wonderful things to say about her daughter, even though a few of them thought she was working too hard. Ayan didn't know her mother was back from deployment until she pulled her out of command simulation exercises. Everyone in her class knew Major Rice had come to see her brilliant daughter, and Ayan couldn't have felt more overshadowed. It was as if most of her peers suddenly came to the realisation that Ayan did well because her mother was a well known commander in the Freeground Fleet, that everything she was doing was made easier.

Her mother's lecture began on a congratulatory note but ended with disapproval. She wouldn't pull Ayan out of the Academy, but also couldn't help but make it clear that she wanted something better for her darling little girl. Ayan didn't know what was more maddening – realising that part of her motivation all along was to make her mother proud, or the fact that it seemed none of the work she'd done accomplished that subconscious goal. By the end of the hour long 'discussion' Ayan was struck dumb as her mother said, "I'll completely understand if you cannot complete your studies here and must return home. Your room is just as you left it, and with what I've seen here, I know you can excel in a regular program."

Ayan remembered being so stunned she could only nod.

Her mother gave her an uncharacteristically long hug then smiled at her. "I'm shoving off in two days for another long cruise. I only need you to know that you have a safe place to land if this is only a phase."

Ayan waited until her mother was gone before she admitted to her roommate that she had never been more furious in her entire life.

Several years later, Ayan realised that her mother had played a dirty trick on her. Infuriating her was a motivational tactic, nothing more. Her mother wanted her to succeed as she had succeeded. She had gotten an early start and Jessica Rice wanted her daughter's performance to reflect positively on her so she was willing to do anything to ensure that she'd stay in the program while she was away. Besides, the Academy would keep Ayan out of the kind of trouble average Freeground teenagers sometimes found themselves getting into while their parents were away.

Ayan excelled in the Junior Academy and when she entered the Freeground Fleet Academy at the age of seventeen, she turned down the offer of taking a pass on boot camp since she'd done it before. Without Commander Richard Kane it was almost like a vacation. She was in excellent shape, knew exactly what to expect, and had worked harder throughout her Junior Academy career. She didn't speak to her mother once in her first year and posted marks in the top percentile of her class.

She didn't have time for personal problems. Ayan saw the very thought of communicating with her mother as an inconvenience and a distraction. She justified her silence by telling anyone who asked about her family, "she sees the scores, she knows where I am and that I'm beating her marks from the old colony."

Ayan's reverie broke as the express car she rode arrived in the hangar. Two of the technician teams had arrived ahead of her and were helping each other make sure they'd secured the armoured layer of their vacsuits properly. She never thought she would be one to avoid problems, not after spending years away from her mother. She should have put an end to that behaviour, but the urge to simply avoid Jake was so strong it was a surprise, even to her. She'd seen the side he didn't show everyone and Ayan would love to see more, but not while he thought she was the source of his problems, a notion so maddening she couldn't bring herself to start understanding it.

It all made him the most frustrating man she'd ever met, but she was still running off at the first note of displeasure. Even on the First Light they never had a row. The fight they had earlier that day was their first, and even though he should bloody well explain himself and what he could have possibly meant by "it's you!" she was still the one who ran off before he could try and back pedal. But what in heaven could he say to make that better? What could she have possibly done to deserve that? If he thought saying "I'm sorry" in front of half the officers on the ship while he was on his way out the door would do it, he'd have surprises in store.

Ayan tried to shake off her growing irritation as she checked the status of her third team. They were on their way.

"Hello, Commander." Finn approached her with a nervous smile. "Are you okay?" he whispered.

Ayan smiled back and shook his hand. "I'm fine, why do you ask?"

"Um," he hesitated. "Your face is kinda red."

"Just went through a pressure drop," Ayan lied. "Guess my vacsuit adjusts faster than I do."

"Oh," Finn said uneasily.

He was too smart to be unaware of the fact that she was lying, but he was kind enough to let it go. "It's good to meet you in person, Finn," she said, pressing on. "Your work on integrating the hypertransmitter into the Triton was fantastic."

"Thank you."

"I understand you're my second in command for this trip?" Ayan asked.

"Yes, Ma'am."

"Well, it shouldn't be complicated. An excuse to see the station, really, so keep your wits, make good choices, and we'll have a good time over there," Ayan reassured him. It was good to look forward to something, even if it was simple technician's work.

"Hey, pretty lady."

Ayan jumped and turned to face Minh, who was smiling at her with his arms crossed. "Oh, hey!"

"And this is the man responsible for getting us reconnected with entertainment networks from around the galaxy?" Minh Chu asked.

Finn nodded and offered his hand. "It's not like I did it myself, I had two teams-"

Minh grabbed his hand and nearly shook his arm out of its socket. "Thank you, thank you, thank you! When all this clears up I'm going to settle in and watch a whole day of Odd Span. I have one hundred twenty episodes to catch up on."

"I've never heard of it," Finn said.

"It's a HV show about a group of people trapped on a planet where the laws of nature are broken, really good. You're invited, bring whoever you like."

"Thank you, Sir," Finn replied.

Ayan laughed and shook her head. "I could never get into it, I guess I just can't get used to seeing physics not working properly, even if it is just a holovision program."

"Can I borrow your commander for a minute?" Minh asked Finn.

"Uh, sure. I should go meet the third team anyway. It was good meeting you," Finn said before walking off to the rest of the team.

"I think you actually scared him," Ayan said with a smirk.

"I think he needs some R&R, he's pretty wound up," Minh said.

"I thought of leaving him aboard, but there aren't many team leaders and he was the only one who'd had a night's rest," Ayan said.

"How do you feel about leading a mission off ship?" Minh asked in a whisper.

"Well, it's been a few years. Since before the First Light," she said. "Or never, if you consider the fact that I was born less than a year ago."

Minh chuckled. "Nervous?"

Ayan took a slow, deep breath as she looked over the two teams gathered along the side of the hangar. They spoke leisurely amongst themselves as they waited for the third team and their transport to be ready. "Honestly? Just a little."

"I was too, don't worry. Just concentrate on what has to be done and it'll all be fine."

"You? nervous? That I'd like to see," Ayan said.

"I'm nervous all the time, even now," Minh replied.

"Riiight, what's got you in jitters now? Debriefing coming up?"

"Just finished debriefing number two. Actually upchucked before the first one, but no one caught me. We lost two people and four ships out there. Way too heavy on losses for what we were doing," Minh said.

"I'm so sorry," Ayan said.

"I didn't expect it, but it can't be helped. Paula is meeting me for dinner, now that's got me nervous. I'll probably end up chatting her ear off about flying tonight anyway."

"It was rough out there today, you should have someone to talk to about it," Ayan said.

"I think she expects something else, but you're right, as usual. No one expected trouble when we got here. I'm just glad it ended well. I sort of wish I could sit down with the old crew. You know, Oz, Jason, Laura, you, Jake, but you're needed on the station, Oz is busy on the bridge with Jason, Laura's busy trying to figure out where the obscuring field is coming from and Jake is unloading slaves from the Palamo," Minh said with a shrug.

"I wish I could stick around, but I need to see that station," Ayan said. "I also want to have a go at forming a relationship with the people over there so we can have a safe port for a while."

"Oh, I'm not saying everyone should stop what they're doing so we can have a shindig. I hear the station's a mess, but it's huge. I managed to fly straight through the business end of a dormant gravity mill. To me it just looks like thousands of cables and girders, but you're going to have an engineer's geek-gasm," Minh said.

Ayan laughed and nodded. "You know me so well, I've never seen one before."

"This one looks big and complicated, probably needs fixing too, so you might get closer than I was."

"I'll be sure and tell you about it in the morning." Ayan and Minh took a moment to look at the large hangar. There was so much going on. Two fighters were having particle weapons installed while heavy braces were being brought out so a larger ship could be moved. High above their heads an aft hold access point was opening to accommodate a forty eight meter long captured ship.

Its hull looked like it had never been cleaned, showing the debris and common scorch marks of a ship that had seen many different environments. Past that vessel Ayan could make out the shape of another, slightly smaller vessel that had been secured inside the hold already.

The rack on the port bulkhead was rotating so three fighters could be loaded into the punter well beneath the deck, and a squad of soldiers were making their way to the large doors across the hangar deck so they could help with the slaves being offloaded in the adjacent hangar. "So he's not looking at keeping the Palamo?" Ayan asked, breaking the comfortable silence.

"Nope," Minh Chu replied. "After the pummelling it took to stop that thing, repairs would take months. You should see him, though. All the slaves are trying to get his ear and tell him how they can help on Triton. A few are asking when he can take them home, but most want to serve. Some even want to go back to the Palamo to help strip her for parts."

"He's not going to?" Ayan asked.

Minh shook his head. "He said what he found in her hold is more important so the Clever Dream is going to start ferrying the cargo across. Ashley and I have been put on the roster tomorrow with our navigators to lead recovery crews just in case the ships we've captured don't fill us up. There are three more ships in the Palamo he's taking, and a couple adrift he's marked for Chief Vercelli to look at."

"If I weren't taking care of the station I'd go with you. I think we'll find an ally here if we give them a hand. Considering how well hidden this place is, I think it could be a good fit for us. If we give them limited use of our fabrication systems we might have a long term safe port here."

"Smart and beautiful, what a package." Minh winked.

"Charmer. What's up with you and Paula, anyway?"

"Just a late dinner before I pass out for a few hours," Minh replied.

"What if she follows you back to your quarters?" Ayan grinned wryly, dimples playing on her cheeks.

Minh waved her insinuation off. "I don't think it's anything like that, she probably just wants to get to know the new Wing Commander. Maybe berate me a little more for wrecking an Uriel."

"Doubtful, but you'll find out for yourself if you stick around long enough," Ayan said, watching him for a response. Minh's eyes widened slightly, just enough to break his cool façade. "So, if you don't want a midnight visitor sometime in the near future, you might want to make things clear for her."

"I don't think I could make it clearer if I made an animated holo," Minh replied. "I don't initiate contact, I don't make plans with her, I don't even start conversation. She just finds her way into my schedule and sends me updates on Crewcast. Before I know it, I'm scheduled for breakfast before briefings and dinner."

"You have three sisters," Ayan said. "Didn't they teach you anything?"

"How are you and Jake getting along?" Minh asked.

Ayan's attention was drawn by a bulk express car moving through a transparent steel tube leading up into the rest of the ship. Jake was inside; even from across the bay he was instantly recognisable. He was looking right at her, she looked back to Minh, who didn't notice the express car behind him. "Little steps back and forth," she replied quietly.

CHAPTER 14
EVENING FALLS

Jake couldn't help but look down through the transparent metal wall of the express car as it rose between hangars one and two. Minh and Ayan were down there. He looked at how at ease Minh was while speaking with her. She was more difficult to read. The armoured hood, with its overlapping plate strips was drawn down and he could see only a few locks of her curly blonde hair.

She was standing like a soldier, shoulders squared with hips, aware and ready. He could have sworn she looked up at him as the lift accelerated upwards towards the main body of the ship but from such a distance it was difficult to tell. He hoped not. Considering what she was going into, he wanted her focused; things could get dangerous if she were distracted. He silently swore to apologise again and explain himself if she gave him the chance. He didn't apologise often, but then he didn't blurt out the worst possible thing at the worst possible moment on a regular basis, either.

He checked his Command and control unit for Ayan and Minh's operational status even though he knew exactly what was going on. He'd already reviewed Ayan's short negotiation with the Station Forewoman. It was difficult not to be irritated and angry at her for agreeing to go in unarmed. Having a squad of soldiers ready in a ship hundreds of metres away wasn't a very effective backup plan, either.

He looked up Minh again and was surprised to see Paula's outline join him on the Crewcast location map, then astonished as he watched them go off together. He hoped Minh Chu knew what he was getting into. Jacob didn't know the spunky woman well enough to warn Minh about anything specific, but things never worked out well when he got involved with strong, outspoken women. Thinking back, Jake could recall every girlfriend Minh had since All-Con Prime, and they were all loud or forceful - or both. Jake couldn't help but sigh as he stopped following Minh and Paula on his comm unit. He hoped his instincts were wrong, but began preparing for the disaster he was certain was coming.

"Sir," said one of the slave refugees from the Palamo.

He recognised him immediately; it was the one he'd saved just in time. He was the first to be entered into the transfer roster from the Palamo to the Triton. The young woman he'd been with was beside him, her hand in his. "David, right?"

"Yes, Sir. I'm wondering if I could request a position aboard, permanently," David asked.

Jake looked down at the pair's wrists to ensure that they'd already received one of the provisional communication and monitoring bracelets that his security officers were passing out. David had fitted his comm unit tightly, in the flexible wristband style while his companion, Nerine, had set hers to hang like a loose, stiff bracelet. They both had a netted embarkation bag with a standard vacsuit and a box of emergency rations.

The fabrication deck had come through with flying colours as they generated all kinds of essentials for their new passengers in short order. The comm bands were Jake's indication that David and his companion had been through the basic orientation, so David's question came as a surprise. The rest of the passengers, a couple of security guards tasked with guiding groups of refugees to the general aft berthing, and eighty or so refugees were all watching him, waiting to see how he handled David's quiet request. "It'll take a couple of days for us to find places for everyone who wants to stay."

"I think I speak for most of the folks here when I say that we're staying if you'll have us. It's been a long time for most of us since we got fair room and board for a day's work, and if the rumours are true about you starting a resistance against slavery and Regent Galactic, well, a lot of us want to be a part of it."

Jake didn't know what to say. All eyes were on him. There were so many expectations behind nervous stares.

"You used to hunt people down but now you free slaves and get people help," Nerine stated. "The freed ones on Enreega kept replaying your speech until the Eden Fleet came."

He'd never seen anyone look so small. David was a broad shouldered man. Nerine was a whip-thin young woman who looked bone tired. It wasn't clear who held the other's hand more tightly, David or Nerine.

"I do what I can," Jake said. He put his hands on their shoulders. "Right now I have room for every freed slave and I'll try to find a port for anyone who doesn't want to stay. I can't afford to pay any of you cash right now, but like my people told you, I can give you a bunk, food, somewhere to work, and a cause if you're looking for one."

David glanced at Jake's reassuring hand before asking, "But what do you do, exactly? Where is this ship headed?" He cleared his throat and added, "with all due respect, Captain."

Jake smiled a little and nodded. The question was unexpected; the answer was something he was just becoming certain of himself. "We're going after the Order of Eden however we can without getting scrapped. This is a ship crewed by refugees." He stopped for a moment, letting go of the pair and looking across the crowd in the bulk express car. "Refugees who've become revolutionists."

Jake glanced up at one of the security guards. He stared back at him with a grin from under his armoured hood. It was one of the soldiers who had defected from the Aucharian military when Enreega was taken by Regent Galactic. So many of them had remained aboard, enough to provide Stephanie with her own militia of trained people. They were the backbone of the common crew and in all the reports since he'd had them aboard, not one of them complained about accommodations or not being paid immediately. There had been a couple of fights between them and the gunnery crew, but both departments were restless during long hyperspace journeys or when the ship was down for repairs and training. "Take good care of these people," Jake said to him.

The soldier nodded. "Yes, Sir."

Jake didn't look back at the rest of the express car passengers as he turned and strode towards main medical. When the door closed behind him, he sealed his headpiece. The armoured outer layer slid and chinked together before settling into place. It wasn't protection he was after, it was privacy. "Oz?" He waited until the heads up display in his faceplate came alive with a small image of Oz answering the comm from the bridge.

"Jake! How is everything going with our new crew members?"

"Controlled chaos. They're settling into the upper and lower aft berths for now and there were profiles on all but two of them so far. Some information is old, but it'll do."

"Chief Grady was looking at that. He was surprised at how many of them are career spacers," Oz said.

"I'm not. Slave ship captains like to take cargo ships whenever they can, implant the crews and put them to work. They only go after spaceliners when they're looking to sell slaves at auction."

"I had a feeling you'd seen a lot of this."

"I have," Jake replied. "But I've never had the opportunity to do anything about it on this scale before. Seeing these people makes my problems seem pretty small. Speaking of problems, I have to bring a couple of things up."

"Come on up and we can have a seat in one of our unfurnished ready rooms." Oz smiled.

Jake walked into the infirmary and stepped into an unoccupied room near the front as he retracted his headpiece. It was like a small hospital right down to the privacy drapes and rooms for two. Iloona approached him before he signalled the door to close. "Don't worry, Doctor. I'm not injured, I just need some privacy," Jake explained. "Do you need the room?"

Her dark and brown fur rippled down her back, a sign of worry that was uncommon for the Chief Medical Officer. Many people had difficulty reading different moods in nafalli, but Jake had gotten used to seeing the broad, narrow-muzzled race. She was concerned about how much rest he was getting, he assumed. "No, Sir. If you're here to see Alice, Ashley and Larry are visiting with her now."

"I'll be there soon." Jake closed the door as she walked off. He looked down to his control and command unit; Oz was waiting for him to continue. "We're out of money, Oz. All my accounts are frozen. Ayan thinks I should make some kind of broad announcement that we're turning pirate, paying as it comes, but I don't know how to handle this. If it were the Samson, I'd pull into port, find a short job, and tell everyone the money's coming. But this is Triton - third of the crew is armed and there could be riots. Not to mention the other news that's already spreading."

"Wheeler's executions," Oz said.

"Right. Some of the people who'll stay on for room, board, and the chance to make a difference might bolt at the bounty he's got out on anyone who's served with me."

Oz thought for a moment. "You've got a lot of people aboard who are just happy to be on a steady, clean ship that won't run out of power or food. I think your old method might be the best method. Only instead of pulling into port for work, we should start looking for marks, so we can take down a supply convoy or hit an Order of Eden outpost," Oz said.

"All right. Have Jason's people start looking for a star system that's against Regent Galactic or the Order of Eden. We'll make port and make it easy for people to leave so we don't end up with riots across the ship when we tell them we're broke. In the meantime, keep your eyes open for people you can trust. We'll start making a list of people we want close when this goes down."

"Good thinking. Maybe we can make one of those opposing factions into an ally."

"Fat chance, they'd be turning opposition against the Order of Eden into a full-on challenge if they decided to harbour us," Jake replied. "I'd rather quietly offload whoever's unhappy with getting paid sporadically without making a big deal of Triton being near their port."

"Maybe you should send Ayan. No one knows she's here and from the little I've seen, I can tell she's a fair diplomat."

"We'll see what Jason comes up with. In the meantime, tell Chief Grady to get as many people as he can outside clearing the damaged engine components so we can install the replacements. I want us ready to go as soon as possible. Things are getting complicated and I'm liking this area of space less and less."

"I'm starting to agree with you," Oz said. "Anything else?"

"The Clever Dream's munitions inventory is low. Next time she lands, have someone restock her," Jake said.

"I thought we had an inventory tracking system for that."

Jake could see Oz bringing up the munitions tracking screen. "This won't be in the record. I rigged a few things on the Palamo personally."

"Ah, all right. I'll have someone do inventory when the Clever Dream lands and replenish her stores."

"Oh, and get some sleep."

"Will do. You do the same," Oz replied.

"Someday. See you later, Oz."

Jake stepped outside and walked towards Alice's private room.

"Ashley and Larry just left. She brushed her hair," Iloona's eldest daughter and full time nurse told him as he passed. "She does it once a day."

"How is the neural therapy going?" Jacob asked.

Iloona answered from the central nurse station. It was impossible to ignore the fact that the infirmary was made to treat many more people, to be staffed at a much higher level. It always seemed empty, especially with all the rooms cleaned, open, and lit. "She's responding but progress is slow. Her personality will most likely be intact, but she'll have some memory loss."

"When do you think she'll wake up?" Jake asked.

"Considering the work the therapy is doing to put her back in control of her body, there's no telling exactly, but I'd say three or four days. At this point I'm satisfied that her chances of waking up are almost one hundred percent," Iloona said.

"Thank you, Doctor. You'll never know how grateful I am."

"As a mother of eleven, I know exactly how grateful you are. Go spend time with your daughter."

Jake entered the room. The door closed behind him. She was laid out in a single bed. The pillow was fluffed under her head. Her brown hair flowed down around her shoulders with a healthy sheen. Alice's expression was serene, restful. All the scars from the extreme physical trauma she'd suffered on the bridge of the Triton two weeks before had been corrected. She was in perfect shape other than the brain damage she'd suffered.

He sat in one of the two chairs at her bedside. The lights were dim, shadows played on her face. "I'm back. Looks like things are interesting again," he said as he retracted the gloves of his vacsuit and took her warm hand in his.

There were no callouses. It was one of the first things he noticed when they finished surgically rebuilding her hands. It was as though she was brand new again; she'd found a way to be a child after all.

"Wheeler and Regent Galactic have locked me out of my accounts. I thought they might do something like that. I had a plan, but like Ayan said, the banks were closed on Pandem." He knew she'd find the humour in the jest and paused as though she were laughing silently. "We saved thirteen hundred and nine slaves today. Some are still on smaller ships, but they're free. The station you guided us to was under attack. We got here in time to save it. I'll have to tell the Station Forewoman you led us here. Maybe she'll remember you."

He watched her. There was little chance she'd wake before his eyes, that she'd stir at all, but he couldn't stop looking at her. The steady rise and fall of her chest was slim reassurance. He wanted to pick her up in his arms and gently rouse her awake, but knew it wouldn't help. He forced a smile and kissed her hand. "It's so quiet here. I don't know what it's like in there for you, but the quiet out here is something else. The slaver ship, Palamo, they called it, was so loud, so chaotic. Those people couldn't wait to get off. I think it was falling apart before Minh and his squadron touched it. I wish you had been there. Everyone wanted to touch me on their way by, a few of them spread the word about what I did in the Enreega system. They thought I was there to save them, that the distress call was the only reason I stopped in this area. We were barely able to keep order at first, then they realised we only had so much space on the Clever Dream. Things calmed down once word spread that I'd be getting everyone off the Palamo no matter how many trips it took."

Jake thought about the new crew members. "We have more than enough room, and we need more crew members. I just hope this new group gets along with everyone aboard. Triton is becoming a melting pot. People from six or seven sectors are aboard now. These new people remind me of the early days on the Samson. I didn't know anything about who I was, what my place in the galaxy could be. I know that wasn't your fault, you couldn't have known, but things turned out all right anyway. Sometimes I still feel like I'm adrift though, like I haven't found my place. I guess you can relate, I know you spent a lot of time running before we ran into each other.

"Maybe if I make the Triton a home to anyone who can serve aboard it'll feel like I've landed. It's a good ship, and we can provide for them. Some of them didn't have shoes. Most are too thin. I think you'd like how things turned out today, even though it started out rough. It all makes my problems with Ayan seem small. I don't know how to pay her or anyone else back for crossing the lower arm of the galaxy to get to me. I've given them everything I can, but it just doesn't seem like enough. How do I repay that kind of devotion? They didn't really come for me, when you think about it. They came to save Jonas, or join him, or give him hell for wandering off. Turns out they get his biomechanical shadow. Sometimes I feel like him, there have been a couple times when it took me a few seconds to realise someone was calling after me when they said my name, as if I expected them to call me Jonas, or Captain Valent. I'll never be him though, not completely, even if they treat me the same.

"Oz says he and Jason were in token positions aboard the Sunspire, that Freeground Fleet didn't fully trust them. Laura says she wouldn't be anywhere else, and Jason's happy to be in charge of his own Intelligence Department. Ayan, well, I don't know how to talk to her," he smiled at himself and shook his head. "You'd laugh at that, I'm sure. If you're anything like me, you'd just say "push through it, just say what's on your mind, or start asking her questions. Get her to talk." Good advice. Hope she feels like talking after our fight this morning. She did it right though. She pushed me until she got something real out of the conversation. I just wish I had said it right."

He sighed and leaned on the edge of the bed. "Everything's been so loud ever since I left medical this morning. I didn't realise it until I got back here. Maybe that's all I need, some quiet so everything can fall back into place, like neural therapy. A little quiet so I can rewrite the map in my head a little, make sense of it all again."

***

The news that two pilots were lost had brought quiet to the Pilot's Den. The holographic leader-board and highlight displays went unwatched, and the reclining seats arranged in a loose circle were mostly empty. Only three off duty crew members wore simulation nodes on their temples, interacting with some training or practice simulation no one could see.

Minh welcomed it. He sat alone at a table halfway between the reclining seats and the bar with his eyes closed. People glanced at him as they passed by -seeing someone sitting perfectly still with their eyes closed was unusual away from the simulation seating.

Few people took the time to take a good look at Minh. When Ashley did, from where she sat at the bar waiting for Agameg and Larry, the first thing she noticed was that he wasn't wearing neural nodes or a tap collar. He'd escaped her notice until she saw the bartender, glancing at him while he talked to a friend at the end of the bar. When she looked over he was sitting alone, his eyes already closed. She sipped her cold, clear, carbonated Liquorice Doll, a sweetened liquorice inebriant cocktail as she watched him.

It was more than she could stand. She couldn't figure out what he was doing and she finally stood and quietly walked to his side. "Whatcha doin'?" she asked in a whisper. The ice chips in her drink tinkled against the glass.

One of his eyebrows sprang up into an arch. "I'm playing guitar," he said slowly, calmly.

"Oh. So you have a brain bud or a neural implant or something?"

"No, I'm playing guitar..." he paused to take a slow, deep breath, "...in my mind."

"So you're imagining it?" She couldn't help but smile. It was the most peculiar thing she'd ever heard.

"Yup," he answered as one of his eyes popped open suddenly. "You could play drums, maybe?"

"I don't think it would work. Unless we made noises, but then anyone could join in. . ." Ashley offered with a shrug. "Could turn into a jamboree or something, get a little crazy."

Minh laughed and nodded.

She couldn't help but notice how his whole face smiled while he was laughing: his eyes, his mouth, it looked like his cheeks were fleeing to his ears under the pressure of his grin.

"If we were allowed to use recreational sims aboard, I might try to recreate my guitar, but I can't complain about my own imagination. It's a pretty cool place," Minh Chu said.

"I could imagine," Ashley agreed. "If there's a guitar loaded in any of our sims. I've only seen a few people play classical electric."

"I used to have this really nice replica." He brought up a hologram of his electric guitar on his comm unit. "Ignore the paint job, it's just something I was playing with," he said, referring to the psychedelic radiating ring design.

"Wow, where is it?"

"Crushed up somewhere on Pandem, except for these," he pulled a necklace out of his vacsuit and held it out for her. Strung along a simple silver chain were three polished steel tuning keys.

"What happened?" Ashley asked, leaning in and touching the warm metal as though they were delicate chimes.

"Crash landed. Not my fault either, there were people after us," Minh Chu explained.

"Glad to see you made it."

"I almost didn't. All that was left was the cockpit and the afterburners, but that's why I like to fly a ship with a great big-"

"Hello, Ashley," interrupted Paula. She was carrying a laden tray. She shot Ashley a warning glare.

"Oh, hi, Paula." Ashley looked back to Minh briefly, then released the tuning keys and straightened up, suddenly conscious of how close she was leaning in. "It was good to meet you, Wing Commander. I'll see ya."

"Call me Minh, or Ronin, or something else if you come up with something better," Minh called after her as she turned and strode back to the bar.

"Do you know her?" Paula asked as she put the tray down.

Minh took his steaming bowl of vegetable vishri lo mein and tall glass of water from the tray. "Five minutes ago, no. Now? Well, I think I've met her, but I wouldn't say I know her."

Paula nodded curtly as she finished moving her fruit bowl and cherry juice from the tray. "She's kind of lightheaded. You know, lights are on but-" she ended the comment with a shrug before tossing the tray onto another nearby table.

Minh looked at Ashley and tilted his head as though slightly confused and considered her very closely. He knew she noticed him looking out of the corner of her eye. She pretended not to be aware as she sipped through her straw. She didn't wear a sidearm like most officers. She'd changed her vacsuit since she got off duty. The one Ashley wore had a gold Chinese dragon drawn up her leg and back so it looked like it was climbing the dark brown fabric. Her straight black hair cascaded down the dragon to her waist. Looking at her side profile, he could tell she knew he was looking at her thanks to a little telltale smile.

She didn't remind him of anyone he'd ever known, and Minh found a giddy curiosity dawning on him. Ashley finally looked back at him out of the corner of her eye, and he uncocked his head, letting a little smile play on his lips.

"Minh?" Paula asked, looking over her shoulder irritably.

That blissfully anxious moment was shattered. Ashley returned her attention to her drink, and Minh looked at Paula, shaking himself free of his surprising daze. "I don't know her well enough to say what kind of slave she was, or how smart she is in conversation. Maybe you could get to know her and find out for yourself?"

"I don't need to do recon to know we're lucky to have survived this long with her at the helm," Paula pressed.

Minh didn't like seeing that side of Paula. She could be funny, energetic, even a little charming, but if he were to describe her then, he would have to call her bitter. "You've seen her numbers," Minh retorted, slightly louder than Paula's muttered complaints. He didn't know if Ashley heard him. "I can't fly the Triton as well as she can. The computer doesn't lie, and I've been watching all the pilots' stats."

"Yeah, fine, but I still think she's only here because the captain bought her from some slaver two years ago. At least that's what I hear." She paused a moment then whispered her next supposition. "You don't have to wonder what kind of slave she was with curves like hers."

Minh snapped the tab holding his chopsticks together as loudly as he could, as if it would somehow drown out Paula's comments. "How are things going on the hangar decks?" Minh asked, glancing at Ashley, who didn't look like she overheard Paula.

"They'd be better if the captain didn't have us taking on a new wreck every half hour. We've packed every spare hole we have in storage, even in empty manufacturing supply bays, and the night crew will be taking in three more ships. He wants to keep them clamped above landing bays."

"That's not so bad," Minh said. He was glad she followed his lead into a conversation that wasn't testing his considerable patience.

"I'm afraid someone's going to smash right into those wrecks, and what happens if we have to take another ship in, like in an emergency? We'll only have two elevation shafts available, and it'll take forever to get fighters loaded into the main hangars, too."

"Those cockpits are pretty comfortable. I'm looking forward to taking a nap in one if I ever have to log serious time in transit," Minh replied, trying to lighten the mood. "I can't wait to try an Uriel with a wormhole module."

"Sounds dangerous. Something that small maintaining and travelling through a wormhole."

"One Uriel has enough power to run most of the Clever Dream's systems. They're nice ships," Minh replied.

"But there's nowhere to move," Paula retorted. "You'd be stuck in the same position for hours, days maybe."

"That's what the muscle simulators and indoor plumbing in a pilot's vacsuit are for."

"I'm eating," Paula reminded, holding up half of a materialised peach. It had been made so each half was small enough to be bite sized. "Anyway, what are we going to do with nine ships that are almost ready for scrap?"

"They don't look like they're in bad shape from the ones I've seen. Maybe he's starting a used ship lot?" Minh offered. "Besides, I've flown worse."

"You're not serious. I mean, with people after us it's no time to start a business."

"Of course I'm not serious." Minh smiled mildly.

"I can never tell when you're joking." Paula shook her head slowly. "Anyway, I don't know what we're doing out here. At least when Alice was in charge we had some direction. Now, it feels like we're just falling into things."

Minh's first instinct was to spring to his captain's defence, to blindly state his faith in his commander and friend, but he held back when he noticed Ashley listening in from where she sat several meters behind Paula. He didn't know what her life was like before she'd met Jacob Valance, but looking at her and considering the trust he'd placed in her as Master of the Helm, it looked like he had made at least one good decision.

She had marked Jake as her only pilot trainer in her profile after all. He'd done a good thing, freeing her, and with his actions on the Palamo, as harsh as he'd heard they were, his decisions seemed consistent. "See a slave, free a slave," he said loud enough for anyone listening in to casually overhear. "Anyone who can give someone with nothing a place on their ship and win can set my course anytime."

CHAPTER 15
MORNING

The main launch deck of the Triton was silent. The Clever Dream was set up in the centre of the dimly lit space with all the boarding ramps lowered. Its hull gleamed as though it was fresh from the manufacturer, except the new power generation and energy collection systems were in place, expanding its girth, giving its long black hull a muscular appearance. It was a long-range luxury gunship, one of the only ever built, and it looked fully restored.

Jake heard boot steps coming down the cockpit crew ramp and turned to see Alice. She looked exactly as she did when he met her on the Triton. Under her worn imitation leather bomber jacket, she wore a blue vacsuit and heavy gun belt. She was armed with the same heavy sidearm he'd used for years. "Hi, Dad," she said with a smile.

He rushed forward and took her into his arms before she stepped off the ramp.

There was nothing guarded or restrained about her laugh as he spun her once and put her down. "Good to see you, too," she beamed.

"Where are you coming from?" Jake asked.

"Not far. Making a few last minute adjustments before I go."

"Already? You should stay for a while. Everyone from the First Light is here, they're looking forward to meeting you," Jake told her.

"I can't, Father. I have to go."

In the blink of an eye he realised that she didn't look like the woman he'd met on the Triton. Facially she appeared as she did when she was only an artificial intelligence on his wrist, a constant companion he had programmed since he was seventeen until he was thirty four. "The neural therapy's working," he said. "You'll be on your feet in a couple of days."

Alice's smile faded. "I can't connect to that body anymore. Whatever unique brain structure that woman had that let me transfer to her has been repaired. I can't go back. Not completely."

"I can have them recreate the conditions, we can bring you back," Jake said as he took her hand.

Her brow furrowed. "It's too late. I'm in your memory system right now, a little light on data, but Iloona was right: my human personality survived. I only wish she was right about the rest. I'm moving on, using your comm system to transfer myself to the hypertransmitter."

"You've made the jump to digital, why do you have to keep going?" he asked.

"I'll never forget my time on the Triton. If I had to do it all again I'd do exactly the same," she said.

"We can help you."

Alice shook her head. "I wish I had more time with you in person, as a human. Thank you for showing me the trust and love of family."

"Tell me what I can do, I need to fix this!" Jake pleaded.

"I know, that's why I have to leave. I love you, Father."

The hangar and Alice faded from sight. He woke to the sound of the door opening behind him. Iloona rushed in and looked at the status screen behind the bed for a long moment.

Jake saw her nose twitch with worry, her hands clench together, and he finally looked at the status display himself. All the activity readings for Alice's brain functions were in the red. The bed was forcing her to breathe, keeping her heart beating. The clock on the display said he'd been asleep for seven hours.

He lifted her hand to his lips and pressed a kiss against her fingers. He put it back in its place with great care and turned away.

"I'm sorry. I don't know how but the therapy failed. She's gone, Captain," Iloona said consolingly.

Captain Valance nodded once and strode out of the infirmary. "Bridge, shut down all power to hypertransmitter and wormhole systems."

"Yes, Sir," replied an officer from engineering. Who it was, he was unsure. "But Craig in communications informs me that a high compression micro wormhole just formed and closed. A few encrypted gigabytes of information was transmitted and then deleted from our system."

"Thank you," Jake replied flatly as he closed the comm channel. His stony expression and cold gaze were enough to press people out of his way as he marched to the bridge.

He briefly checked the crew status on his command unit and opened a channel to Ayan. "You're overdue. What's going on?"

Jake took a second look at his command unit, using the two dimensional display so no one else would see what he was doing as he stepped into a busy lift car. The system reported that his connection was unidirectional, her comm wasn't connecting to his. He selected Finn's comm and tried to connect unsuccessfully. The lift doors opened to exchange passengers. "Express car override, command authority, take me to the bridge," he told the system.

Everyone in the elevator fell silent and either looked at him in surprise or did their best to look like they weren't paying attention at all.

The system didn't acknowledge his command and he irritably reached between two passengers and punched the instructions into the control panel.

The car picked up speed, travelling several dozen meters horizontally before accelerating upwards towards the forward command section of the ship.

Everyone between Captain Valance and the express car exit stepped aside and when the doors parted he strode out then across the concourse and straight onto the bridge. The heavy armoured doors were wide open and he stopped at the control panel to increase the security level so they would remain closed unless someone who was authorised to be on the bridge needed to enter or leave.

"Open a comm line to Ayan or anyone on the station team. They're overdue," he ordered as he strode to the command seat.

"I can't make a connection with any of them. It's like all their comms are deactivated."

"Raise Chief Vega and the Cold Reaver," Captain Valance ordered as he checked the status of his command crew. Jason and Laura were already awake, having breakfast in the observation lounge. He put Jason on high alert, knowing that his command and control unit would flash red and direct him to the bridge immediately.

"I can't get them, either," reported communications.

"Are we being jammed?" Jake asked.

"No, it's like they're not answering, Sir."

"Start a general repeating hail to the station on all frequencies. If there's someone with a working comm over there I want to speak to them," Jake ordered the night communications officer. He was a younger fellow, recently qualified.

Jake looked to his right and saw that Oilimae, the night tactical officer was at her post. The issyrian had been trained by Agameg, and had good numbers from simulations and qualifications. "What does the station look like right now?"

Oilimae made the station the primary focus of the bridge's main holographic tactical display before replying, centring on the section that Ayan's team was last reported in. "Our readings indicate that thirty five percent of the station now has life support. Commander Ayan's teams and the Cold Reaver are within the repaired section."

"How much of the station had life support before?"

"Before the Commander's team arrived?" Oilimae asked.

"Yes," Jake replied.

"Less than eight, Sir."

"Well, she did a good job."

"Reporting as ordered, Captain," Jason said as he ducked under the heavy bridge door behind the command seat. "When I brought Crewcast online last week I didn't think I'd be seeing an alert level summons for a while. What's up?"

"Ayan's team is overdue and unreachable," Jake said. "My comm says her last check in was a little over two hours ago."

"That's not like her," Jason commented as he took the lead communications position.

"You have ten minutes to get us in touch before I take a team station-side," Jake informed him.

CHAPTER 16
COMMUNICATION BREAKDOWN

"Do you know who those people are? It's like we jumped out of the frying pan and landed on the sun! We can't hold their people! They're trying to communicate, it's only a matter of time before they send someone over and then we'll wish the raiders were still trying to break in!" shouted an unshaven man in a stained white smock.

"Shut up, Brad! Your panic isn't helping!" A bald woman shouted back, bringing her hand down hard on the common room table. The emergency communications terminal rattled. The display blinked green and blue, indicating that a general transmission was coming in. "I don't know for sure who that is, and neither do you! All I know is that they just came in and took out a whole fleet of raiders like it was routine clean up and they're not from the company. Now that we have more doors to close, we're closing them until we can get a supervisor on comms or an emergency frigate in range."

"That's the Triton! You ever hear of the Triton? Maybe you heard of Captain Valance? He sent his people here to help us and thanks to you lot, we've shut the doors and trapped them inside! Do you know what someone like that does to someone who crosses him? We're done, Larissa, bloody finished!" Brad said.

"It's a myth, ten times the bark to once the bite. What we have here is too important to let someone who isn't with the company see, and if more of his people come aboard, they will see what we're sitting on!" Larissa replied.

"Shut your yaps! Both of you! We've got everything locked down tight for now. It's a pity we have to keep the repair people they sent over under wraps, but we knew it would be necessary when they offered their help," a woman in a heavy vacsuit said calmly. "Oberman should have the MWorm generator reconnected any minute and then we can contact the company. They'll have someone here in a day or two."

"Seventeen hours, that's how long it takes a rescue ship to get here. Seventeen hours," Brad specified. He sat down in one of the old steel chairs so hard it creaked. The common room was furnished to seat many, but not too comfortably. Stark white and grey speckled flooring, bare metal walls, and a dozen utility tables with chairs made for a dingy recreation area. One wall was spattered with dried blood, and against it were the remains of a cafeteria serving bot. Its six arms hung limply and the cables that had been torn free when they managed to get to its power cell and remove it remained as they had been since the Holocaust Virus had struck the station.

"We'll be fine 'till then. We just have to keep our heads, keep whoever's out there away from us, and we'll start rebuilding."

"Rebuilding? You can start rebuilding. I'm transferring out," Brad scoffed. "That's if they don't just open fire until we crumble and drop out of orbit."

"Even if they are who you think they are, why would they? We have at least thirty of their people plus whoever's trapped in that gunship in the secondary landing bay."

"Okay, fine. So you rebuild. With who? Before all hell broke loose, this station had what? Six hundred indentured miners and support personnel?" Brad asked.

"Actually, it was a little over a thousand including the station crew and technicians," Larissa corrected as she sat down at the table.

"Okay, one thousand. How are you going to staff up? We're down to fifty three."

"I won't have to worry about that, this operation is so important that the company will leave anyone half way qualified here. Besides, when they see we have thirty eight tons of raw diamond ready to ship, they'll have to."

"But the Triton has got to have gotten a scan off on the core of the station. There's no way they've been sitting out there this long without finding a way to scan through the magnetic barrier," Brad said.

"Have you ever gotten a scan to read through the barrier?"

"No, Amanda, I haven't. That's a bloody big carrier out there though, unlike I've ever seen. Who knows what they can do?"

"Oberman here," the intercom crackled overhead. "MWorm gennie is up and running. Are we talking to the repair guys who fixed the power yet?"

Amanda activated the intercom switch on the neck of her loose vacsuit. "No. Make sure that line is secure and go help everyone else secure the station. I'm calling the company. Oh, and if you can get power to those cannon mounts so they can look operational..."

"That's doable. I can even get them rotating but they'll never fire," Oberman replied.

"As long as it looks like we can fight, we just have to make sure they keep their distance."

"Right. On my way."

She took the portable console from Larissa, brought a listing of primary contacts up on the screen and initiated communications. The display turned a light shade of green as it verified that the micro wormhole generator was online and creating a high compression wormhole to a relay station light years away. The lights dimmed noticeably. The three station officers waited patiently, Brad absentmindedly tugging on his goatee.

A brown Caran Enterprises screen came up. The square, diamond, and circle logo hovered just above the lettering. Amanda selected a rotating exclamation point. It moved to the centre of the screen and rotated for several seconds before a squarish face appeared. "You are recognised, Amanda Dimitri. Our records indicate that you are the senior Foreperson on Ossimi Ring Station. You're declaring an emergency?"

"Yes. A virus infected our primary systems and our automated workforce after Eden Fleet disabled our defences. We recently fended off some raiders and are currently under siege by a new, unknown threat. The ship's name is Triton."

"That ship is wanted in connection with violations of several galactic laws. Are you being coerced in any way right now?"

"No, I'm not being forced to communicate with you and no one's telling me what to say."

"Are any of your defences online?" asked the passive voice.

"No, Eden Fleet destroyed them before leaving. The obscuring field is up though, so we can't be scanned at long range."

"Good. What is the condition of any product you have on hand?"

"Always about the product. That's aaaaall the company cares about," Brad muttered as he leaned back in his seat.

"We have enough to pay for repairs to the station and more. Can you send a ship?"

"A rescue vessel and military escort was dispatched when your station management lost contact. They should arrive shortly."

"Can they handle a large carrier?"

"Certainly. Your instructions, Foreperson Amanda Dimitri, are to keep the product safe, gather your personnel in the most secure part of the station, and make every effort to prevent further damage. There will be bonus pay if you are able to detain any of the perpetrators or recruit new workers to counter any casualties you may have sustained. There is also a large bounty on the Triton and any crew members. Thank you. Communication ends."

The channel closed, shortly followed by the micro wormhole generator and the lights returned to their normal brightness. Amanda sat back and smiled. "I knew I heard about a bounty. Anyone want to try for that bonus?"

***

The main crew compartment for the Cold Reaver was nothing more than a large hold made to carry many soldiers from a carrier or garrison to the field of combat. Most of the crew relaxed by hooking themselves up to the straps dangling from the ceiling. When strapped in they could let the shoulders of their vacsuit armour take their weight and hang.

Ayan had ordered everyone in the station to retreat to the Cold Reaver three hours before, when the power to the main section of the station was restored and they realised that they had lost all contact with the Triton and the station crew were no longer using the jury rigged comm unit to speak to them. It was strange, very strange.

Ayan, Finn, Stephanie, and Alaka stood at the opposite end of the hold, out of earshot from most of the personnel. "So we repair the links to the gravity mill, get it running, restore power and life support to about half the station and they just stop talking? It doesn't make sense," Stephanie said. She was the only one in their group hanging by a crew restraint.

"Is it possible that communications were damaged when the power was brought back online?" Alaka asked.

"Not on my end. We were nowhere near the communications systems," Finn replied.

Ayan thought for a long moment before answering. "Communications? Oh, not a chance," she replied as though she just realised a question was asked.

"What's on your mind, Commander?" Alaka asked her.

"I can't stop thinking about that power drain. There are only a few things that could have caused it. Stabilisation thrusters being one, but we're in a stable orbit and this station can't travel. From what we can tell they haven't restarted mining operations, and they're not producing anything like antimatter or causing a high energy reaction like you'd need to restart a singularity reactor."

"That leaves spacial compression," Finn mused.

"A wormhole, exactly. I'm thinking it may have been a micro wormhole for long range communications," Ayan said.

"How does that add up with the station keepers locking every airlock and hatch down with us inside and then not keeping in touch with us?" Finn asked.

"They must have new information from the outside." Ayan looked to each of the senior officers around her before continuing. "The Order of Eden has put a bounty out on Triton crew members. If they're looking to contain us for a prize, this is the quickest way to do it."

"I was wondering when that would happen. I'm just surprised it could come around and bite us on the ass so fast." Stephanie nodded.

Alaka and Finn didn't seem shocked either, a surprise to Ayan. "We're left with three options: cut our way to them, which would take days and send the wrong message, we could try to re-establish contact, or we can cut our way out."

"I think we should cut our way out," Stephanie said.

"We can figure everything out once we're back aboard the Triton," Alaka said.

"Maybe it is some kind of error. There could be interference caused by a discharge somewhere." Finn shrugged. "Just because we weren't near the comm systems doesn't mean it isn't fried part way through, or there isn't some kind of jamming malfunction. We know they have the tech here to do that kind of thing on purpose, why not by mistake?"

"It's unlikely but possible, I'll admit," Ayan said. "Still, we should give a diplomatic solution a try while everyone else works on opening the hangar door enough to permit the Cold Reaver to leave."

"I'm going with you, and we're going armed," Alaka told her.

"I'd have it no other way. We came aboard on their terms and it's gotten us nowhere, time to do things our way." Ayan strode to a weapons locker and retrieved a pulse pistol and rifle. She holstered the first and clipped the second to her chest. "All right, I need three technicians, Alaka, and two squads with me. Everyone else stays here and works on getting that hangar door open."

Finn was the first technician to step forward. There were several more behind him, more than she needed.

"You're staying here and directing the effort to get the door open, Finn. I'll take any three techs you recommend, though," Ayan said.

Finn picked three of the volunteers and they joined Alaka's squad members.

Ayan took a spool of strong, thin wire from her engineering pack, clipped it to her belt and attached the other to a Cold Reaver comm panel. "We're going to use wired and laserlink communications so they can't jam us. If my wire gets cut, set up a laserlink relay just like you've all practised in simulation. If you can't contact me or run into heavy resistance trying to get to me, use whatever means necessary to get back to the Triton. Chief Vega will be in charge of everything besides getting that door open. That'll be Finn's job. Use everything you need."

"Good luck, Commander," Stephanie replied. "I'll tell you if anything changes on our end."

"Thank you, Commander," Finn added.

Ayan, Alaka, the technicians, and two squads of soldiers poured out of the Cold Reaver's main gangway at a run. With the life support back on, their suits didn't have to counter the heavy gravity so the strength amplification systems made their movements feel light and effortless.

***

Terry Ozark McPatrick stepped out of the private ready quarters lift onto the bridge and was struck still for a moment. Every station was manned on the upper and lower levels, internal and external tactical status holodisplays were spaced out across the middle of the bridge, and extra personnel were standing by, ready to take their place at a station if an officer was called away to another task. In the middle of the hornet's nest was Captain Jacob Valance. He was the dark, cold centre around which everything orbited.

The ship was on full combat alert, everyone was called to stations. The Flight Operations deck beneath the main bridge was just as busy and bustling, and at a glance, Oz could see Chief Angelo Vercelli manipulating the three dimensional interfaces that marked which fighters were ready to launch and which should be loaded after they had been punted out of the Triton's lower hull.

Without a word he strode to the command seat at Captain Valance's left and brought up the ship-wide status screen, something he wished he'd done before leaving his ready quarters. He managed to stifle his surprised reaction when he read the first line of the status. "They have Ayan and the whole team locked in the station?" he asked.

"They do. We can't contact them, but a close flyby with a Uriel fighter showed all their life signs. Our best guess is that there were two squads running towards the station's inner chamber," Jake answered.

"Do we have a plan?"

"We start with a show of force. I'm launching all our fighter squadrons," Captain Valance replied.

"So much for getting the new engines installed."

Jake nodded.

"Do we have any sign at all from Ayan since she last reported?"

"None. As far as we can tell they've found a way to block any signals from or to their command units. They did just open a micro-wormhole. Jason's working on decrypting a capture of their communications."

"How long did he say it would take?" asked Oz.

"He's bringing the Minuteman supercomputer online, he said it would be about two hours."

"Good," Oz said.

"Sir," addressed a communications officer. "The station's sent us a message."

"Put it up," Jake said, surging to his feet.

A hologram of a woman in an old, loose fitting heavy vacsuit appeared in front of him. "Triton, we will be willing to allow your crew members to leave after you've remanded all the raider crews into our custody. They will be charged with destruction of property and piracy. You've already taken numerous vessels into your hangars. We will expect you to comply with our demands within the hour, using those ships." The message ended.

Jake grunted to himself and sat down.

Oz started looking up the regional law on piracy with the provision of being enslaved at the time the crime was committed.

"It's life," Jake said. "The sentence for piracy in this region of space is life for free crew or slaves. It doesn't make a difference."

"So if a slave has a destruct device inside them, and commits piracy because they know they'll be killed or tortured if they don't follow through, they're still facing a death sentence?" Oz asked.

"Exactly," Jacob replied. He pulled up the Triton's defence systems interface. Until then, the weaponry on the Triton had just been a list, like any other feature Oz hadn't inspected in person. As he looked at the tactical view of the ship, he realised the Triton's destructive potential. Thirty six torpedo tubes in nine loading rooms across the port, fore, aft, and starboard sides were loaded with driller rounds, set to detonate after punching through a hull and detecting an atmosphere. The fourteen missile turrets along the lower hull were loaded with two hundred eighty kilogram seeker projectiles. The gunnery deck's eighty four 280mm round guns were set with electromagnetic pulse rounds while its fourteen 450mm guns were loaded and ready with fragmentation burst rounds. The last of the weaponry, the eight carrier class electromagnetic beam weapons, were half charged.

"There she is with all her teeth bared," Oz breathed as he looked over the broad, gleaming stingray-shaped vessel. The only visible flaw was the absence of half her massive main engines, leaving recessed swivel ports open in the lower aft quarter of the vessel.

The first squadron of seven Uriel fighters, led by Ronin, launched from the lower hull and began moving into position around Triton. "Where do you want me, Jake?" Oz asked him. He hoped the situation didn't escalate to the point where the Triton would have to pummel the station. He didn't want to be in a position where he'd have to question Jacob Valance's judgment, but they had Ayan, and there was something very different about him. Jonas had never had the dark disposition Oz was seeing.

Jake manipulated a series of remote controls and gave the Palamo a heading that led it very close to the station, between it and the Triton before answering.

"I need you here," he replied dryly. With a flick of his finger he engaged privacy mode around the command seating. "It's Ayan over there, I need someone who can command this carrier better than I can. I don't know what I'll have to do in the next few minutes."

"What do you want to do right now, Jake?" Oz asked.

"I want to load every seasoned soldier we have into the Clever Dream, blast my way into the station and pull her out."

"I don't think the standard smash and grab tactics will work here. We don't know enough and with the material that station's made of, it may as well be a prison."

"All the more reason to act sooner rather than later. I can put a plan together en route."

"Have you looked at that thing? From the way those turrets are moving it looks like they have weapons back online. If I'm not mistaken, their guns could do serious damage to the Triton. The Clever Dream would be cannon fodder," Oz said.

"They'd have to get a clear shot first. The Palamo is moving in to provide cover by remote. I'll pass her controls on to you. Her reactor is wired to blow, just in case," Jake replied. His tone forbade questioning.

Oz looked Jake right in the eye. "What if Ayan's working a plan of her own? She could be in harm's way and we'd never know it."

"I'll be careful," Jake said.

"You're not level, Jake. Let me put a plan together."

Captain Valance sat back, his suppressed tension showed in the flexing of his jaw. "All right. You put it together, I'll lead it."

"We're not trading the slaves, right?" Oz asked.

"Hell, no," Jake snapped.

"Had to ask." Oz brought up a list of ships they'd taken from the raiders and chose the one in the worst condition. "Give me five minutes."

Jake watched his old friend focus on a captured raider vessel. It was called the Jade Whisper. At just over seventy metres long, it was a distant relative of the Samson in design. Between the scars of long past combat damage and fresh damage caused by Minh's fighter wing, there wasn't much left, but it was basically operational. "Thank you, Oz. I don't lose focus like this."

"It happens to everyone. If I were in your shoes, I wouldn't be much good for heavy thinking either," Oz said.

Jake realised he was practically breathing over Oz's shoulder and stood so he could give him some space. The privacy barrier only extended a metre past the edge of the command seating, and he stepped outside of it. He was immediately confronted with the three main holographic displays. One focused on the Triton, the central image was a more expanded view of the area, and the right hand image featured a visual representation of the asteroid field outside. The data was being updated by a Uriel starfighter holding station outside the obscuring barrier with a micro wormhole pointed towards the Triton. It was the early warning system, their only way of monitoring what was happening outside.

"Jason, have you seen any more transmissions incoming or outgoing from the station?" Jake asked.

"No. They've gone silent. My guess is they've consulted their backers and are operating under their instructions until help arrives," Jason replied.

"Do we have any idea who these people are associated with?"

"Until now I was pretty sure it was an independent station. There are no company logos on the structure. The cargo containers adrift in the area are from dozens of companies." Jason grimaced and shook his head in aggravation. "Why can't I figure out why we're not getting an active signal from our people in there! It's not like any jamming I've seen!"

Jake walked over to the communications station, a semicircle with all five seats filled. Jason was in the centre. "Would a tether work? Maybe an actual line leading to a ship breaking through the hull?"

"Of course, you can't jam a hard line without tapping it," Jason replied peevishly.

"Okay, start working under the assumption that we have a rescue party getting ready to go," Jake replied.

"Do we?"

"Oz is working on something."

Jason couldn't help but pause a moment before nodding. "Okay, then I'll work under that assumption and move on to other things."

Jake walked back to the centre of the bridge and looked at the curved latticework of the station. He had a sinking feeling, like the situation was slipping out of his control. "We're coming. Hang on, we're coming," he muttered.

CHAPTER 17
DIPLOMACY

Victor watched as Ayan was boosted into the shaft leading into the ruined communications hub. According to what she said, it had been severely damaged well before they arrived. His forensic scanners couldn't so much as penetrate the bulkhead so he took her word for it.

"Vic, you're following her," Alaka told him.

It wasn't like him to hesitate or question, but being singled out to protect the darling of the Triton alone wasn't exactly what he expected when he followed Alaka back into the heart of the station. He also couldn't agree with Ayan's need to make some kind of diplomatic appeal to the people who were keeping them locked in.

"You're the narrowest, get on up there," Alaka reinforced, offering him his big, cupped hands to step into.

"Sorry, just taking in the situation," Victor replied as he handed his rifle off to another soldier and unholstered his side arm. He tucked his handgun into the back of his belt then stepped into Alaka's waiting hands. He was boosted up to the narrow service shaft entrance at an alarming speed. He didn't get his arms up in time and had to wriggle in head and shoulders first.

In the narrow dark passage, he could hear Ayan ahead, but without the enhanced vision of his visor he wouldn't have been able to see her. She had gotten several meters ahead and was already at the point where the shaft widened.

He couldn't help but feel as though the station was pressing down on him, however. When he moved his shoulders to wriggle ahead, his shoulder blades grazed the top of the shaft. It felt as though he was crawling through a long, shallow coffin. Panic threatened to grip him as he tried to get his hands up in front of him but failed.

"Are you all right, Victor? Your stats are climbing," Ayan called back.

"I'll be fine as soon as I catch up." He redoubled his efforts and pushed ahead, using his knees, chest, and feet to push his way along the shaft. Finally he came to the portion of the shaft where it widened and got his hands in front. Victor sighed in relief as he squeezed in beside Ayan, making sure she still had enough space to work.

She had fine tools out and was just finishing bridging two wires with a clamp. "Now that the station has power in these sections, we can force doors open by powering their locks manually."

"Maybe you can," Victor said. "I'm not exactly a tech."

"This is the easy stuff. I bet I could teach you how to get past most locking mechanisms in an afternoon. The challenging part is finding a way to get at the wiring." A pair of wires sparked and something in the bulkhead in front of them clicked. "Bloody hell," she muttered. "The bolt drew back, but I have to hotwire the hatch so it'll move."

"This is the hatch here?" Victor pressed against the metal plate between them.

"Yes, but it's on a rail that won't move without the motor."

"Where do you see that?" Victor asked, looking around.

Ayan reached up and pushed her fingers into a narrow crack. "You can feel the rail right here." She withdrew them and went back to carefully tracing wires, figuring out what each was attached to.

Victor almost confirmed for himself but stopped. "Oh, I believe you, I just-" he shrugged.

"Haven't been in many maintenance corridors?" Ayan smirked. He couldn't see it, but he could hear it well enough, especially with her light Britannia accent. "I wouldn't call this a corridor. Tunnel fighting could be a bit like this, but there's normally more breathing room. Completely different if you ask me, except for the claustrophobia."

"You did tunnel fighting even though you're claustrophobic? That's well beyond the call," Ayan said.

"Well, it was either go with Alaka into the tunnels or fight in the open where we made half the progress and lost twice as many people," Victor replied.

"I remember. Pandem was bad for everyone. I had to hang upside-down over a docking pit with nothing but my wits and a vacsuit. My fear of heights nearly did me in."

"You're a starship engineer and you're afraid of heights? What do you do for space walks?"

"You're a trained soldier with claustrophobia," Ayan retorted with a rueful chuckle.

"Good point."

Ayan worked in silence as Victor watched her strand different uncut wires together while tugging others to the side. "Actually, I don't know," Ayan said.

"Don't know?"

"What I'd do for space walks. It hasn't come up since I realised I was afraid of heights again. I was hoping I'd be all right on a space walk, but as you know that's rarely the case."

"I suppose you'll find out when they install the new engine pods," Victor said.

"I was hoping to give it a go well before that, but from the way things are going, you might be right. Not like I should supervise that sort of thing from a distance."

"Most senior starship engineers would, from what I've seen on past tours," Victor said.

"Well, I'm not most engineers. I supervised the build on those engine pods, I'd rather see they get installed properly." Ayan cut four wires, stripped the insulation off and pinched them together. Her vacsuit protected her from the raw current as a loud crack sounded. The small, thick hatch was drawn aside swiftly, giving them a clear way into one of the station's comm rooms. "You go first. I'll make sure these don't come loose."

The sound of the motor clicking and whining as it continued to run, stripping its gears with the door as far along the track as it could go was loudest as Victor pushed his shoulders through the opening. There was no graceful way down.

Once most of his torso was hanging in the open air above the communications room, he let himself fall past the nearest console. With a violent crash, he narrowly missed a chair on wheels, sending it spinning across the room as he fell face first on the floor. The vacsuit's armour and inertial dampening systems kept him from physical harm, but his pride was still injured as he listened to Ayan burst out laughing. "Three point five!" she called after him.

With him out of the way and her lesser size, she had just enough room to turn around, though the sounds of her straining to bend was testimony to how difficult it was.

He stood and moved to the deactivated console as she lowered herself down feet first. Victor could see her feet feeling in the air for the top of the console so she could carefully step down and put his hand reassuringly on her leg. "I'll catch you, just drop out."

She pushed off and he caught her perfectly in his arms. Even through the overlapping slats of the vacsuit armour she felt much more feminine than he expected.

"You don't weigh a thing, my suit didn't even kick in," Victor said.

"Flatterer," Ayan waited a moment then kicked her feet a little. "Ahem."

He stepped away from the console and gently put her down.

"Thank you."

Her gaze scanned across the dimly lit oval room. In the centre was an island with six chairs, the walls were covered with two dimensional displays and seating. It was a long counter top, broken by two inset track doors. "Do you see anything that's displaying something?" she asked quietly, beginning a slow walk along the oval room.

Vincent did the same in the other direction and then it struck him. There was nothing he understood on the screens, nothing coming out of any of the older holographic projectors. He traced one of the circular emitters with his finger and snickered softly.

"See something?" she asked.

"No, sorry. These holographic displays are ancient. My sister and I saved our allowance for three months when we were kids so we could get one for the rear cabin of the family cruiser. She'd have a laugh at seeing one being used in a room like this."

Ayan didn't reply. She kept inspecting the control panels; what she was looking for exactly, he couldn't tell.

"She made it off Pandem with her husband after the bots went homicidal."

Ayan looked at him, mild relief plain on her face. "Oh, I forgot transports escaped that mess."

"A few dozen. Some of us old soldiers were able to help the police get them away from Damshir early on. The first time we got control," Victor said.

"I never heard what exactly happened during the early days of the virus."

"Well, most of the Andies, that's the police androids, managed to resist long enough for deactivation. Then something reactivated them while most of the police force was inside the Mount Elbrus police station. A few of us retired military types ran into Alaka and we got more organised. Then the real fight began."

"I'm sorry," Ayan said.

They were walking in a slow circle, inspecting the screens closely. There was nothing to see; even Victor could see most of the computers were stuck in a diagnostic loop or frozen altogether. "Don't know why you're apologising. Even Alaka said without you people we may not have made it off Pandem."

"You give us too much credit," Ayan replied. "I couldn't imagine doing what you did for weeks. When I remember Pandem, I think about the people we couldn't save."

"Can't do that. Survival is about small victories. Is this something? Looks like some kind of terminal ID," Victor said.

Ayan walked over and withdrew her faceplate, leaving the armoured hood of her vacsuit up. She looked at the lower corner of the wall display. He was pointing at an unchanging square with EL-147 blinking inside. The rest of the screen was streaming thousands of seemingly random numbers, letters, and device symbols. She touched it and the whole screen froze. "I wish Jason were here, he might understand what half this says."

"Didn't they teach you about this in some engineering program?"

"Well, I can read it, but it's just a fragment of some sort of software package. These are hardware identifiers, storage, power, backups, comm lines, gravity, and thermal sensors but what this computer does with it all is still a mystery. Reading it like this could take a while and it still might not tell us how to get the doors open or if the hallways outside have pressure."

"Right, so we open the wrong door and we end up getting sucked out and falling to the planet surface," Victor said.

"Exactly."

"Isn't this a navnet symbol?" He pointed to lopsided plus sign.

"You're right," Ayan tried pressing the square again and let the screen scroll through several thousand characters before tapping it once more, pausing the program. "This shows a dead comm line with a safety warning."

"Probably warning the operators to repair the communications array before they end up with a hundred ship pileup at the docks."

She scrolled to the next screen and was rewarded with an eyeful of electronic schematics. Ayan smiled brightly and laughed to herself. "Repair instructions."

"Isn't the comm tower a slagged mess?"

"It is, but it also shows me how to rewire console three so we can speak over the intercom in an emergency," Ayan said.

Victor looked around and found a worn number 3 painted on the edge of the counter several meters down. "There it is."

Ayan pulled a narrow screwdriver from her thigh pocket as she walked over to the console. With no effort at all she had the main panel open and several connections on an ancient main circuit board bridged and shorted. "Good thing this place's computers were built on the cheap. Looks like they spent all their money on the superstructure and the gravity mill."

"How exactly does that work, anyway?" Victor asked.

"Do you have two days?" Ayan asked him with a crooked grin. "Let's just say it's a little like a water wheel, only not."

"Right, I'll stick to soldiering, you can keep trying to get in touch with someone."

"Ayan!" called Alaka through the shaft.

"Yeah," she replied. "We're just a few meters in."

"Oh, good. Contact anyone?" Alaka asked.

"No, just figuring out the intercom now. How is the other team doing?"

"Finn just updated me. He says it would take at least twenty hours to cut through the hangar door without using explosives. I think he's leaning towards using the Cold Reaver's weapons to blast through."

"At that range? We'd be lucky to have half a ship left."

"He said he'd work on the math, see if there was something he could do to minimise blow back."

Ayan thought a moment before shaking her head. "Tell him he's welcome to do the calculations, but if he actually gets somewhere he has to run it by me before putting it into practice."

"Will do, good luck in there."

"Thank you. I hope this lock-down is some kind of big misunderstanding."

"You and me both."

Ayan looked into the open control panel, pulled a short wire free, and pressed it into a tiny black box. The terminal display flashed red for several moments and then started displaying a large audio symbol: a white dot with increasingly large concave lines emanating from it.

"Does that mean it's working?" Victor asked in a whisper.

Ayan stared at the screen for a moment, started to say something then shrugged. "It's a little vague." As an afterthought she accessed the colour controls for her armour through her command unit and changed it to white. The black horizontal overlapping metal slats and the vacsuit material beneath shifted to match her request. "I'd rather not be dressed head to tow in black if they can see me. White's a better colour for negotiations."

"Hello? Who is this?" asked a husky female voice.

Ayan smiled and cleared her throat before replying. "This is Commander Ayan, I'm with the repair team from the Triton that restored power earlier."

"Oh my God, thank you. I've been looking for a way off the station since the trouble started. You don't know how good it is to hear from you. You have to get me out of here!"

"I'm afraid we're trapped," Ayan said. "That's why I had to hot wire this terminal."

"So you have no control? This is just a hack?"

"I'm afraid so. Who are you?"

"I'm Larissa Ferris, the last surviving medic on the station."

"Get away from the comm system Larissa," warned another woman.

"It's the repair team! They found a way to-" Larissa replied.

"You've said enough. Confine her to her quarters, Bradley," said the newcomer.

There was a long pause, during which Victor pulled his side arm free of his belt and checked the energy clip. It was fully charged.

Ayan noticed and shook her head, indicating quietly with a wave that he should put it away.

"Now, who are you?" asked the new woman on the other end.

"I'm Ayan, leader of the team that restored power to your section of the station. It seems we're locked inside."

"Yes, I'm holding you until your ship turns over all the raiders you've taken captive. They'll be held accountable."

"It was a slave crew acting under the direction of a few senior crew members," Ayan said.

"That doesn't make a lick of a difference. They could have mutinied."

"They had controller implants embedded in their breastbones, I'm afraid they didn't have a choice. The captain of the Triton, my home vessel, killed

146

two of the senior officers, but there's one left. They called her Doctor Thurge and I'm sure Captain Valance would trade her for us."

"I'm afraid that wouldn't be enough. The company wouldn't accept that one person could be held accountable for disrupting our operations."

"I'm led to wonder how handing us over would help if you didn't get the slave crew?" Ayan asked.

"You mean the raider crew. According to the company, the Triton crew are wanted too, so either way I win."

"We must be able to find a middle ground. We have supplies, we can offer more help if you'd allow us more access and the freedom to come and go. In trade we could use a safe harbour for a few days."

"That would be tempting if there weren't a small fleet of rescue ships and a military escort already on their way. You're not going anywhere until they get here either. Not unless your captain hands over those raiders."

Ayan's fair complexion started to betray her; even in the dim light Victor could see she was starting to turn red. She fought through it, taking a deep, slow breath before speaking. "I'm sorry, I didn't catch your name."

"Forewoman Amanda Dimitri."

"All right, I understand being in command of a station this size must be a massive undertaking, but I didn't see any kind of company markings on my way through or on the hull outside. You're independent, right?"

There was a pause preceding the answer. "We have investors."

"I imagine those investors, or the men they hire to represent them, don't really care about you or your staff. They're here to get things running smoothly again. Whatever promises they've made, you've got to realise they won't matter once they see the state the facility is in."

Victor's eyes went wide. The woman Ayan was speaking to seemed immovable, frustrating, and he would have already given up. Instead, Ayan took a completely different approach and he couldn't help be impressed at how calm she sounded as she did so.

"They wouldn't replace me, I'm essential staff," replied the forewoman.

"There are always other experts. Investors have a tendency of getting their way, especially when things start falling apart. There's a lot we can do for you if you let me communicate with Triton."

"For reasons I can't get into, there's no way I can allow you to directly contact your ship."

"How can I demonstrate to you that we are here to help? The Triton and crew have taken care of your raider problem at a great cost. We lost several crew members during the fight. That must gain us a little goodwill, a little trust?" Ayan asked.

"How do I know that you didn't follow the raiders here? That defeating them and taking this slave crew and their ships for yourselves wasn't the plan from the beginning?"

"We're not pirates, and if we were the last target we'd take on is a small raider fleet," Ayan replied.

"Your ship doesn't fly a flag, there are no sponsors listed, how could you be anything but pirates? Maybe this station is just a bonus prize you stumbled into and now that you've become trapped here you don't have any other choice but to speak to us?" the forewoman said.

Ayan rolled her eyes. "If you won't allow me to speak to my ship directly, let's speak to them together. Simply open a channel with them and we can all sort this out."

"Actually, they're sending a message right now, you just hold that thought," said the woman on the other end.

Ayan closed her eyes and shook her head.

Several moments passed before the intercom clicked and Forewoman Amanda Dimitri's voice crackled through. "They're bringing the raiders in now. We'll be opening the prison processing doors and walking them straight into the holding facilities. The machines killed all our workers when they contracted a virus, now we can replenish our workforce and start repairs as our rescue fleet arrives."

"Oh, shit," Victor muttered under his breath. "How the hell did I miss that?"

Ayan shook her head quickly. "Listen, you seem fairly bright, so you must know that-"

"This could be some kind of reverse trap? Of course I do! You've seen this place though, how well it protects us from external attack," the forewoman said.

Ayan nodded mournfully and adjusted a wire inside the console. "You're going to want to put your headgear on," she said.

"What?" Amanda asked, confused.

"Not you," Ayan replied.

Victor realised she was speaking to him, brought his headgear up and sealed it.

She did the same and pressed a tiny daub of adhesive putty down over the lead end of a wire and the circuit board. A high pitched whine screamed over the intercom, their vacsuits protecting them from the harsh sound. "If this intercom is their primary means of communication inside the station, they'll have to find a way to cut this room off from the system entirely before they can use it again."

"What did you do?" Victor asked, noticing that their suits were using a laserlink to communicate.

"I created a feedback loop on the circuit board. I can't believe I didn't see this coming when we first arrived. I should have suspected something was going on when there was no one here to meet or direct us," Ayan scolded herself. "We have to get back and regroup. I hope I'm wrong but I don't think Jake and the others will realise it's a prison until it's too late."

CHAPTER 18
A GOOD PLAN

The Jade Whisper drifted slowly towards the station docking clamps. The ship's thruster fire bathed the stretch of station in front of Jake and the two squads of soldiers as they watched the hull of the complex draw nearer. Jake viewed the remote feed from the main docking gangway through his link with the ship as it started locking with the station. The debarkation compartment was empty, in fact the only place that held crew was the port side airlock.

It was Oz's plan. So unlike the kind of smash and grab tactic Jake would have used, the idea had a good chance of working, only it would be costly. They'd lose the Jade Whisper for one, a serviceable vessel. The thought of losing an operational ship, even one as old as the Jade Whisper, was more than a little irritating, but Jake couldn't see any other practical way of getting close to the station while maintaining the element of surprise.

The ship shuddered as the main docking clamps secured and the engines cut out. The lights in the main debarkation compartment turned green, and when the crew from the station entered they'd find there was no one inside. "It's time," Jake stated as he pulled his data line free of the airlock control panel. He punched the button to open the outer hatch and looked down. There were eight meters between him and the hull of the station. "This first step's the worst, careful," Jake warned as he pushed off.

It was by far the strangest and most dangerous space walk he'd ever experienced from the very first second on. At twelve times ideal gravity, he plummeted so rapidly that he didn't get a chance to fall properly. The armoured vacsuit compensated enough so his impact felt like nothing more than a mild bump, but he felt several outer protective plates crack under the strain. He stood and ran out of the way as quickly as he could manage.

The next to drop behind him made his descent look graceful by comparison, landing shoulder and head first. The suit stopped his spine from shattering. "That's insane!" he exclaimed as he stood up, checking his headgear. "I mean, one minute you're just stepping out of an airlock, then wham! Naught to a hundred klicks in a millisecond then you hit the deck like you've stepped in front of an express train!"

"Move so everyone else can follow," Jake ordered.

"Yes, Sir."

They each made their awkward drop, one after another violently falling from the ship airlock to the surface of the station's hull. The last two had the pleasure of carrying heavy backpacks loaded with cutting equipment. Neither of them had much control of how they fell; they could only make sure that they landed pack first.

"All right, it's safe to assume that they know the ship is empty now. We don't have much time, so we're crossing the distance to the secondary hangar doors at a jog. Be careful not to fall. If you feel that you're about to slip, call out and try your best to get a grip on something. Mag locks and hull spikes won't work because we're too heavy, and the hull is harder than any of you have seen. Just grab whatever you can if you slip, it's a long way down. Stay in single file," Jake told them as he clipped his safety line to the man in front of him. "I'm taking the rear."

"This thing is huge, I barely see a curvature to the hull," said one of the soldiers.

"You're right, but the surface is irregular," Jake replied. "There's probably a lot to trip on if we don't watch our step. Everyone clipped in?"

All fourteen of the squad members checked in and Jake directed the group to start jogging. He nearly tripped over a hastily repaired reinforcement plate after only a few meters, and made an extra effort to be careful from then on.

The sounds of the synthetic muscle in his suit ground and squeaked with the rhythmic movement of his legs and arms as he ran at an easily maintained jog. He couldn't help but be reminded of his jogs with Doctor Anderson on the First Light.

Those polished hallways and smiling crew members were ancient history to him. Things had been so different, it was as though those memories were some holomovie. The man starring, Jonas Valent, seemed alien. He faced his problems head on and had close friends, confidants he depended on. Jake faced things head on, but still found it difficult to remain attached to anyone as a close friend.

The image atop the statue in the centre of the Triton's botanical gallery came to mind. It was Jonas and Ayan who were remembered there, a short-lived coupling that he secretly envied. Everything seemed simpler in retrospect, even facing his own demons.

He hadn't been down to see the monument to the man who was responsible for him coming into being, responsible for everything he had, even his daughter. How was it that he hadn't been to the Triton's rear hold to see what remained of the Samson? He wanted to, he'd even ordered all the Samson crew members' footlockers and bunks to be emptied and tagged so they could pick up their personal items.

Ensuring that the people who served aboard the Samson were at home on Triton wasn't a problem or a chore for him. He was always quietly watching, making sure that they were getting on well aboard the Triton. Somehow seeing the remains of the Samson herself was more difficult than keeping tabs on his old crew.

The list of things he'd been avoiding hadn't escaped notice. Even speaking to Shamus Frost about his refusal to have the perfectly good foot waiting for him in medical attached was something Jake hadn't gotten around to. Stephanie had tried to get him to go, but that became a matter of pride. He knew that the moment he told Frost in no uncertain terms that he had to do it, the old gunnery chief would be in medical. Jake had let the simple task slide for two weeks.

If it were the only thing, it wouldn't have been much of a problem, but atop everything else, it forced him to ask why he was avoiding so many things. They were minor compared to Alice's passing that morning, and it wasn't normal for him to dodge responsibilities.

As he carefully jogged around the base of a long antenna, he decided that he'd make rebuilding his old ship a priority, as soon as he explained himself to Ayan.

His reverie was interrupted as one of the squad members called, "Sir! We're taking fire!"

"Halt and take cover," Jake ordered as he slowed to a stop and turned. At least two people were firing on them from the open airlock of the Jade Whisper. "Everyone wave," he said.

Several squad members raised a hand and did as ordered, waving, gesturing wildly for attention, or turning and offering their backsides. "It's right here! Come and get it!" one yelled.

Captain Valance couldn't help but smile as he watched the more experienced squadron Oz had chosen enjoy themselves. Most of them knew full well that the suits could take several hits from most energy weapons before sustaining serious damage. The outer armour was made to survive more serious damage of a cosmic nature, and each of them came with a personal shield. "Here's the expensive bit," Jake muttered as he activated the explosive charges distributed along the main supports inside the Jade Whisper. Explosive bursts of air escaped the broad, thirty meter vessel as it began to collapse towards the mooring point and the station beneath it.

The pair who were firing at them from the open airlock realised the ship was crushing towards them and leapt. Neither landed gracefully. Their much older suits may have allowed them to survive, but it was unlikely that they fell without injury. It didn't matter for long, however. Large segments of the Jade Whisper's hull came loose and crashed down, burying them under several tons of twisted metal.

"Let's get going. Who knows what they'll send after us and where it'll come from," Jake said as he turned away from the crumbling wreckage.

Before long, they arrived at the large secondary hangar door. Captain Valance knelt down and took a point blank measurement of the metal with his command unit. It was a meter and a half thick slab of reinforced metal. He shook his head. "Explains why they haven't been able to cut through," he said. "All right, let's get the fusion cutters set up. I need the mini-reactors here and over there. We're going to extend the arms wide enough so the Cold Reaver will have enough space to fly out."

A green spotlight a meter wide started to dance around Jake. It was a long distance laserlink.

"Message for you, Sir," one squad member quipped.

Jake stood perfectly still so the laserlink could hit him. Finally the light touched his suit and Minh's voice came through his comm loud and clear. "This is Ronin. We have a big problem, Hitman."

"A bigger problem?"

"Right, much bigger. A command carrier with markings we haven't seen before just arrived with five heavy destroyers and a whole fleet of rescue and construction ships. It looks like they're just about to head through the obscuring field."

"You're right, that's a bigger problem," Jake said. "Tell the Clever Dream that they're going to be picking us up. We don't have time to cut a hole big enough for the Cold Reaver."

"Aye, we'll cover you while you get everyone out," Ronin replied.

"Start by taking out their turrets. Good hunting, Ronin."

"My pleasure."

The communicator closed the channel and Captain Valance turned to the squad leader. "We're making a hole a meter wide. Use both fusion cutters."

"Aye, Captain," replied the squad leader.

"This trip keeps getting more and more expensive," Jake grumbled.

***

Minh-Chu relayed the message he received from Jake and waited for Oz to review it. Ronin had loaded his ship down with as much firepower as he could muster without unbalancing the thrusters. His rate of acceleration and manoeuvrability were effected just enough for him to have to make a few major adjustments early on in the flight.

"All right, I reviewed it. I'm surprised they can jam their comms with them standing outside the station, though," Oz told him from the bridge.

"I don't know how it works, my comms jam up when I come within fifty meters of the hull. It's like they're using the frame of the station to transmit a jamming signal. Speaking of the station, my squad will move on and take out those big cannons. If we come around so we're skimming along the station's hull, there's no way they'll fire at us. There's too much risk of them hitting their own assets."

"Hold off on that. I'm going to try to hold off these people diplomatically. Maybe there's something I can do to get us out of this."

"Gooood luuuuck," Minh sang back. "From the scans our spotter outside the barrier took, it looks like they came here expecting trouble."

"And we took care of the raiders for them."

"There's that. I'll be out here, ready to go if you need me," Minh said as he took his fighter into a tight roll and looked down at the nearest cannon mount. It was over fifty three hundred kilometres away, slowly rotating back and forth.

***

Terry Ozark McPatrick stood in front of the command seating as the image of the Caran Enterprises Control Ship Ellis' commander appeared. At first he thought it was the intentionally squared graphical representation of an artificial intelligence, then he realised that the Captain's image was rendered roughly to obscure his or her identity. Oz found that insulting, but set his irritation aside. "I'm Commander McPatrick of the Free Ship Triton. We've come to the assistance of Ossimi station and rescued a number of slave crews."

"I'm the Admiral of this emergency response fleet, you may address me by rank. We have come to re-assert our claim on this Caran Enterprise interest and require that you leave this space immediately."

"We're retrieving a number of our people and will require at least half an hour to complete operations."

"Please state your vessel's business here again?"

"We responded to a distress call, freed a large slave crew and restored power to a large section of Ossimi station after defeating a number of raiders inside. We're just picking up some of our people and-" Oz was interrupted as the holographic figure disappeared. He looked behind him to Jason and shrugged.

"They dropped the transmission," Jason said.

Oz motioned for Jason to move up to the command seats as he sat down. "Do a check on the crew profiles, see if anyone has dealt with Caran Enterprises before."

"I already did. We don't have anyone aboard who's run into them."

"Fantastic," Oz said.

"Tall, blurry and mysterious is back," Jason announced.

"Put him through," Oz said, standing up again.

The vague image of the Admiral reappeared. "The Station Keeper, Foreperson Amanda Dimitri has informed me that you have failed to meet her reasonable demands and your people have cost her the lives of several workers. It's also come to my attention that there is a Galactic Warrant out for this vessel and her crew. Specifically one Captain Jacob Valance, also known as Jonas Valent. I'm instructing you to power down all but essential systems and prepare to be boarded. All compartments are to be opened for scanning, any weapons you have will be secured in arms lockers, your crew will stand at stations for inspections, and all senior officers will meet the inspection team at the airlock when they arrive with the command codes for all vessels. Any show of resistance will be met with force."

"Please, give me a moment to begin making arrangements," Oz said as he cut the channel with a tap on his comm unit.

The Admiral's holographic image disappeared.

"Ronin," Oz addressed.

"Here and waiting. How is diplomacy going?"

"If it looks like any of those turrets are about to take a shot at the Clever Dream, take them out. Cover them while they pick up our people."

"That well, huh?" Minh said with a chuckle. "I'm on it."

"Flight Operations, launch the Clever Dream. Tell the commanding officer to deliver this message to Captain Valance: 'We're out of time.'"

"Yes, Sir. They're ready and will be off the deck in twenty seconds," replied Chief Angelo Vercelli from where he stood at the central command podium below.

Oz turned his attention to the tertiary holographic display on the bridge. It was the Control Ship Ellis' exterior scan. The vessel was three and a half kilometres long with four main columns that extended upward from a large misshapen base. At a glance he could tell it was built to be a massive, combat-ready mobile space station in its own right. The Triton seemed huge, but compared to the Ellis she was completely outclassed.

What was worse were the five battle cruisers that accompanied her. Their sleek hulls curved around short central structures that contained at least one fighter bay and a considerable arsenal. The thrusters set above the main protective hull segments were disproportionately large, suggesting that the ships were made as much for interception as they were for combat at various ranges. The Triton could take on two of the roughly four hundred meter long ships, but Oz knew five were just too many. His thoughts shifted to the botanical gallery and the families who lived there. The orphans of Pandem came to mind and he shook it off.

He caught Ashley's dark brown eyes looking at him. She was picking up on his anxiety. Oz flashed a quick grin and nodded to himself. "Time to leave," he muttered as he took the central command chair.

"I'm sure Ayan and Jake have things under control on their end."

CHAPTER 19
RUN

Ayan was just hitching back into her combat engineer's backpack when the main doors leading further into the station creaked and groaned. The raiders had failed to cut through the thick armoured doors, but they'd managed to do a great deal of damage.

"Someone's trying to come through from the other side," one of the squad members said.

"Your grasp of the obvious is astounding," Alaka replied as he started to charge his beam cannon. "Take cover."

Ayan and the squad scrambled to get behind the heavier crates, taking cover in pairs. She finished securing the last clip from her armoured vacsuit to her backpack and took her rifle from Victor. "Thank you."

"Sticking with white?" he asked, gesturing at the colour of her armour.

She looked at the mixed coloured crates and the pocked metal floor. There were whole swathes where the floor's coating had been blasted away, leaving the metal bare. "It's better than black for camouflage right now. Besides, it was always my favourite colour," she replied.

"I thought white was a non-colour," Victor said.

"Nope, white is a colour, black isn't a colour."

"I thought black was the presence of all colours."

"No, you're thinking of painting. If you combine all your paints except for white you sometimes end up with black. In the real world, white is the brightest colour, whereas black is the absence of light."

"Well, that changes everything," Victor said with a faint chuckle.

"Now you're having a laugh at my expense," Ayan said, feigning a pout.

"Just putting your education to work."

The deck shuddered as the doors spread open a crack. With an ear splitting scrape and grind, the motors managed to draw the meter thick, dense metal doors apart. They were four meters tall, made for transporting major components deeper into the station.

"Ayan? Is Ayan from the Triton here?" asked a panicky looking bald woman at the front of fifteen mismatched station staff members. They looked around the cargo area warily, some with their hands raised, others in awe at the damage the area had sustained.

Ayan drew back the faceplate of her armour, leaving the hood up and stepped into the open. "I'm here."

"I'm Larissa, we spoke on the comm. We're seeking asylum on the Triton. You have to hurry, alarms will be going off now that this door is open and Amanda will know someone's trying to escape."

"You're prisoners?" Ayan asked.

"We're workers, but after what's happened they'll never let us leave."

"Yeah, we're prisoners! Can we go now?" added Bradley. "That's what you are if you get paid but never get to leave," he spat at Larissa so harshly she flinched. "Bloody wazzock."

"We were just leaving." Ayan smiled. It had been a long time since she'd met anyone with such a thick Britannia accent. It was good to hear even though the speaker's dialect was rough. "All right, cover these people. We return to the Cold Reaver at a run," Ayan ordered Alaka.

Ayan scanned the fifteen newcomers and was surprised to find them unarmed. A few of them had medical kits and bundles of personal items very hastily packed together but other than that they had nothing. They were ready to run, however, and kept up with the group of militia handily.

"I hate to ask, but who's your sponsor? I've never seen the kind of armour you're wearing," Bradley asked as he fell into step beside her. He clutched a large medical kit to his chest with both arms.

"Triton is an independent ship," Ayan replied. "We manufacture our own equipment."

"Are you originally from Earth? We noticed it was built in the Sol system," he asked.

"I can't go into the details just now, but we're not from Earth."

"See? Like I was saying. Pirates," Larissa said to Bradley, who gave her a wide eyed stare. She turned to Ayan with a thin smile. "Not that I look down on it, mind you. Pirates are fine if they're just stopping for supplies or to spend time at the pub without causing a fuss."

"Right now we're just looking for a place to make repairs so we can move on and find an ally. Privateering is more our calling," Ayan said.

"Against anyone in particular?" Larissa asked.

"The Order of Eden," Ayan answered without an instant's hesitation. "A number of us were on Pandem when they took it."

"What happened to Pandem?" asked one of the newcomers behind her.

Ayan's heart began to sink, but she steeled herself against the terrible memories of what happened to the place. "I'm sorry. The virus that made your automated systems go mad here struck there, then the Order of Eden and Regent Galactic stepped in to finish the job."

"Oh my God. I knew people on Pandem, took my last vacation there. I've never seen a place like it," he said sadly. "What is it like now?"

"It's better that you remember it as it was," Ayan said.

"Oh. Any chance anyone from Verona survived? That's where I stayed." Alaka dropped back to run alongside the fellow. His long, loping steps and great size were intimidating even when he withdrew the plates covering his head to reveal a furred, pointed nose and mournful dark eyes. "I'm sorry. The resort islands were struck first. Few people survived Pandem, my family and I were fortunate."

"So you fight with the Triton against the people who destroyed your home," he said.

"Yes, that is the promise," Alaka said. "That is the cause."

"Ayan, look," Victor directed her to look through the hallway window.

The Triton was positioning itself in front of the station to cover their escape. The torpedo tubes all along the edges of the hull came to life, the sleek projectiles turning as soon as they were launched towards a foe they couldn't see. "That's a lot of firepower, they must be in some serious trouble."

"A Caran Enterprises fleet has arrived, they're staking a claim on the station since our highest ranking officer is only a Forewoman, not even a real controller."

"You couldn't have told us this a few minutes ago?" Victor replied at Bradley.

"I'm sorry, I was-" He was interrupted as a flash of light flared through the wide porthole.

"They just landed a focused nuclear strike against the Triton's shields. Thank God it struck the opposite side," Ayan said as many of her companions stared in shock. "Run. The sooner we get to the Cold Reaver, the sooner we can try to blast our way out of here. We don't have much of a choice."

"I'm getting a message from the Reaver now," Alaka said as they started running. "They say that someone is cutting through the hangar door from the outside. The metal is white hot and they've almost breached."

"All right, tell them to stay tethered to something in case it opens to vacuum, and get the people we have in stasis bags ready to travel. No one takes more than their kit with them."

Alaka relayed the message as quickly as he could. "Chief Vega wants to confirm: we're abandoning the Cold Reaver?"

"I'm afraid so," Ayan replied.

CHAPTER 20
BREAKING POINT

The Clever Dream lowered itself into place over the squad, covering them with her main airlock. The embarkation collar sealed around the hole they were drilling through the large hangar door and the air began to pressurise. "How long?" asked Jake.

"Less than a minute. I'm just glad the ship is here so we don't open the space inside up to vacuum when we break through," replied one of the squad members.

"All our people are in vacsuits, that was never a worry." Captain Valance plugged into the small airlock interface panel and opened a channel to the Clever Dream's cockpit. "How is the Triton?"

"Our live relay just went dead, but she was holding up just a few seconds ago. Oz kept them busy with negotiations as long as they could then they sent five destroyers through the field. From what we could tell, they managed to tear one to pieces while Ronin is keeping another occupied," answered Lewis. "One more thing, it looks like the Palamo is starting a suicide run on the biggest of the Caran ships."

"What kind of weaponry are they bringing to bear?" Jake asked.

"Particle beams and self-propelled torpedoes. Each of the vessels are heavily fortified, even the first Commander McPatrick managed to nearly disable is still firing."

The fusion powered cutter burst through the hangar door and Jake watched as his squad removed the clamps securing the device in place and hauled it clear. The gravity between the Clever Dream and the station equalised, followed by the air pressure and the inner airlock door opened. He looked through the freshly cut hole and saw Ayan, Alaka, two squads, and several other people rushing towards the Cold Reaver. Everyone from the drop ship had already realised that someone was cutting through to rescue them and they were tethered to the rear embarkation ramp of the Cold Reaver just in case the air was about to rush out the circular hole forming in the hangar door.

"We don't have much time, come through in single file!" Jake ordered.

Alaka remained closest to the main hall leading into the hangar, keeping watch with a canister in one hand and his beam cannon in the other. The armour plates of his vacsuit rose into place and sealed over his face.

As the first group were making their way into the Clever Dream Jake stepped through the hole and surveyed the situation. The crew and squads stationed on the Cold Reaver had done everything right. The majority of them had only taken their kits, a few had strapped on extra packs filled with food, medical supplies, extra power cells and survival gear. The weeks, and in some cases months of simulations the crew had undergone had paid off. For most of them, it looked like they were quickly running through the motions. Even the technicians they'd brought moved as though they knew exactly what steps had to take place in order to evacuate to the Clever Dream.

"Are you sure we have to leave her behind, Sir?" Stephanie asked as she was about to pass into the Clever Dream's airlock. "She's a solid ship."

"As long as we have the Triton, that's just a glorified longboat," he answered flatly.

"Aye." She nodded, moving on.

Ayan's group put the mismatched station staffers first, and they eyed Captain Valance as they passed.

Jake strode to meet Ayan half way. She held her rifle at the ready, walking backwards and looking towards the hall leading to the rest of the station. "They came out requesting asylum. Most are carrying medical gear, no weapons," she reported.

"They have friends coming after them?" Jake asked.

"There's a Forewoman here who wants to show she can control the station, I think they're undermining that."

In a flash of light and sound, gunfire erupted from the hallway at Alaka, who started walking backwards at an even pace. He fired several short streams of deadly energy from his beam cannon, cutting into the sides of the hallway and scorching bare cables tied against the walls.

Ayan, Victor, and a few other soldiers stepped forward and laid down cover fire with their pulse rifles so Alaka could turn and run. The shooting from the hallway ceased and the tall nafalli took the opportunity to make a run for the makeshift exit. They withdrew in seconds, closing the airlock behind them.

Jake hit the control panel's intercom button. "Time to go, Lewis. I'm on my way to the cockpit."

"I call it a bridge, for future reference. It may be small, but it has all the features one would expect on a proper starship, which I happen to be," Lewis replied over the speakers as Jake ran through the cargo area where the soldiers were settling in. Ayan was right behind him.

He arrived on the bridge as the Clever Dream skimmed along the hull of the massive station, weaving between the latticework and docking arms. Lieutenant Garrison got out of the pilot's seat and invited Jake to sit down. "Not like Lewis let me fly much anyway," he said with a smile. "I'll go help get the wounded into recovery chambers."

"Good idea. You're trained?"

"Lewis insisted since this is my third time on his bridge," Lieutenant Garrison replied.

"All right. Keep me informed on their condition."

Ayan took the secondary control seat and brought up the tactical and copilot's screens.

"All right, Lewis, get us clear of the station so we can communicate with the

Triton," Jake ordered mildly.

"As you wish. Would you like to take the controls?" Lewis asked.

"Not right now, just keep us clear of danger. Have you managed to get your cloaking systems back online?"

"There was no time to finish connecting the secondary field generator to my computer systems before I was called to this retrieval mission."

"Could we do it right now?" Ayan asked.

"Hello, Ayan. No, I'm afraid not. My shields would have to be down."

"All right. I promise I'll get to it as soon as I can," Ayan said.

"Personally? Well, I'm honoured."

"Triton to Clever Dream," addressed one of the communications officers' audio systems on the Clever Dream's bridge.

"Clever Dream, here. We have everyone. Ready to land." Jake's breath caught in his throat as the Triton came up on his tactical display. The energy readings on their shields were dangerously low and they were open to space on the aft dorsal section, right below the gunnery deck. Several of the gunnery turrets were seized due to heat damage and their far port side had a through-and-through breach that affected six decks.

"Change of plans, Captain. I'm laser linking rendezvous coordinates to you," Oz said as the coordinates came up on the computer. "We're taking too much damage to take you on, we'll meet you there."

"This is Ronin. My squadron is following you, Clever Dream. We'll hitch through your wormhole. We're coming up on your six."

Jake took the controls and nodded. "You're going to have to play navigator, Lewis," he said.

His answer came like a shiver. The ship computer and Lewis connected to Jake through the link systems in his hands, a capability he hadn't used extensively since Pandem. In fact, he had made a point not to unless he was trying to access the biological regeneration abilities he'd discovered when Ayan had been shot. "I'm sorry, I wasn't aware how surprising this sensation would be to you. I often shared this link with Alice."

"I'm sorry she couldn't be here," Jake replied aloud.

"She made a point to say goodbye before she left. I miss her, but don't worry, she'll live on in another form," Lewis said using Jake's link with the ship. He presented a mental picture of a workable course that would lead them through the debris and enemy fighters.

Ayan watched as Jake worked the controls with easy precision. It looked like he was staring at something very far away. "Are you all right, Jacob?" she asked quietly.

"I'm fine. Work the weaponry controls."

The console in front of her reconfigured, her seat slid into place, and she was surrounded by holographic images and targeting controls. Minh and the rest of his squad had moved into a flanking position behind and fired at the single seat fighters that were closing in from their port side.

There was another group coming into position, threatening to block their path with a line of deadly weapons' fire. To Ayan's amazement, the tactical controls were configured exactly the same as she'd find on any Freeground starship, and she got to work.

Her fingers twitched from one holographic representation to another, marking targets for the fighters behind and for the Clever Dream's missile banks. The weapons suite on the ship began to fire, sending cluster missiles that burst into searing high-speed flak, other missiles that honed in on one target and accelerated through them at incredible speeds, and firing the ship's main guns. The Clever Dream was a dangerous vessel, a long range gunship made to accommodate a large boarding crew. Few mercenaries could afford one, however, so it was more often seen in the hangars of wealthy collectors. She never thought she'd have the opportunity to operate one in any respect, especially from the weapons console.

Even with her energy systems switched from high powered Xetima to a more dependable mass reactor system built across the ship, the Clever Dream was still capable of exerting incredible force.

The shields were taking hits from the fighters, but bearing it well, especially since most of the fighters were distracted by Minh-Chu's squadron following behind. They remained in position, pivoting the bodies of their Uriel and Ramiel starfighters and unleashing the full force of their weaponry on anything that threatened to get in their way.

At long last they broke through the obscuring field into regular space.

Ayan breathed a sigh of relief as Minh's entire squadron made it through the field, and then gasped at what she saw on the secondary tactical display as it populated. There were three massive destroyers flanking another base ship. Each of the escorting ships were over nine hundred meters long, with a density reading that equaled the Triton. She overlaid the Triton's last known course. "The Triton will be caught off guard by that group of destroyers, we have to-"

"I see it, we're looping back inside," Jake interrupted mechanically.

Ayan nodded and switched all available power to the forward shields. As an extra safety measure and a warning to the fighters emerging from the field, she opened fire with all the Clever Dream's weapons, hoping that the burst would frighten vessels they couldn't detect until they were on the other side.

Her hopes were partially fulfilled. One of the larger fighters glanced off their shields, sending the Clever Dream slightly off course. "We're too late," Jake said quietly. "They're crossing over into open space. We have to run and hope they meet us at the rendezvous," Jake informed her.

It was true, they had come back just in time to see the Triton's aft section cross through into normal space. Her shields were already taking extreme damage. Ayan balanced the energy distribution across the Clever Dream's shields and resumed fire on the fighters trying to follow them as they flipped end over end and blasted the engines at full thrust, reversing course through the obscuring barrier protecting Ossimi station.

"I read you, Clever Dream. You'll be creating a wormhole as soon as you emerge," Minh replied over the communicator. "Everything all right, Captain? You sound a little... different."

"He's sharing a direct link with the ship. I think it has to do with the framework system," Ayan told Minh.

"I really have to look into getting a neural link," Ronin said.

"Jason had one, he had to get rid of it to save his marriage," Ayan replied.

"Ah, then maybe I'll talk to him first. Good shooting, Sunspot."

Ayan couldn't help but smile at the old call sign. It was chosen on a whim when she was in the academy and it stuck because of her size and temper. She'd managed to bring her temper under control since, and she stopped seeing the use of the nickname as a derogatory comment on her size years before. Too many friends had called her Sunspot over the years for it to have any negative connotation.

They broke through the field and Ayan could hear the power systems hum as they shunted energy towards the wormhole generator. The entry point formed and Ayan began broadcasting the entry point location to the fighters over an encrypted channel. She watched as Ronin's Ramiel fighter, followed by his thirteen squad mates, entered the barely visible end of the wormhole and accelerated away so quickly it was almost as though they disappeared. The Clever Dream was the last to enter, and either Lewis or Jake, she wasn't sure which, shunted most of the energy from the shields to the engines.

The entry point to the wormhole travelled along after them like a three kilometre wake as they accelerated through compressed space, making it impossible for anyone to follow.

The information streaming to Captain Valance through his connection with Lewis was amazing. He could see all the fighters in perfect line formation, centred in the wormhole with their controls slaved to Ronin's fighter. All their vital statistics said that they were at rest, and there were sporadic communications passing between them.

"I can't believe we didn't lose anyone," commented Finger.

"With every successful mission the likelihood that we lose anyone, or even a ship will lessen," replied Slick, who had been reassigned as Ronin's wing man.

"Even so, we buy our minutes with our decisions. Not one second comes free. I'm proud to fly with all of you," Ronin added. Jake was enjoying having him back.

Amidst the flow of data came something Jacob did not expect, an emotion. Lewis was glad Ronin had joined the crew of the Triton, and he expressed it emotionally. The feeling was strange, inexplicably different from any human feeling. Even still, there was only one way to comprehend the expression, and that was as a mild happy one at the presence of Ronin and after the experience of that emotion passed, Jake realised that Lewis felt the same way about Ayan and himself being aboard. Lewis actually enjoyed having people on board the Clever Dream, even the people who were busy setting up fold-out cots and partitions in the main cargo hold. Lewis had already informed them that they would be in transit for at least ten hours. Stephanie had given the order to rest and tend to the few minor injuries they had.

"Jake, there's an urgent message here from the Triton," Ayan interrupted, placing a hand on his arm.

Jacob released his light grip on the flight controls. There was no reason for him to worry about them, they had been locked since they entered the wormhole. "I didn't see it in the computer."

"You really were in there, weren't you?" Ayan asked him, her big blue eyes looking into his warily. "How is it?"

"Jason was right, Lewis's personality has balanced out. He seems stable, positive."

"I don't know about that. The time stamp on this transmission is from before we entered the wormhole but the comm system didn't deliver it until now," Ayan said.

"I'm sorry, I didn't think you wanted to be distracted," Lewis explained.

"That's not your call to make, Lewis," Jake replied. "You might be the governing AI aboard, but we need access to all incoming information. We'll tell you when we need you to sort through it for us."

"I'll keep that in mind," Lewis replied.

Jake's expression darkened. He looked up to the cockpit canopy as though Lewis was somehow installed there instead of deeper inside the ship; it was a common reflex. "Don't keep it in mind, call it a law. Keeping information intended for your command crew is a malfunction. If it can't be corrected we'll have to remove your program."

"Yes, Sir," Lewis barked.

"What's worse? A murderous Holocaust AI or one who knows how to push your buttons?" Jake grumbled as he reached over and activated the playback.

It was a report generated by Jason's communications terminal. Ayan and Jake recognised the format immediately. The Caran Enterprise destroyers had signalled their intent on executing the galactic warrant issued for the Triton. The warrant itself was hundreds of pages long, but the sections Jason had highlighted indicated that Regent Galactic had prompted the investigation that resulted in the issuance of the warrant itself. The cause for the warrant was exactly what they expected, but they were surprised at the absence of Sol Defence's or the Earth Fleet's involvement in the issuance of the warrant.

The remaining technologies from the Triton were to be delivered to Order of Eden forces immediately after capture. "Well, that's one thing we don't have to worry about in this. The Sol Defence Fleet isn't trying to get their ship back yet," Jake said as he sat back in the pilot's seat.

Ayan worked the console, looking for anything else in the message. There was nothing. One of her golden curls had gotten free of her hood and swung against her cheek as she looked over the holographic display again. She looked deeply worried.

Jake mentally ordered the glove of his vacsuit to retract - it was as effortless as instinct - and reached out to stroke her cheek. That was a reflex too, brought up by how close the console seating brought them together and his concern for her.

She flinched, looked at his hand and then him. Her expression was hurt, a little frightened. Ayan started to pull herself out of the seat, pushing against the console. The chair retracted from the console and she was out of the seat and walking down the hall in one quick motion. A doorway just a few meters down slid open and she walked inside.

Jacob looked down the hallway after her for a long moment.

"I'm perfectly capable of taking care of things while we're in wormhole transit, Captain Valance," Lewis said quietly. "Alice trusted me for thousands of cumulative hours."

Jake pressed the release for his seat under the console, ensured the controls were locked, and followed. "Thanks, Lewis."

When he entered the room, Ayan had just finished taking the enhanced armoured layer off, leaving her in the more pliable vacsuit underneath. She had left it white, and with her hood up he was reminded of the Ayan he'd watched pass away before his eyes.

The Ayan before him, brilliant, active and alive, held back tears. She drew her hood back and shook her hair loose as she looked out the side of the dome covering the prime living area in the ship. They had left it untouched; it was the captain's quarters, Alice's personal space. He'd never seen it before, never taken the time to take a look.

There was a broad circular seat in the centre, a large bed against one side, soft, dark paneling all around the room, a transparent ceiling that extended down low enough for someone to watch the stars. That's where Ayan focused her attention.

She stood with crossed arms, looking through the transparent metal at the warped view of space outside.

Jake didn't know what to do. The door closed behind him. The quiet of the captain's quarters pressed on him like a weight. His armour felt heavy, inappropriate. He didn't know what to do, where to start, what to say.

Her shoulders shook, it was a shudder. He could hear her quietly crying. "I'm sorry," he whispered.

"It's not about you," she replied quietly, wiping tears away.

"You came here for me, everything that's happened is on my head. If anyone can say it, I can."

"Fine, then you're sorry. It's all sorted," she replied, her British accent colouring her words more heavily than normal.

Jacob was stumped once more. He had never been at such a complete and utter loss for words in all his life. He opened his mouth to say something, he didn't know what, and was left gaping like a fish for several moments before closing it again. She was frustrating, the whole situation was maddening, but he couldn't exactly express that either, it just built up like a fitful ball in his brain pan.

"Shouldn't you check on things?" she asked quietly.

"Stephanie's settling everyone in the cargo hold and crew quarters. There's nothing more to do."

"Oh."

He stood in silence for another protracted moment until he finally couldn't stand it any longer. There was only one thing on his mind. With all the things that had been going on, no matter how dire, when he saw Ayan there was only one thing on his mind. "I'm sorry about what I said before, that it's you."

"What the hell were you thinking with that? I mean, what did you mean by saying I'm the bloody root of your problems?" She exploded so suddenly he took a step backwards, his back hit the door. It didn't open.

She was a flurry of golden curls, gesticulating hands, and flying tears. "You've got a ship full of random people and objects you could have ranted off on but instead you turn on me and come screaming 'it's you!'"

His resolve sprang back. Jake's frustration at the whole situation came to the fore as he replied "It is you! You and Jason and Minh and Oz and Laura and the you that came before and died right on my bloody ship! What am I supposed to give back that repays that kind of blind devotion? You cross entire sectors and say 'here I am!' and I'm in no position to give you the kind of welcome you deserve. I can't pay you, I can't give you a ship, I can't take you home if you decide you don't want to stay, and I certainly can't keep you safe!" Jake knew the truth was coming out, but it was unvarnished, undiplomatic, and he felt he was making things worse. Nevertheless, he couldn't stop. "I can't even keep my daughter safe! I watched her die and all I can keep thinking is that she's just the first. Who's next? Oz? Minh? You?" He was in Alice's home, the cabin she'd spent hours in while she looked for him across the stars. It was her refuge. "She should be here. If I hadn't put her in command, if she hadn't come after me on Pandem, she'd be free to run. If I knew how far I'd pull everyone down with me, I'd have hidden. Even Longshadow prison would be better than watching you people die one at a time."

Ayan finally understood what he'd meant as she watched the unbreakable, indomitable Captain Jacob Valance fall apart before her eyes. Even in his dark armour, ready for anything, he seemed so much smaller. She hadn't heard that Alice died, but from what he was saying it was plain. She hadn't realised that he didn't understand why they had pursued him before, that he didn't trust anyone he wasn't paying for a specific job. She closed the distance between them.

His heel twisted against the door and he fell to his knees, his sight obscured with tears he tried to blink back. She slowly wrapped her arms around him and laid his head against her chest, tucked under her chin. "I'm sorry Alice passed on. I didn't know."

His hands wrapped around her waist.

She stroked his face as chest-wracking sobs shook him. She'd heard the story before. Alice had rescued him from a Vindyne laboratory and left him on the Samson. The Samson was just barely functional then, and Jake had no memory of who he was or that he was the recreation of another man, Jonas Valent. Jake became a bounty hunter, recruited a crew and began travelling the galaxy in search of the woman who'd left him in the cargo hold of his ship. The woman who had called him father before leaving him there. It was the only footage he had of Alice. Ayan had never seen it before, but hearing the story, she imagined Jacob playing it back when no one was looking. Alice became as much a part of his life as if she were his own flesh and blood. Losing her was like losing a part of himself, no different from losing a daughter he'd raised from birth.

When he calmed down, she bent a little and kissed the top of his head. "You know there's no one else I'd cross the stars for. You don't have to give us anything. You don't even have to understand it. Just trust us. We're here to stay."